# 英語
# English

陳朴 編著

# 一日一題

# √365

5 6 7 8 9 10 11
12 13 14 15 16 17 18
19 20 21 22 23 24 25
26 27 28 29 30 31

臺灣商務印書館 發行

# 前　　言

　　學英語的人莫不想把英語學好，而要學好英語就得做到四會——會聽、會說、會讀、會寫。四會中說與寫是主要的，也是比較困難的。聽與讀當然也重要，但如果能做到會說會寫，則會聽會讀也就比較易於解決。

　　本書編寫目的就是想對具有一定英語基礎的人士提供一些學習英語寫作和會話的素材。題目內容廣泛，包括生活和社交的各個方面，有對話、有造句。根據不同題材，有些方面對話多一些，有些方面則造句多一些。至於句中出現的語法，雖不系統，也不全面，但重要部分，如動詞的各種時態、語態、虛擬語氣、冠詞以及某些介詞的用法，都有接觸，特別是對於某些詞的習慣用法和常用句型作了比較詳細的介紹，務使讀者看過之後清楚明白。

　　由於題材不同，每天的問題有長有短，有難有易。學的時候似不必拘泥於一日一題，儘可按照自己的程度和時間作適當的安排。譬如比較短的和容易的，每天不妨多學幾則；比較長的難的，則兩三天學習一則也未始不可。開始學習，在看過問題及說明之後，可先口頭試譯，再把句子寫在紙上，然後與書中譯例仔細比較，看看有何出入。在充分理解之後，再做後面翻譯習題，這時候一定會感到比較容易。做習題時也要先試譯，再參考書末答案。如有錯誤，加以改正。這樣學習，其效果可能會比較好些。

　　學習要持之以恒，不宜間斷。每隔一段時間——如一星期或十天複習一次。有些會話的句子，最好能把它記熟，在適當場合予以實際運用（即與別人用英語對話）。經過這樣反覆練習，口語能力一定會逐漸提高。

本書在編寫時曾參考了國內外出版的一些書籍，如日本岩田一男的《英文作文一日一題》、《英語九百句》、《情景對話》、《英美貿易書信大全》以及其他一些同樣性質的書籍。

在編寫過程中承李中行先生提出了一些寶貴的意見，並校閱了全稿，謹在此表示感謝。

本書編寫時間比較倉促。在內容方面或文字方面如有不妥和錯誤之處，衷心希望讀者提出批評和指正。

編者

# Contents

# 第1月
# 時間、歲月、年齡

## 第1天

"勞駕，請問現在幾點鐘了？""現在4點鐘。"

### 【說明】

"勞駕"可用 Excuse me (, but…)，這是客套話, 在向別人詢問時常要用到。

"請問現在幾點鐘了？"可說 Please tell me the time, 或用疑問句 What time is it? / What time do you make it? / What time do you have? 都可以。

"現在4點鐘。"即 It is (It's) four (o'clock)。如要表明正好4點鐘, 可說 It's just four o'clock 或 Four o'clock sharp。如快要到4點鐘, 可說 It's close on (或 upon) four o'clock, 或 It's getting ( 或 going) on for four o'clock。如剛過4點鐘, 可說 It's just past four o'clock。如爲4點20分, 可說 It's twenty (minutes) past four, 或簡單地說 It's four twenty (4:20)。如爲4點半, 可說 It's half past four, 或簡單地說 It's four thirty (4:30)。如爲4點50分, 可說 It's ten (minutes) to five, 或簡單地說 It's four fifty (4:50)。

### 【譯例】

(a) "Excuse me. What time is it now?" "It's just four o'clock."
(b) "Excuse me, but please tell me the time." "It's four o'clock

1

sharp. "

    (c) "What time do you make it, please?" "Oh, it's just four. "

# 第2天

這手錶是兩年前在瑞士買的。走得很準。從來沒有快慢。

## 【說明】

"兩年前" 要說 two years ago。

"瑞士"(國名)是 Switzerland;"瑞士製的"是 Swiss made。

"走得(不)準" 可說 It keeps good (bad) time。

"從來沒有快慢" 要說 It never loses or gains, 或 It's never fast or slow。如錶走快(慢)了, 可說 It's gaining (losing) time;如每天快(慢)半分, 可說 My watch gains (loses) half a minute a day, 或 My watch is half a minute fast (slow) every day;如不快也不慢, 可說 It neither gains nor loses。

## 【譯例】

    (a) I bought this watch in Switzerland two years ago. It keeps good time. It never loses or gains.

    (b) The watch I bought two years ago is Swiss made. It keeps good time. It's never slow or fast.

# 第3天

學校8點半開始(上課), 3點半放學, 午休1小時。

"8點半開始"是 begin at half past eight 或 begin at eight thirty (8:30)。

"3點半放學":"放學"是結束的意思,所以可說 end at half past three。"鐘點"作爲狀語前面要用介詞 at,表示"在"。此外如 at noon(中午),at midnight(午夜),at night(夜裏)都要用 at。

"午休": a noon recess; a break at noon.

【譯例】

(a) School begins at half past eight and ends at half past three. We have an hour's noon recess.

(b) School begins at eight thirty, and ends at three thirty. We take an hour's break at noon.

# 第4天

我通常早上8點10分到學校去。路不遠,步行只需5分鐘。

【說明】

"早上"作爲狀語要說 in the morning;同樣"下午"是 in the afternoon;"晚上"是 in the evening;"夜裏"可說 in the night 或 at night。

"到學校去": go to school; leave for school

"路不遠"可說 It's not far (away 或 off),也可說 It's no distance (at all),或 It's within walking distance(步行可到)。如"相當遠"可說 It's some distance, 或 It's a fairly long way; 如"很遠"就說

It's a great distance, 或 It's quite a long way。上面句子都可加上 from…to…在後面。

"步行"是 on foot; "乘公共汽車"是 by bus; "乘無軌電車" 是 by trolley bus 或 trolley coach; "乘電車"是 by car 或 tram, 名詞 前都不用冠詞。注意 foot 前用介詞 on, bus 等詞前面則用 by。

"步行只需5分鐘"可說 It takes me only five minutes to go on foot, 這裏 take 是 "需要"或 "花費"的意思; 另外也可簡單地說 It's only five minutes' walk, walk 在這裏是名詞。

## 【譯例】

(a) I usually go to school at ten past eight in the morning. It's not far away. It's only five minutes' walk from my house.

(b) I usually leave for school at eight ten(8:10)in the morning. It's no distance. It takes me only five minutes to get there on foot.


# 第5天

我的家在郊區, 步行到車站要30分鐘以上, 乘公共汽車却只需6 分鐘。

## 【說明】

"郊區"outskirts 常用複數, "在郊區"要說 on the outskirts of the city, 注意 outskirts 前用介詞 on。

一個建築物 "在"什麼地方, 動詞可用 be, 也可用 stand 或 be situated。

"30分鐘"可說 thirty minutes, 但通常說 half an hour, 往往也

4

可說 a half hour; "以上"可說 more than 或 over。

**【譯例】**

(a) My house is on the outskirts of the city, so it's more than half an hour's walk to the station though it's only six minutes by bus.

(b) As my house stands on the outskirts of the city, it takes me more than half an hour on foot to the station though by bus I can get there in six minutes.

(c) The station is situated over half an hour's walk from my house on the outskirts of the city, though it can be reached in six minutes by bus.

# 第 6 天

離開車還有一段時間，我們進去這裏喝點茶吧。

**【說明】**

"還有一段時間"可說有 plenty of time; 也可說有 time enough 或 enough time（時間充裕）。"還有一段時間"表明未來的時間，所以動詞可用將來時態 there will be plenty of time, 但用現在時 there is… 也可以; 或以說話人為主用 we shall have（或 have）…也通。

"離開車"是"車開之前"的意思，所以要說 before the train starts, 這是狀語從句。注意: 用 before, after, when, if 等連詞所引起的狀語從句其動詞要用現在時態替代將來時態，所以我們不能說 before the train will start。

"進去"可用 drop in 表示"就便進去"的意思。

"喝點茶"是 take some tea, 或 have a cup of tea。

【譯例】

(a) There will be plenty of time before the train starts, so let's drop in here and take some tea.

(b) We shall have time enough before the train starts, so let's drop in here for a cup of tea.

# 第7天

我急急忙忙地到車站去趕頭班列車，但因遲了 2 分鐘沒趕上。

【說明】

"頭班列車"是 the first train, "末班列車"是 the last train; 也可按開車時刻說, 如 9 點 15 分列車 the 9:15 train, 4 點 30 分列車 the 4:30 train 等, 或不用 train 字樣也可, 如: If you take the 9:15, you'll be there at 16:40。

"趕"這裏要用 catch; "趕上火車（公共汽車）"說 catch a train (a bus); "沒有趕上"是 fail to catch, miss 或 lose。

"遲了 2 分鐘"是 two minutes late, 但如用 fail to catch 或 miss 表明未趕上則後面加上 by two minutes 就可以了; by 在這裏是"相差"的意思。

【譯例】

(a) I went hurriedly to the station to catch the first train, but I was two minutes late, so I missed it.

(b) I hurried to the station for the first train, but lost it by two minutes.

(c) Though I hurried to the station (so as) to be in time for the first train, I failed to catch it by just two minutes.


# 第8天

只要不下雨，我們就能在下午3時前到達目的地。

【說明】

"只要不下雨" 可譯作 as long as（或 so long as）it doesn't rain, 也可說 unless it rains, 改爲短語則爲 weather permitting。

"下午3時前"：before three o'clock in the afternoon

"目的地"：destination

【譯例】

(a) As long as it doesn't rain, we shall be able to reach our destination before three o'clock in the afternoon.

(b) Unless it rains, we shall be able to get to our destination before three o'clock in the afternoon.

(c) Weather permitting, we shall be able to arrive at our destination before three in the afternoon.


# 第9天

你有點傷風。只要在11點之前回來，你可隨便到什麼地方去玩。

【說明】

"傷風" 要說 catch cold 或 have a cold; 也可說 get a bit of

a cold。a bit of a…是 "有點" 的意思。

　　"11點之前" before 11 o'clock; 也可說 by 11 o'clock。by 是 "不遲於" 的意思，與 before 稍有不同。

　　"隨便到什麼地方" 是 to any place 或 anywhere，也可用連接副詞 wherever。

## 【譯例】

　　(a) You have a slight cold. You may go to any place you like if you get back before eleven.

　　(b) You have got a bit of a cold. If you come back by eleven, you may go anywhere you please.

　　(c) You have caught a slight cold. Can you promise to return by eleven? Then I will let you go wherever you want.


# 第 10 天

　　*我們家裏人起床都很早。我的父親起得最早。他起床從不超過6點鐘。*

## 【說明】

　　"家裏人" 用 family，指合家的人，所以是複數；如作 "一個家庭" 解就作單數用。

　　"起床" get up 或 rise；"早(遲)起" get up early (late)；"早起的人" 是 an early riser, 也可說 an early bird。（從諺語 The early bird gets the worm: 早起的鳥能捕到蟲子──早起三朝當一工。）

　　"不超過6點鐘" 是 "不遲於6點鐘" 的意思，所以可說 not later than six (o'clock)。

(a) All my family are early risers. My father is the earliest. He never rises later than six o'clock.

(b) Everybody in my family is an early bird, but my father is second to none, never getting up later than six.


# 第 11 天

我的朋友是個非常守時的人，聚會時總是按規定時間5分鐘前出席。

【說明】

"守時的"是 punctual；'我的朋友是個非常守時的人"可照字譯，也可譯作 My friend is punctuality itself。

"聚會"：a meeting；a gathering

"規定時間"：the appointed（或 fixed）time

"5分鐘前"是"早5分鐘"的意思，所以要說 five minutes earlier（than…）。

"總是"：always 或 without fail；如改用動詞，可說 never fail to。

"出席"可說 be present (at)，present oneself (at)，或 attend。

【譯例】

(a) My friend is very punctual. He is always present at a meeting five minutes earlier than the appointed time.

(b) My friend is a very punctual man. He never fails to present himself at a meeting five minutes earlier than the fixed time.

(c) My friend is punctuality itself and will attend a gathering without fail five minutes earlier than the time appointed.


# 第12天

那個人工作非常努力。他往往從早到晚工作，從不請一天假。

## 【說明】

"工作非常努力"：work very hard, 或 be very hardworking

"從早到晚"：from morning till night; all day long

"請假" ask for leave; take a day off

## 【譯例】

(a) That man works very hard. He often works from morning till night and never asks for a day's leave.

(b) That man is so hardworking that he often works all day long and has never taken a day off.


# 第13天

你來得正好。如再晚5分鐘的話，我們就出去了。

## 【說明】

"正好"這裏是"時間正好"的意思，所以要說 just in time, 或 in the nick of time。

"如再晚5分鐘"可用 if-clause 的虛擬語氣. 也可譯作 Five minutes later, and… 。

"5分鐘的話"是個假定的說法，所以可在 five minutes 前加個 say, say five minutes 是"譬如說5分鐘"的意思, 但不加也通。

## 【譯例】

(a) You have come just in time. If you had come, say, five minutes or so later, we should not have been at home.

(b) You are in the nick of time. Five minutes later, and you would have found us absent.

# 第14天

"他什麼時候走的？""他剛剛走。他要我在你來時告訴你他會在車站的候車室等你。"

## 【說明】

"他什麼時候走的？" When did he go away (或 leave)？注意: 用了疑問詞 when, 動詞不用現在完成時,如不可說 When has he left?。

"剛剛走" left a moment ago 或 went away just now; 也可說 has just left, 但不能與確指過去時間的狀語連用, 如不可說 has just left a moment ago。

## 【譯例】

(a) "When did he go away?" "He went away a moment ago. He asked me to tell you when you came here that he would be waiting for you in the station waiting room."

（b）"When did he leave？" "He left just now. He asked me to inform you when you got here that he would be waiting for you in the waiting room of the station."

# 第15天

*俗語説"時者金也"。時間一去不復返。我們必須好好利用時間。*

## 【説明】

"俗語說"用 The proverb says…, The saying goes that…, 或 The proverb has it that… 都可以。

"一去" once it is gone 或 as soon as（the moment, the instant）it passes; 這裏 once, as soon as, the moment, the instant 都是連詞, 表示 "一……就…… "。

"好好利用時間" 可説 make good use of one's time, employ one's time well（或 profitably）, 也可説 turn one's time to profitable account。

## 【譯例】

（a）The proverb says, "Time is money." It will never come back once it is gone. We must make good use of our time.

（b）The proverb has it that time is money. Never will it come back as soon as it passes, so you should employ your time well.

（c）The saying goes that time is money. The moment it passes, it will never come back. Hence one should turn one's time to profitable account.

# 第 16 天

光陰似箭，我到這裏差不多 3 個月了，這使我感到吃驚。

## 【說明】

"光陰似箭" 可照字譯 Time flies like an arrow, 也可簡單說 Time passes swiftly ( 或 quickly )。如用感嘆句可說 How time flies!

"我到這裏差不多 3 個月了" 可說 I've already been here for almost three months, 也可說 Nearly three months have passed since I came here, 或 It's nearly three months since my arrival。Since 是 "自從……以來" 的意思，可作連詞，也可作介詞。注意: 用了連詞 since, 從句裏的動詞要用過去時，主句裏的動詞一般用現在完成時，如 Nearly three months have passed since I came here, 或用現在完成進行時，如 It has been raining since yesterday; 如只說多少時間則多用現在時，如 It's nearly three months since my arrival。

"感到吃驚" 要說 I'm surprised ( 或 astonished )，不可說 I'm surprising。

## 【譯例】

(a) Time flies like an arrow. I'm surprised that I've already been here for almost three months.

(b) Time passes swiftly. I'm surprised that nearly three months have passed since I came here.

(c) How time flies! I'm astonished that it's almost three months since my arrival.

# 第17天

他們結婚已3年，但還沒有生過孩子。

## 【說明】

"結婚" 是 be married 或 get married;"結婚已3年" 可參照前例，用三種方法譯出。

"沒有生過孩子" 可簡單說 have no child, 或 be childless；也可用被動語態表達，如 No child has been born (to them)。

## 【譯例】

(a) They have been married these three years, and yet they still have no child.

(b) Three years have already passed since they were married, but they are still childless.

(c) No child has been born to them, though it is already three years since they got married.


# 第18天

"你明天忙嗎？" "是的,我明天正巧有事, 後天才有空。" "好吧, 後天請過來玩。"

## 【說明】

"忙" 是 busy; 如說 "有事", 可用 be engaged, be occupied 或 have something on。

"有空"：be free, be clear, 或 have time, have time to spare。

"正巧": happen (to)

"才……" 要說 not… till（或 until），如"他明天才回來"是 he will not be back till tomorrow。

"好吧"在這裏是嘆詞，可說 well。

"來玩"是 come and see us 或 drop in; 這裏"玩"並不指遊戲，所以不可譯作 play。

## 【譯例】

(a) "Are you busy tomorrow?" "Yes, I happen to be engaged tomorrow, and won't be free till the day after tomorrow." "Well, then, come and see us the day after tomorrow."

(b) "Are you engaged tomorrow?" "Yes, I happen to have something on tomorrow and won't be clear until the day after tomorrow." "Very well, then, drop in the day after tomorrow."

# 第19天

我的姪女隔天跟一位音樂老師學習兩小時左右的小提琴。

## 【說明】

"隔天"是 every other day 或 every second day; 每隔2天是 every third day; 每隔3天是 every fourth day, 餘類推。

"音樂老師": music teacher（或 master）

"跟"是"在……（的指導）之下"的意思, 所以要說 under（the guidance of）…。

"左右"表示概數, 可用 about 表示; "兩小時左右"也可說 a couple of hours。

15

(a) My niece learns the violin for about two hours every other day under a music teacher.

(b) My niece is now learning to play the violin for a couple of hours every second day under the guidance of a music master.

# 第20天

"今天是幾號？（星期幾？）" "今天是6月3號（星期二）。"

## 【說明】

"今天是幾號？" 可說 What day of the month is it? 或 What's the day of the month today? 也可簡單地說 What's the date? 或 What's the date today? Date 是 "日期"、"日子"。這裏是指 "幾號"，但也可包括星期，所以答句可單說 "幾號" 如 It's June 3 或 Today is June 3，也可包括星期說 It's Tuesday, June 3，或 Today is Tuesday, June 3。

"今天是星期幾？" 可說 What day of the week is it? 或 What's the day of the week today? 也可簡單地說 What day is it? 或 What's the day today? 這裏 day 只指 "星期" 不包括 "幾號"，所以答句只可說 It's Tuesday, 或 Today is Tuesday, 而不能說 It's Tuesday, June 3 或 Today is Tuesday, June 3。

## 【譯例】

(a) "What day of the month is today?" "Today is June 3."

(b) "What day (of the week) is today?" "Today is Tuesday."

(c) "What's the date today?" "Today is June 3." (or "Today is Tuesday, June 3.")

16

# 第21天

"星期六你在哪裏?" "看電影去了, 下午3點才回來。"

**【說明】**

星期名稱如 Saturday 用作狀語時前面要加 on, 是 "在" 的意思 ( 比較 at four o'clock )。On Saturday 根據句中動詞的時態可指 "上星期六" 或 "下星期六", 如 Where were you on Saturday? 和 Will you come on Saturday? 也可統指 "星期六", 如 His son often comes on Saturday。如說 "星期六早上 ( 下午, 晚上 )" 前面也要用 on, 如 on Saturday morning (afternoon, evening)(比較 in the morning, in the afternoon, in the evening )。另外, 在特定的一天前面也要用 on, 如 on National Day ( 國慶日 ), on one's birthday ( 生日 );但前面如有 last, next 等字樣則不可加 on, 如 last Saturday, last Saturday morning, next Monday, next Monday afternoon 等。

"看電影": go to (see) the movies; be at the movies

**【譯例】**

(a) "Where were you on Saturday?" "I went to the movies. I didn't come back till three o'clock in the afternoon."

(b) "Where were you last Saturday?" "I was at the movies and didn't get back till three in the afternoon."

# 第22天

父親3月3號到美國去了, 要到4月底才回來。

17

"3月3號"可寫作 March 3 或 March 3rd, 但都要唸作 March (the) third, 3rd 表示third (同樣, first, second, fourth 都可寫成 1st, 2nd, 4th); 比較正式的也可說 the third of March。序數詞前要有定冠詞 the。如作狀語用也像星期名稱一樣前面要加 on, 如 on March 3 或 on the third of March。

"4月底"是 the end of April, 用作狀語前面要加 at; "到4月底"要說 till (或 until) the end of April。

【譯例】

(a) My father went to the States on March 3. He will be back at the end of April.

(b) My father went to the States on March the third. He'll remain there till the end of April.

(c) Father left for the States on the third of March and won't be back till the end of April.

# 第23天

他是1950年出生的。今年剛好30歲。

【說明】

年份作狀語, 前面要用介詞 in, 如 in 1950, 或 in the year 1950。

"出生": be born

"剛好": just, exactly

"30歲" thirty years old 或單說 thirty 也可以。

(a) He was born in 1950. He is just thirty years old this year.
(b) He was born in the year 1950, and is exactly thirty this year.

# 第24天

"你猜猜看我幾歲。""照我看来，你最多是25歲。""我已經過了30週歲了。""眞的嗎？你看上去還不到這年齡。"

## 【說明】

"猜"是 guess; 後面"我幾歲"是個從句，所以不可說 how old am I，要說 how old I am; 如不用 guess，也可說 How old do you think I am? 注意: 這個類型的句子，do you think 不可放在句首。

"照我看來"可說 It seems to me that…，或 I take it that…。

"最多"是 at (the) most，"最少"是 at (the) least。

"過了30週歲"可說 be already over thirty，或 was thirty on one's last birthday; 這是說已經過了30歲的生日。

"眞的嗎？": Really? Is that so?

"看上去不到……"可說 look younger than …，或 look young for one's age。

## 【譯例】

(a) "Guess how old I am." "It seems to me that you are twenty-five at most." "I'm already over thirty." "Really? You look younger than your age."

(b) "How old do you think I am?" "I take it that you are twenty-five at most. " " I was thirty on my last birthday. " " Is that so? You look young for your age."

# 第25天

上星期碰到 5 年不見的外甥。他還是十幾歲的孩子，却長得那麼高，我幾乎不認得了。

## 【說明】

" 5 年不見 " 可照字譯，因爲是隔了 5 年又遇到，所以也可說 met after a five years' interval （或 after an interval of five years ）。

" 十幾歲的孩子 " 可說 a boy in his teens; teens 是指 13—19 的年齡；也可說 a teenager （或 teener ）。

" 那麼……以致 " 的意思可用 so…that 的句型來表達。

" 認得 "： recognize

## 【譯例】

(a)Last week I met my nephew after a five years' interval. He is still a boy in his teens, but he had grown so tall that I could hardly recognize him at first.

(b)Last week I met my nephew after an interval of five years. He is still a teenager, but at first I failed to recognize him as he had grown so tall.

# 第26天

她告訴我15年前曾經見過你的母親。那時候她還是個6歲的孩子。

## 【說明】

"15年前"在這裏指的是過去某一時候的15年之前，所以要說 fifteen years before，而不可說 fifteen years ago。ago 是從現在算起15年之前，如 She saw your mother fifteen years ago，因此在這例句裏我們只能說 She told me that she had seen your mother fifteen years before。

"那時候"： at that time

"6歲的孩子"可說 a child of six, 或 a six-year-old child 複合詞中間的名詞不可用複數，故 year 不可加 s。

## 【譯例】

(a) She told me that she had met your mother fifteen years before. At that time she was only a child of six.

(b) She told me she had seen your mother fifteen years before when she was only a six-year-old girl.

# 第27天

"你看那個女人有幾歲?" "那我不清楚，大約30多歲吧。" "是30與40之間，還是靠近40?" "不，大約是30出頭吧。"

## 【說明】

"30多歲" in one's thirties, thirties 是30—39的年齡。

"30與40之間"可說 in the middle of thirty, 或 in one's middle

thirties。

　　"靠近40"可說 in the latter part of thirty, 或 in one's late
thirties。

　　"30出頭"是 in the first part of thirty, 或 in one's early
thirties。

## 【譯例】

　　(a)"Do you know how old the woman is?""That I don't know.
Somewhere in the thirties, I think.""Middle or latter part?""No, I'd say
about the first part."

　　(b)"How old do you think the woman is?""Oh, I'm not clear. In her
thirties, I think.""Middle? latter?""No, may be in her early thirties."


# 第28天

　　我的哥哥快25歲了。他比我大3歲。我的妹妹最小，今年還不到
20歲。

## 【說明】

　　"快到25歲"是 will soon be twenty-five, 或 be getting on for
twenty-five。

　　"大3歲"可說 three years older than…, 或 older than…by
three years。

　　"還不到20歲"be still under twenty, 或 be not quite twenty。

## 【譯例】

　　(a)My brother will soon be twenty-five. He is three years older

22

than I. My sister is the youngest. She is not quite twenty.

(b) My brother, who is older than I by three years, is getting on for twenty-five. The youngest is my sister, who is still under twenty.

# 第29天

我的祖父年紀大了。他早已過了70歲, 但看上去還不很老。

## 【說明】

"年紀大了" 可說 be growing old, 或 be getting on in years。

"早已過了70歲" be well past (或 over) seventy, be already on the wrong side of seventy; 如未過70可說 on the right side of seventy。

## 【譯例】

(a) My grandfather is growing old. He is well past seventy, but he doesn't look so old.

(b) My grandfather is getting on in years. He is already on the wrong side of seventy though he looks younger than his age.

# 第30天

他家裏的人都是長壽的。他父親活到80歲。母親依然健在。下一生日將是90歲了。

## 【說明】

"長壽" long-lived; 用動詞可說 live long。

"活到……": live to the age of…

"健在"可說 be still in good health (in one's old age), 或 carry one's age wonderfully well。

## 【譯例】

(a)His family are all long-lived. His father lived to the age of eighty and his mother is still in good health. She'll be ninety her next birthday.

(b)All people in his family live long. His father died at the age of eighty and his mother, who carries her age wonderfully well, will be ninety on her coming birthday.

# Words and Expressions

| | |
|---|---|
| excuse [iks'kju:z] me | 勞駕，對不起 |
| four o'clock sharp | 4 點正 |
| gain (lose); be fast (slow) | （鐘）快（慢） |
| keep good (bad) time | （鐘）（不）準時 |
| begin at half past eight | 8 點半開始 |
| noon recess [ri'ses] (或 break) | 午休 |
| five minutes' walk | 步行 5 分鐘 |
| It's no distance. | 路不遠 |
| get there on foot (by bus) | 步行（乘公共汽車）到那裏 |
| It takes (me) five minutes to… | （我）得用 5 分鐘…… |
| on the outskirts ['autskə:ts] | 在郊區 |
| drop in (on somebody, for something) | 就便看望（某人，爲某事），就便進去 |
| (fail to) catch a train (a bus) | （沒）趕上火車（公共汽車） |

| | |
|---|---|
| be two minutes late | 遲到 2 分鐘 |
| destination [ˌdesti'neiʃən] | 目的地 |
| catch cold; have a cold | 傷風 |
| be present ['preznt] at; attend | 出席 |
| from morning till night | 從早到晚 |
| ask for leave | 請假 |
| in the nick of time | 正是時候（恰好）趕上 |
| went away just now; left a moment ago | 剛剛走 |
| make good use of one's time | 好好利用時間 |
| How time flies! | 光陰如箭 |
| It is three months（或 Three months have passed）since… | 自從……已 3 個月 |
| get married | 結婚 |
| have something on | 有事 |
| have time to spare | 有空 |
| every other day; every second day | 隔天 |
| a couple ['kʌpl] of hours（days） | 兩三小時（天） |
| go to（see）the movies['mu:viz]（或 film） | 看電影去 |
| be born | 出生 |
| It seems to me that… | 照我看…… |
| at most（least） | 至多（少） |
| after an interval ['intəvəl] of five years | 隔了 5 年之後 |
| teenager ['ti:neidʒə] | 青少年 |
| at that time | 那時候 |

| in one's thirties, (forties, fifties, etc.) | 30(40, 50等)多歲 |
| be getting on for twenty-five | 快到25歲 |
| three years older (younger) than… | 比……大(小)3歲 |
| be getting on in years | 年紀大了 |
| be on the wrong (right) side of seventy | 已過(未到)70歲 |
| live to the age of… | 活到……歲 |
| be in (good) health | 身體健康 |
| long-lived ['lɔŋ 'livd] | 長壽的 |

# Exercise 1

Translate the following into English:

1. 甲：勞駕，現在幾點鐘？

   乙：現在是兩點二十五分。（第1天）

2. 我的錶走得不大準，每天要快1分鐘。（第2天）

3. 甲：你到學校去，步行還是乘公共汽車？

   乙：學校離我家不遠，我總是走去的。（第4天）

4. 甲：你到學校去，得用多少時間？

   乙：步行只需10分鐘。（第4天）

5. 他的家在郊區，到車站得用很長的時間。（第5天）

6. 公園離這裏不遠，乘公共汽車不用許多時間就可到了。（第5天）

7. 離開電影放映時間還有半小時，我們進去這裏喝點咖啡吧。（第6天）

26

8. 甲：電影什麼時候開始？

   乙：噢，還有一段時間。（第6天）

9. 昨天他急急忙忙地到車站去，因為他要趕2：15的火車。（第7天）

10. 他因為遲了5分鐘而沒有趕上末班列車。（第7天）

11. 甲：我們什麼時候可以到達目的地？

    乙：只要天不下雨，中午前就可到達。（第8天）

12. 今天我有點不舒服；大概昨晚受涼了。（第9天）

13. 他們一家人每晚睡覺從不遲於10點鐘。（第10天）

14. 甲：你明天什麼時候來？

    乙：恐怕不會早於8點鐘。（第10天）

15. 那學生很守時，每天上課從不遲到。（第11天）

16. 甲：他在工廠裏工作怎樣？

    乙：他是個好工人，工作努力，從不請假。（第12天）

17. 我們來得正好。如果遲了3分鐘的話，就會趕不上火車。（第13天）

18. 他剛剛在這裏。如果你要找他的話，可在這裏等他。（第14天）

19. 時間過得真快，我學習英語已有3年。我一定要好好利用時間把它學好。（第15，16天）

20. 甲：他明天會回來嗎？

    乙：不，他要到下星期才回來，這星期不會有空。（第18天）

21. 我的兄弟每隔兩天跟一位英國教師學英語，到現在已有4個月了。（第16，19天）

22. 星期天我去看個朋友，晚飯後才回家。（第21，22天）

23. 甲：你是哪一年出生的？

    乙：我是1948年出生的，今年32歲。（第23天）

24. 甲：你今年幾歲？

乙：我今年50歲。

　　甲：眞的嗎？我以爲你只有40歲。（第24天）

25. 昨天碰到20年不見的一位同學。他老得幾乎使我不認得了。（第25天）

26. 我告訴他20年前我們同在一間學校唸過書。（第26天）

27. 20年前他見過我的父親。那時候他還是個10來歲的孩子。（第25，26天）

28. 他的哥哥已經40出頭，比他要大四五歲。（第27，28天）

29. 甲：你的祖父今年幾歲？

　　乙：他已經過了70歲。

　　甲：眞的嗎？他看上去還不到這年齡。（第24，29天）

30. 他的父親年紀大了，但身體還是很好。下一個生日將是80歲了。

　　（第29，30天）

# 第 2 月
# 天氣、寒暖、季節

## 第 1 天

"今天天氣怎樣？"

"今天天氣很好，但天氣預報說明天天氣要變。"

"只要不下雨就好。"

### 【說明】

"天氣"：weather，也可用 it 來替代，如 It is fine today。"天氣怎樣？"可說 How is the weather? 或 What is the weather like?。

"天氣預報"是 weather forecast 或 forecast；"天氣預報說"：The weather forecast says，或改成詞組 according to the weather forecast 也可。

"天氣要變"：it will make a change，或 there will be a change。

### 【譯例】

(a) "How is the weather today? " " It's fine. But the weather forecast says it will make a change tomorrow. " "It'll be all right as long as it doesn't rain. "

(b) "What is the weather like today? " "Fine. But according to the weather forecast there will be a change tomorrow. " "It ll be OK so long as it doesn't rain. "

# 第2天

"按時節來説現在是冷了點，是嗎？""是的，而且今天似乎比昨天還冷，以後甚至可能會變得更冷呢。"

【説明】

"按時節來說"可說 for the time of year, 或 at this time of year; year 之前可以有冠詞 the, 但不用的多。

"以後"說 later, later on, hereafter 都可以。

"可能"maybe, probably, possibly, 或 It is probable that…, It is possible that…。

"變得更冷"：turn colder, get colder

【譯例】

(a) "It's rather cold for the time of year, isn't it?"
"Yes, and it seems colder today than yesterday. Maybe it's going to turn even colder later on."

(b) "Isn't it a bit too cold at this time of year?"
"Yes, and it seems that today is colder than yesterday. It's possible that it will get even colder hereafter."

# 第3天

今年春天不知爲甚麼來得這麼遲。郊區桃花還未開。我記得去年此時早已開了。

【説明】

"不知"可譯作 wonder 後跟 why, where, when, if, how, what 等疑問詞。這個句型在口語中是常用的，如：

"我不知他爲甚麼還不來。"I wonder why he hasn't come yet.

"我不知他們從哪裏來的。"I wonder where they came from.

"她不知他甚麼時候回來。"She wondered when he would be back.

"來得遲"：be late (in) coming

"花開"：come out, open, be in blossom 都可以；如以桃樹爲主語，也可用 blossom 或 flower 作動詞。

"去年此時"：this time last year；"去年此時桃花已開"要說 The peach blossoms had already opened by this time last year，這裏動詞用過去完成時表示過去，也即"去年此時"，已經完成的動作。

## 【譯例】

(a) I wonder why spring is so late in coming this year. The peach blossoms on the outskirts haven't come out yet. I remember they had already opened by this time last year.

(b) I wonder why spring is so late in coming this year. The peach trees on the outskirts haven't yet flowered though they had already blossomed by this time last year, I remember.


# 第4天

春天來了，天氣一天天地暖和起來了。公園裏的花即將盛開。

## 【說明】

"一天天"：day by day; from day to day。

"暖和起來": grow warmer; get warmer and warmer。

"即將": soon, before long; 改成句子可說 It will not be long before…。

"盛開": be out 或 be in full bloom

## 【譯例】

(a) Spring is coming. It's growing warmer day by day. The flowers in the park will soon be in full bloom.

(b) As spring is coming, it's getting warmer and warmer. The flowers in the park are going to open before long.

(c) Spring is in the air. It will not be long before the flowers in the park are out, as it is growing warmer day by day.

# 第5天

春光明媚，如此良辰，呆在家裏實在太傻了。

## 【說明】

"明媚"對天氣來說可用 charming; enchanting。

"如此良辰"在這裏作狀語可說 such a fine day, 或 such magnificent weather。

"呆在家裏": stay at home; keep indoors

"實在太傻"可說 it's really too foolish to…。如要指誰太傻，可以在 foolish 之後加上 of you, of him 等字樣即可。

## 【譯例】

(a) Spring is charming. It's really too foolish to stay at home on

32

such a fine day.

(b) The scene of spring is enchanting. It's foolish of you to keep indoors in such magnificent weather.

# 第6天

今天天氣多好啊！到郊外去作一次春遊怎樣？

## 【說明】

"郊外"：suburbs，作狀語要說 in the suburbs。（比較：on the outskirts）

"春遊"：spring outing

"怎樣？"是向對方建議，可說"What do you say to…?"（注意：這個 to 是介詞）；How about…? 或 Do you feel like…?也可說 Feel like…? 。

## 【譯例】

(a) What fine weather today! How about having a spring outing in the suburbs?

(b) How lovely the weather is today! What do you say to a spring outing in the suburbs?

(c) How splendid it is today! Feel like having a spring outing in the suburbs?

# 第7天

在風和日麗的春日裏，沒有比漫步海濱更為愉快的了。

## 【說明】

"在風和日麗的春日裏"可說 on a warm and sunny spring day 或 on a sunny spring day with a warm wind blowing, 也可說 in spring when the weather is warm and sunny, 這裏用關係副詞 when 連接起來作爲從句去說明 spring。

"沒有比…更 …": Nothing is more … than …, 或 There is nothing so…as…。

"海濱"on ( 或 along ) the beach ( 或 seashore )

## 【譯例】

(a) Nothing is more pleasant than to take a walk on the beach on a warm and sunny spring day.

(b) There is nothing so pleasant as to take a walk along the seashore on a sunny spring day with a warm wind blowing.

# 第 8 天

天像要下雨。你最好把傘帶去。

## 【說明】

"天像要下雨"可說 It looks like rain, It is likely to rain, It is threatening to rain, 也可說 The weather is threatening (to rain), 或以 rain 作主語寫成 There is rain coming。

"最好": You had better, 後面加沒有 to 的不定詞, 在會話裏也可省去 you had, 只說 Better…。注意: had better 沒有時態的變化。

34

**【譯例】**

(a) It looks like rain, so you had better take an umbrella with you.

(b) You had better take your umbrella with you; the weather is threatening.

(c) There is rain coming; better carry an umbrella.

# 第9天

從前天晚上起，雨下下停停，停停下下，不知哪天轉晴。

**【說明】**

"下下停停、停停下下"可用副詞詞組 off and on 或副詞 intermittently（間斷地）；intermittent rain 則是"間斷雨"是形容詞加名詞。

"轉晴"：clear up

**【譯例】**

(a) It has been raining off and on since the night before last. I wonder when it will clear up.

(b) There has been intermittent rains since the night before last. I wonder when we shall have fine weather.

(c) The weather has been unsettled with intermittent rains since the night before last. I wonder when we shall see the sun again.

# 第10天

我們明天出發到郊外去遠足，風雨無阻。

"出發": set out; start

"遠足": excursion; trip

"風雨無阻" 可說 rain or shine, 或 whether it rains or not; 也可說 whatever the weather may be。

【譯例】

(a)We are going to make an excursion to the countryside to-morrow, rain or shine.

(b) We are setting out on an excursion to the countryside to-morrow, whether it rains or not.

(c) Whatever the weather may be, we'll set out on a trip to the countryside tomorrow.

# 第11天

昨天我在學校回家路上遇到驟雨，成了落湯鷄。

【說明】

"在學校回家路上" 可說 on my way home from school。

"遇到驟雨": be caught in a shower; 如說 "突然下起驟雨", 也可譯作 All of a sudden it started showering, 或 Suddenly the rain poured down。

"成了落湯鷄" 是一句俗語, 是 "淋得濕透" 的意思, 所以不能照字譯, 要說 be wet through and through, be drenched to the skin, 或 be thoroughly soaked。

(a) Yesterday I was caught in a shower on my way home from school and was wet through and through.

(b) I was on my way home from school yesterday when all of a sudden it started showering and I was drenched to the skin.

(c) Yesterday the rain suddenly poured down while I was on my way home from school; naturally, I was thoroughly soaked.

# 第12天

春雨過後，空氣清新，微風吹拂，眞想到一片新綠的山上走走。

## 【說明】

"春雨過後"：after the spring rain。

"清新"：pure and fresh; pure and refreshing; 單說 fresh 也可。

"微風"：gentle breeze; light wind; soft wind。

"吹拂"：blow

"眞想…"是表示說話人的願望，可說 I should like, I wish, 或用感嘆句 How I wish…! 也可。

"一片新綠的山"：hills covered with soft green grass。

## 【譯例】

(a) After the spring rain, the air is pure and fresh, and the light wind is blowing. I should like to walk on the hills covered with soft green grass.

(b) After the spring rain the air is fresh and the gentle breeze is blowing. How I wish I could wander in the hills covered with soft green grass!

# 第13天

電台廣播說："今天白天多雲，傍晚前後有陣陣雷雨。"

## 【說明】

"電台廣播說"： the radio（或 broadcast）says, 或 according to the radio (broadcast)

"白天"： in the daytime; during the day

"多雲"： cloudy

"傍晚前後"： towards the evening

"陣陣雷雨"： thunder showers

## 【譯例】

(a) The radio says that today it will be cloudy in the daytime and there will be thunder showers towards the evening.

(b) According to the radio broadcast, it will be cloudy during the day and we are going to have thunder showers towards the evening.

# 第14天

下午一直下毛毛雨，還不像會停止。我希望明天能轉晴。

"下毛毛雨": drizzle, 這是名詞, 也是動詞。

"停止": stop; let up; 或用名詞 let-up。

**【譯例】**

(a) It's been drizzling all afternoon and it doesn't seem to let up. I hope it will clear up tomorrow.

(b) The drizzle has been going on all afternoon and yet there is no sign of its stopping. Let's hope it will clear up tomorrow.

(c) It has been drizzling all afternoon without any sign of let-up. I wish it would clear up tomorrow.

# 第15天

今年梅雨季節比往年大概早一星期開始, 看來我們要遭遇一段長時間的多雨天氣。

**【說明】**

"梅雨季節": rainy season, rainy 是 "多雨" 的意思。

"比往年早": earlier than usual

"開始": begin; start; set in

"遭遇" be in for, 一般指不愉快的事情, 如不好的天氣、疾病等。這一句型在口語中是常用的, 如 We are in for showers (我們會遭遇陣雨, 也即 "天將要下陣雨" 的意思), I am afraid she is in for a cold (我怕她會受涼)。

"一段時間": a spell, 指某種天氣一段持續時間, 如 a spell

of cold weather, 或 a cold spell；也可指某種疾病發作的一段時間，如 a spell of coughing（咳嗽）。

【譯例】

(a) This year the rainy season has begun about a week earlier than usual. It seems we are in for a long spell of rainy weather.

(b) This year the rainy season has set in a week or so earlier than it usually does. It looks as if we are in for a long spell of rainy weather.

# 第16天

驚雷響過之後，天氣馬上變熱了，過了梅雨季節就是夏天。

【說明】

"雷響"：thunderclaps; thunder rolls 或 rolls of thunder

"天氣馬上變熱"：it has immediately got hot 或 the hot weather has set in at once.

【譯例】

(a) After some awful thunderclaps, it has immediately got hot. The rainy season is over and summer has set in.

(b) After some awful thunder rolls, the hot weather has set in at once. The wet season is gone and summer is with us.

# 第17天

昨晚徹夜雷電交作，我一點也睡不着。

40

【說明】

"徹夜"可說 all night, all night long, 或 all the night through, throughout the night。

"雷電"thunder and lightning, lightning 是名詞;"雷電交作"可說 be thundering and lightening, lightening 是分詞, 注意它與名詞不同的拼寫。

"一點也睡不着"可說 could not sleep at all, 或 could not get a wink of sleep, could not sleep a wink 也可。

【譯例】

(a) Last night, I could not sleep at all, as it was thundering and lightening all night.

(b) Last night, I could not sleep a wink owing to the thunders and lightnings all the night through.

(c) Last night, the thunder and lightning were going on throughout the night, so I couldn't get a wink of sleep.

# 第18天

前晚大雨傾盆, 這是我到這裏來第一次碰到這樣大的雨。

【說明】

"前晚": the night before last

"大雨": heavy rain, heavy rainfall, heavy downpour, 或 torrential rain; "大雨傾盆": The rain pours (或 pelts) down, 或 It rains cats and dogs.

(a) In the night before last, rain was pouring down. This was the heaviest rainfall I have known since I came here.

(b) The night before last it was raining cats and dogs. I've never seen such a torrential rain since I came here.

# 第19天

天氣預報3號颱風訊號已經掛起，預計今天下午有暴雨。

## 【說明】

" 3 號颱風訊號 ": Typhoon signal No. 3

" 掛起 ": hoist

## 【譯例】

(a) The weather forecast says that typhoon signal No. 3 has been hoisted. We are likely in for a torrential rain this afternoon.

(b) According to the weather forecast, typhoon signal No. 3 has been hoisted. Torrential rains are likely to set in this afternoon.

# 第20天

多悶熱的天氣啊！今天氣溫已上升到攝氏40度左右，我在渾身流汗。

## 【說明】

"悶熱": sultry; muggy

"氣溫": temperature

"上升": go up, rise; "下降" 可說 go down; drop, fall。

"攝氏寒暑表": centigrade thermometer 或 Celsius thermometer; "華氏寒暑表": Fahrenheit thermometer。"攝氏 40 度左右" 可說 It's about (或 around) forty degrees, centigrade, 或簡寫為 40℃。"華氏 70 度" It's seventy degrees, Fahrenheit, 或簡寫為 70℉。在 "零度以上" 說 above (zero), 如 It's two degrees above (zero); 在 "零度以下" 說 below (zero), 如 It's five degrees below (zero)。

"渾身流汗": sweat (或 perspire) all over, wet with sweat all over

## 【譯例】

(a) What a sultry weather! Today's temperature has already gone up to about forty degrees, centigrade. I'm wet with sweat all over.

(b) How muggy it is! The temperature today has already risen to around 40°C. I'm sweating all over.

# 第21天

"濃雲密佈，天大概要下雨。""啊呀，已經開始掉雨點，幾秒鐘之後就要下大雨了。"

## 【說明】

"濃雲密佈" 可以說: The sky is clouding over, 這裏 cloud

（雲）是用作動詞；此外，也可用形容詞 cloudy 說 It's coming over cloudy。

"啊呀" 是嘆詞，可用 Oh! Oh, my! 或單用 My 也可。

"掉雨點"：sprinkle

"幾秒鐘之後" 照字譯是 after a few seconds；但動詞如為將來時要說 in a few seconds，如 "一小時之後她會回來" 要說 She will come back in an hour，不可說 after an hour。

### 【譯例】

(a) "The sky is clouding over. Probably we are going to have a shower ." "Oh, it's already begun sprinkling' It will be pouring in a few seconds. "

(b) "It's coming over cloudy. A shower is likely to set in ." "Oh, my, it's beginning to sprinkle, and there will be a downpour in a few seconds. "

# 第22天

"上星期的雹暴多大呀！" "可不是嗎？有些雹子像鷄蛋一樣大，還壞了不少農作物呢。"

### 【說明】

"雹暴"：hailstorm； "雹子"：hailstone

"像…一樣" 可用 as…as 的句型,如 "我的錶像你的錶一樣好" My watch is as good as yours (your watch)。如 "不及…好" 要說 not so…as, 或 not as… as, 如 My watch is not so good as yours。

"農作物"：crop

(a) "What a big hailstorm we had last week! "

"Yes, wasn't it? Some of the hailstones were as big as eggs and they did much harm to the crops. "

(b) "How big the hailstorm was last week! "

"Yes, it certainly was! The hailstones, some of which were as big as eggs, did lots of harm to the crops. "

# 第23天

你到過地中海沿岸嗎?去年夏天我在地中海沿岸避暑, 那確是我所知道的最好的避暑勝地之一。

【說明】

"到過"要說 have  been, 不可說 have  gone。have  gone 是 "去了, 不在這裏"的意思。

"避暑"可說 go for the summer 或 spend the summer。

【譯例】

(a) Have you been to the Mediterranean coast? I was there last summer. It's really one of the best summer resorts I have ever known.

(b) You haven't been to the Mediterranean coast, have you? I spent my holidays there last summer. I bet it's one of the most wonderful summer resorts I have ever known.

# 第24天

"秋天很可愛，是嗎？""是的，特別在炎炎長夏之後，這樣涼快的天氣真使人心曠神怡，我希望能一直如此。"

## 【說明】

"炎炎長夏"the long hot summer, 或 a long spell of summer heat

"心曠神怡"：happy and relaxed

"一直如此"是"天氣一直這樣好"的意思，可譯為 stay like this, 或 keep fine like this。

## 【譯例】

(a) "Lovely autumn, isn't it?" "Yes, it sure is, especially after the long hot summer. Such cool weather makes us happy and relaxed, I hope it will stay like this."

(b) "Isn't it a beautiful autumn day?" "Yes, it certainly is! We feel happy and relaxed in such cool weather, especially after a long spell of summer heat. I hope it will keep fine like this."

# 第25天

風在呼嘯，氣溫在下降，今天晚上一定會極冷。

## 【說明】

"呼嘯"：howl; roar

"冰凍"：freeze

## 【譯例】

46

(a) The wind is howling and the temperature is falling.  It's certain that it's going to freeze tonight.

(b) How the wind roars! The temperature is getting low. I'm sure it will freeze tonight.

# 第26天

雪下得很大。像這樣紛紛揚揚的下去，明天一定會積得很厚。

## 【說明】

"雪" snow 可作名詞，也可作動詞。"雪下得大" 可說 It is snowing hard ( 或 heavily )，也可說 The snow is falling heavily，或 The snow is falling thick and fast。

"紛紛揚揚"：be scattering

"積得厚"：be very thick; be pretty deep

## 【譯例】

(a) It's snowing very hard. If it goes on scattering like this, the snow will be very thick tomorrow.

(b) The snow is falling thick and fast. It will be pretty deep tomorrow if it keeps on scattering at this rate.

(c) How heavily the snow is falling! I'm sure it will be pretty deep if it continues scattering like this.

# 第27天

"你喜歡夏天還是冬天？" "我喜歡冬天，因為冬天雖冷，却是

*溜冰滑雪的好時節。"*

"喜歡哪一個？"要說 Which do you like better? better 之後，如有比較的事物要用 than，如 I like winter better than summer。此外，也可說 Which do you prefer? prefer 之後，如有對比的事物，就要用 to，如 I prefer winter to summer。

"溜冰"：skate

"滑雪"：ski

【譯例】

(a) "Which season do you like better, summer or winter?" "I like winter better, because it's the best season for skating and skiing though the weather is cold."

(b) "Which do you prefer, summer or winter?" "I prefer winter to summer, because in winter I can enjoy skating and skiing though it is cold."

(c) "Which do you prefer, summer or winter?" "I prefer winter. Though cold, winter is the best time for skating and skiing."

# 第28天

因為今天早晨氣溫低至零下5度，昨晚下的雪凍結了，所以路上很滑，腳下不留神就會摔交的。

【說明】

"低至零下5度" be（或 register）as low as 5 degrees below zero; register（儀表）是 "顯示，表明" 的意思。

"滑"：slippery

"脚下留神"：watch（或 mind）one's step

## 【譯例】

(a) As the temperature is as low as 5 degrees below zero this morning, the snow that fell last night has frozen hard. The road is very slippery. If you don't watch your step, you will fall.

(b) The temperature is registered as low as 5 degrees below zero this morning, so the snow that fell last night has become frozen. The road is very slippery. You must mind your step, or you will fall.

(c) The temperature is as low as 5 degrees below zero this morning, so the snow that fell last night has frozen very hard. Mind your step, or you will fall because the road is very slippery.


# 第29天

今年冬天是幾年來最暖和的了。連我這個身體單薄的人也沒得過感冒。

## 【說明】

"幾年來最暖和的冬天" 可說 It's the mildest winter（we have had）in recent years, 這是假定說話時冬天還未過去，如已過去，那麼動詞就要用過去時，如 Yesterday was the coldest day we have had for several weeks。

"連我這個身體單薄的人" 可譯作 even such a weak man as I, even a delicate man like myself, 或 even a man of delicate

49

health like myself。

"得（過）感冒"可說 catch cold 和 catch a cold; 也可說 take cold, 在這裏 cold 之前不用 a; 但如用 have 作動詞，則必須用 a, 說 have a cold; 如 cold 之前有形容詞，也必須用 a, 如 catch（或 take）a bad cold。

**【譯例】**

(a) It's the mildest winter we have had in recent years and even such a weak man as I haven't taken cold.

(b) This winter is the mildest we have had for some years, so that even a delicate man like myself can get through it without having a cold.

(c) We have been enjoying the mildest winter we have had these years, so even a man of delicate health like myself could get through it without catching a cold.


# 第30天

我不在乎嚴寒的天氣。我認為冬天是從事運動的好季節。經過冬天一段時間的鍛煉後，會感到身體很好。

**【說明】**

"在乎"：mind; 這個詞常用於疑問或否定句裏, 如 Do you mind cold weather? I don't mind cold weather; 如表示動作則 mind 之後要用動名詞，如 I don't mind walking some distance, Do you mind my opening the window?（我可以開窗嗎？）

"嚴寒"：bitter（或 severe）cold weather, 或 the bitter（或 severe）cold, 這裏 cold 作名詞用。

50

"我認為"：I think, I believe, I hold, I consider 或 in my opinion 都可以。

"從事運動"：get（或 go）in for sport

"一段時間"：a period

"身體很好"：feel quite fit

## 【譯例】

(a) I don't mind bitter cold weather. I think winter is the best season to get in for sport. After a period of training in winter, I'll feel quite fit.

(b) I don't mind the severe cold. In my opinion, winter is the best time we go in for sport. You will feel quite fit after a period of training in winter.

# Words and Expressions

| | |
|---|---|
| weather forecast [ˈfɔː-kɑːst] | 天氣預報 |
| for the time of year | 按時節來說 |
| be late (in) coming | 來得遲 |
| this time last year | 去年此時 |
| day by day; from day to day | 一天天地 |
| The flowers are in full bloom. | 花已盛開 |
| before long | 即將，不久 |
| on such a fine day; in such magnificent [mægˈnifisnt] weather | （在）如此良辰 |
| in the suburbs [ˈsʌbəːbz] | 郊外 |

| | |
|---|---|
| spring outing | 春遊 |
| What do you say to…? Do you feel like…? | …你以為怎樣?(向對方建議) |
| on a sunny spring day with a warm wind blowing | 在風和日麗的春日裏 |
| It looks like rain. The weather is threatening (to rain). | 天像要下雨 |
| It rains off and on. | 間斷地下雨 |
| intermittent [ˌintə(:)´mitənt] rain | 間斷雨 |
| It clears up. | 天轉晴 |
| make an excursion [iks´kə:fən] to… | 到…去遠足 |
| rain or shine; whether it rains or not | 風雨無阻 |
| be caught in a shower | 遇到驟雨 |
| be drenched to the skin; be wet through and through | 淋得濕透 |
| The gentle breeze is blowing | 微風吹拂 |
| according to the radio (broadcast) | 據電台廣播 |
| in the daytime | 在白天 |
| towards evening | 傍晚 |
| thunder shower | 雷陣雨 |
| It's drizzling. | 天在下毛毛雨 |
| The rainy season sets in. | 梅雨季節開始了 |
| a spell of cold (hot) weather (coughing [´kɔfiŋ]) | 一陣冷(熱)天氣(咳嗽) |
| We are in for showers. | 將下陣雨 |

52

| | |
|---|---|
| all of a sudden | 突然地 |
| all night (long); all the night through; throughout the night | 徹夜 |
| can't sleep a wink | 一點也睡不着 |
| The rain pours [pɔ:z] down. It rains cats and dogs. | 大雨傾盆 |
| sweat [swet] all over | 渾身流汗 |
| The sky is clouding over. | 濃雲密佈 |
| It sprinkles. | 掉雨點 |
| go for the summer; spend the summer | 避暑 |
| summer resort [riˊzɔ:t] | 避暑勝地 |
| the long hot summer | 炎炎長夏 |
| happy and relaxed | 心曠神怡 |
| The wind is howling. | 風在呼嘯 |
| The snow is scattering. | 雪在紛紛揚揚地下 |
| skate | 溜冰 |
| ski | 滑雪 |
| The temperature is（或 registers) as low as 5 degrees below zero. | 氣溫低至零下5度 |
| the mildest winter (we have had) in recent years | 近年來最暖和的冬天 |
| Do you mind⋯ -ing(⋯)? | 你在乎⋯嗎？ |
| get（或 go) in for sport | 從事運動 |
| feel quite fit | 身體很好 |

# Exercise 2

Translate the following into English:

1. 甲: 明天天氣怎樣?

   乙: 天氣預報說明天要下雨。(第1天)

2. 今天天氣倒是好的, 但按時節來說似乎太冷了些。(第2天)

3. 現在已經3點鐘了, 不知他爲甚麼還不來。(第3天)

4. 今年春天來得早, 郊區桃花已盛開。我記得去年此時還沒有開哩。(第3天)

5. 現在是春天, 天氣很暖和。公園裏的花一天天地多起來了。(第4天)

6. 春光明媚, 我們到公園裏去散散步好嗎?(第5天)

7. 如此良辰我們不出去玩玩(enjoy ourselves)實在太傻了。(第5天)

8. 今天天氣好熱! 我們到海濱游泳去(go for a swim at the seaside)怎樣?(第6天)

9. 在這樣風和日麗的日子裏, 沒有比到郊野作一次春遊更愉快的了。(第6, 7天)

10. 甲: 你看今天會下雨嗎?

    乙: 會的, 你最好帶着雨衣。(第8天)

11. 他時斷時續地學了3年英語, 但沒有多大進步(make little progress)。(第9天)

12. 我們打算下星期到郊外去遠足, 但從昨天起一直下雨, 不知哪天轉晴。(第9, 10天)

13. 甲：音樂會（concert）何時舉行（take place）？

乙：下星期三舉行，風雨無阻。（第10天）

14. 上星期我們出去春遊，在回來的路上遇到大雨，每個人都成了落湯鷄。（第11天）

15. 昨天晚上下了一場雨。今天早上空氣清新，眞想到田野裏去散散步。（第12天）

16. 據電台廣播，今天下午多雲，傍晚有小雨。（第14天）

17. 天正在下毛毛雨，不知甚麼時候會轉晴。（第14天）

18. 梅雨季節已經開始。連日來（for the last few days）小雨時斷時續，空氣很潮濕（damp）。（第9，15天）

19. 甲：廣播電台說天要下小雨。

乙：只要不下大雨就好。（第13天）

20. 今年冬天比往年來得早，看來我們要遭遇一段長時間的寒冷天氣。（第15天）

21. 她的嬰孩昨晚徹夜啼哭，我們一點也睡不着。（第17天）

22. 你知道颱風已接近這個地區嗎？昨晚暴雨大概就是因爲颱風的關係。（第19天）

23. 天氣很悶熱，大家都汗流浹背，這是我到這裏來第一次碰到的這樣熱的天氣。（第18，20天）

24. 甲：看呀，天空濃雲密佈，就要下大雨了。

乙：下雨以後氣溫就會下降，這倒是好的。（第20，21天）

25. 昨晚大雨傾盆，根據天氣預報，一二天之後還會有大雨，雨太多怕會損害農作物。（第18，22天）

26. 我到過許多避暑勝地，我認爲地中海沿岸是其中最好的。（第23天）

27. 夏天郊外要比城裏涼快得多，所以我希望能到那裏去避暑。（第23，24天）

28. 雪下得很大，氣溫在下降，明天可能會結冰。天氣雖然寒冷，却是溜冰滑雪的好時節。（第25，26，27天）

29. 下雪以後路上很滑，出去時脚下要留神，否則就會摔交。（第28天）

30. 我不在乎每天跑些路，因爲跑步是很好的運動。經過一段時間的鍛煉我相信身體會很好。（第30天）

# 第 3 月
# 交際、訪問、通信

## 第 1 天

*"久違了。你好嗎？" "托你的福，很好。"*

### 【說明】

"久違了"：這是句客套話，可作不同的理解，如爲"好久不見"的意思，可譯成 I haven't seen you for a long time。如爲"久疏問候，很抱歉"的意思，可譯成 Excuse me for my long silence，或 I'm sorry I haven't asked after you for a long time。

"你好嗎？"：Are you well? / Are you keeping well? / How are you? / How are you getting along? / Are you all right? 都可以。

"托你的福"：這是句客套話，英語裏不能照譯，可說 I'm happy to say (that)…，或只說 Happy to say (that)…也可。

### 【譯例】

(a) "I haven't seen you for a long time. How are you getting along?" "I'm happy to say I'm keeping well."

(b) "Excuse me for my long silence. I hope you are keeping well." "Happy to say, I'm getting along well"

(c) "I'm sorry I haven't asked after you for a long time. Are you all right?" "Happy to say I'm fine."

# 第2天

"最近不大看到你。你搬了家還是怎麼的？" "不，我出去度假了。前天才回來。"

【說明】

"不大看到你"可說 I haven't seen much of you, I haven't seen you for some time, 或 You are quite a stranger。

"最近"：recently; lately 或 of late

"搬家"：move (house)

"…還是怎麼的？"：… or something? 這是比較委婉的問話，如 Are you ill or something?（你病了還是怎麼的？）

"度假"：be away on holiday; spend one's holidays

【譯例】

(a) "I haven't seen much of you recently. Have you moved or something?" "No, I was away on holiday and just got back the day before yesterday."

(b) "You are quite a stranger of late. Have you moved house or something?" "No, I was spending my holidays and didn't come back till the day before yesterday."

# 第3天

"很高興你光臨，請坐。你面色不大好，是病了還是怎麼的？" "是的，前幾天受涼發過燒。現在已經好了。"

【說明】

58

"光臨"是句客套話,在英語裏只說 You come to see me 或 drop in 就可以了。

"面色(不)好": (not) look well (或 fresh)

"發燒": have ( 或 run) a fever; have ( 或 run) a temperature

"好了": be all right; be well

## 【譯例】

(a) "I am very glad that you have come to see me. Please be seated. You don't look very well. Are you ill or something? "
"Yes, I caught cold and was having a fever a few days ago, but now I am all right. "

(b) "Very glad that you have dropped in. Won't you sit down? You don't look so fresh. Are you ill or something? "
"Yes, I had a cold and was running a temperature a few days ago, but I'm well now. "

# 第4天

前天你光臨時我湊巧出去旅行了, 實在對不起。這幾天有空請再過來好嗎?

## 【說明】

"湊巧": happen; "湊巧不在家" 可說 I happened to be not at home, 或 It happened that I was not at home。

"出去旅行": be away on a journey

"實在對不起": be very sorry

(a) I'm very sorry that I happened to be on a journey when you came to see me the other day. Please come again in a day or two when you are free.

(b) I am very sorry, I happened to be not at home when you dropped in the other day. I was on a journey then. I hope you will come again soon if you have time.

(c) How very sorry to have missed your call the other day! It happened that I was on a journey. Would you please come again in a day or two when you have time?

# 第5天

" 對不起，勞你久等了。""不要緊。"

【說明】

" 對不起 " 除了 I'm very sorry 之外，也可說 Excuse me, Pardon me 等。

" 勞你久等 " 是 Keep you waiting; 因為是已經等得久了，所以要說 have kept you waiting。

" 不要緊 "：Never mind, 或 That's quite all right。

【譯例】

(a) " I'm sorry to have kept you waiting. "
" Never mind. "

(b) " Excuse me for having kept you waiting. "
" It's quite all right. "

# 第6天

伯頓先生，我可以把我的朋友瓊斯先生介紹給你嗎？他熱心研究英國文學。他有幾個問題要向你請教。

## 【說明】

"介紹"：introduce；用這個動詞要注意不可有兩個賓語，如不可說 May I introduce you my friend Mr. Jones? 要說 May I introduce my friend Mr. Jones to you?

"熱心研究"：study enthusiastically

"請教"：ask for advice; consult

## 【譯例】

(a) Mr. Burton, may I introduce to you my friend Mr. Jones? He is enthusiastically studying English Literature. He has some questions to ask you for advice.

(b) Mr. Burton, allow me to introduce to you my friend Mr. Jones. He is an eager student of English Literature and wishes to consult you on（或 about）a few questions.

(c) Mr. Burton, may I have the pleasure of introducing my friend Mr. Jones to you? He would like to consult you on a few questions about English Literature which he is now enthusiastically studying.

# 第7天

"你認識庫克先生嗎？""不，我不認識，你可以替我介紹嗎？"
"很樂意為你介紹。"

"我不認識"可譯作 I don't think so, I'm afraid not, 或 I haven't had the pleasure (of meeting him)。這樣說比較婉轉，後一說法更客氣些。

"很樂意爲你介紹"：I'll be glad to, to 後省去了動詞 introduce (you to him)。這種省略是根據前文而來，如 You may leave if you want to。

【譯例】

(a) "Do you know Mr. Cook?" "No, I don't think so. Would you introduce me?" "Yes, I would be glad to."

(b) "Do you know Mr. Cook?" "No, I haven't had the pleasure. I hope you will introduce me." "I'll be very glad to."

# 第8天

好像在哪裏遇見過那個人。到底在哪裏我却怎麼也想不起來了。

【說明】

"在哪裏"在前一句裏是"在某一地方"的意思，所以要譯作 somewhere；在後一句裏則是間接的疑問，要譯作 where it was。

"遇見過"表示經驗，可譯作 I have met him。

"怎麼也…"：for the life of me, 常用在否定句裏，放在助動詞和動詞之間，如 I could not for the life of me solve the problem。（我怎麼也解決不了這個問題。）另外，也可用從句 however hard I try 來表達。

62

"想起"：remember; call to mind

(a) I think I have met that man somewhere, but I can't for the life of me remember where it was.

(b) It seems that I have met that man somewhere, though I can't call the occasion to mind, however hard I try.


# 第9天

昨天在公共汽車上遇見中學同學彼德。我們確是好久不見了。

【說明】

"在公共汽車上"：on a bus

"遇見"指偶然相遇，要說 come across; meet with。

"中學"：secondary school；"中學同學"：a classmate at secondary school, 或 a secondary-school classmate。

"確是好久不見了"可譯作 It's been quite a long time since I saw him last（或 since we parted），或 We haven't seen each other for a long time。

【譯例】

(a) I met with Peter, one of my secondary-school classmates, on a bus yesterday. We had not seen each other for a long time.

(b) Yesterday I came across Peter on a bus. He was at the same secondary school with me. It's been quite a long time since I saw him last.

(c) Yesterday I met with Peter, a secondary-school classmate of mine, on a bus. I haven't seen him for a long time since we parted.

# 第10天

他平時不大說話，朋友也少；但因為很信守諾言，所以受到大家的信賴。

【說明】

"他不大說話"：He doesn't talk much；也可譯作 He is a man of few words。（他是個不大說話的人。）

"他信守諾言"：He keeps his promises（或 word），He is true to his word；或 He is a man of his word。（他是個信守諾言的人。）注意：a man of his word 裏的 his 一字不能因人稱不同而變化；如應該說 I'm a man of his word，不能說 I'm a man of my word；應該說 You are a man of his word，不能說 You are a man of your word。

"信賴"：trust; rely upon

【譯例】

(a) He doesn't talk much and has few friends; but as he always keeps his promises, he is relied upon by everybody.

(b) Though he is a man of few words and has not many friends, he is trusted by everybody as he is always true to his word.

(c) He doesn't talk much, nor has he many friends; but everybody trusts him because he is a man of his word.

# 第11天

我們從小時候起就互相認識。

## 【說明】

"從小時候起"：since childhood, 或改用從句說 ever since we were children 也可。

"互相認識"：know each other; 因為用了 since, 所以動詞要用現在完成時 have known each other 來表示動作繼續到現在。此外，也可說 have been acquainted with each other, 但要注意 acquaint 的用法及後面需用介詞 with。

## 【譯例】

(a) We have known each other since childhood.

(b) We have been acquainted with each other ever since we were children.

# 第12天

在英國逗留期間我認識了名叫威廉的英國人。從此我常常在圖書館裏見到他。

## 【說明】

"在英國逗留期間"：during my stay in England; 也可改成 while I was staying in England, 或 while staying in England。

"名叫…的英國人"an Englishman named…, 或改用從句whose

name is … 也可。

"認識"可照前例譯爲 be (get) acquainted with; 也可說 make the acquaintance of。注意 acquainted 和 acquaintance 之後用不同的介詞。

"從此"在這裏是"從那時開始"的意思，可用 since then, 或 ever since。

"常常"：from time to time; now and then

【譯例】

(a) During my stay in England, I got acquainted with an Englishman named William. Since then I have seen him at the library from time to time.

(b) While I was staying in England, I made the acquaintance of an Englishman whose name is William. I have seen him at the library now and then ever since.

(c) While staying in England, I got acquainted with an Englishman named William. I have often seen him at the library since then.


# 第13天

"在貴地逗留期間承蒙關注，不勝感激。""不要客氣，希望你不久再來。"

【說明】

"貴地"：這是漢語客套，不可照譯，只說 here 就可以了。

"關注"指別人的好意，可譯作 kindness。

66

"不勝感激": thank you very much for…, be very grateful for…, 或 feel very much indebted for…。

"不要客氣": 這是別人向你道謝時的答語, 可說 Don't mention it, You are welcome, 或 It has been a pleasure。後一句的意思是"對你關注是我的樂事", 是一種比較客氣的說法。

"希望你不久再來"是 I expect you to come again very soon, I hope to meet you again very soon, 或 I hope that you can come again very soon。注意: hope 這個動詞後面可接不定詞或以 that 引起的賓語從句, 但不接賓語＋不定詞, 如一般不說 I hope you to come again very soon。

## 【譯例】

(a) "Thank you very much for your kindness during my stay here." "You are welcome, I hope that you can come again very soon."

(b) "I'm really grateful to you for the kindness you have shown me during my stay here." "Don't mention it. Hope to meet you again very soon."

(c) "I feel very much indebted for your kindness while I was staying here." "It has been a pleasure. I expect you to come again very soon."

# 第14天

你幫了個大忙, 我十分感謝。請收下這份薄禮, 略表微忱。

## 【說明】

"幫了大忙": give a lot of help; do a great favour 或 render a big help

"請收下": Please accept…; may I offer…? 或 I beg leave to offer …都可以。

"薄禮": humble gift 或 trifling present

"略表微忱": in token of my gratitude, 或 as a token (或 mark) of my thankfulness

**【譯例】**

(a) You have given me a lot of help. I'm very grateful to you. Please accept this humble present in token of my gratitude.

(b) I'm very grateful to you for the big help you have rendered me. May I offer you this humble gift as a token of my thankfulness?

(c) Thank you very much for the great favour you have shown me. I beg leave to offer you this trifling present in token of my gratitude.

# 第15天

"我們明天駕車到郊外去兜兜風好嗎？""那太好了，謝謝你。""我大約在9點鐘來接你。""好吧，明天見。"

**【說明】**

"駕車兜風": go for a drive

"來接": come over and fetch…, 或 call round for…; 如用汽車接，可說 pick up。

**【譯例】**

68

(a) "Shall we go for a drive in the country tomorrow? "

"That would be very fine. Thank you. " "I'll come to fetch you at about nine. " "Right. See you tomorrow then. "

(b) "How about going for a drive in the country tomorrow? "

"That's fine. Thank you very much. " "I'll call round for you at about nine. " "Ok. I'll see you tomorrow. "

(c) "Would you like to come with me for a drive in the country tomorrow? "

"It's very nice of you. Thank you. " "I'll pick you up at about nine. " "Good. I'll see you tomorrow. "


# 第16天


"今晚你想出去看電影嗎？""我不想去，但還是謝謝你。""那麼我們去喝杯咖啡怎樣？""不，我實在抽不出時間。"

## 【說明】

"去看電影"：go to the films（或 movies, pictures），或 go to the cinema; cinema 是"電影院"。

"我不想去"是"沒有心情做什麼事"的意思，可說 I'm not in the mood for⋯，或 I don't think I will 也可。

"還是謝謝你"：Thank you all the same.

"抽不出時間"can't afford the time，或簡單說 have no time 也可以。

## 【譯例】

(a) "Do you feel like going to the films tonight? "
"I don't think I will. Thank you all the same. "

" Then why don't we just go out for a coffee? "
" No, I really can't afford the time. "

(b)  " How would you like to go to the movies tonight? "
" No, I'm not in the mood for it. Thanks all the same. "
" Then let's go out for a coffee. "  " No, I really have no time. "

# 第17天

"噢，我該走了。""別急，還早呢。""我10點鐘還有個約。"
"既然這樣，我就不留你了。"

## 【說明】

"該走了"可說 I must be leaving（或 going），It's time
for me to leave, 或 It's time (that) I left。注意: 後一種說法是
虛擬語氣，從句裏的動詞要用過去時，如 It's time that we went
（或 should go）to bed。

"別急": What's the hurry? There is no hurry about it, 或
單說 No hurry 也可。

"有約": have an engagement, 或 be engaged

"既然這樣": if so, in that case, 或用從句 if that's the
case 也可。

"留": keep

## 【譯例】

(a)  " Well, I must be leaving. "  " No hurry. It's still early. "
" I have an engagement at ten. "  " If so, I won't keep you any
longer. "

70

(b) "Oh, it's time for me to leave." "What's the hurry? It's early yet." "I have an engagement to fulfil at ten." "In that case, I won't keep you."

(c) "Well, it is time I left." "There is no hurry about it. It's early yet." "I'm engaged at ten." "If that's the case, I won't keep you."

# 第18天

"我是來向你們告別的。""你甚麼時候走?""我乘6:30的火車。""那麼再見了,祝你一切順利。"

## 【說明】

"告別": say ( 或 bid) good-bye to; bid farewell to

"我乘 6:30 的火車"可說 I leave by the 6:30 (train), 或 I'm catching the 6:30 train; 也可說 My train leaves at 6:30。

"一切順利": all the very best, 或說 good luck 也可。

## 【譯例】

(a) "I have come to say good-bye to you." "What time are you leaving?" "I leave by the 6:30." "Good-bye then, and all the very best."

(b) "I come here to bid you good-bye." "When are you off?"
"My train leaves at 6:30." "Farewell then, and good luck."

(c) "I'd like to bid farewell to you." "When are you setting off?"
"I'm catching the 6:30 train." "Well, good-bye, and good luck."

# 第19天

"感謝你來給我送行。""別客氣，祝你一路平安。到家時請代向你家裏人問好。"

【說明】

"送行"：see off

"一路平安"：have a good journey, have a pleasant trip, 或 Bon voyage

"代向…問好"：remember me to…, 或 give my best regards to…

【譯例】

(a) "Thank you for coming to see me off." "Not at all. I wish you a good journey and when you get home, please remember me to your family."

(b) "It's very kind of you to see me off." "Not at all. I hope you have a pleasant trip. Please give my best regards to your family when you are home."

# 第20天

"你以前到過這裏嗎？""是的，曾來過一次。那是1974年我還在大學讀書時的事，是同幾個同學一道來的。"

【說明】

"以前到過這裏"要說 have been here before，不可說 have

72

come here before, 因爲 have come 是現在在這裏, 所以不對。同樣, "來過一次"也要說 have been here once, 不可說 have come here once。但如與確指過去時間的字樣連用, 則動詞要用過去時, 如 I came here once in 1974。

"在大學"可說 at the university 或 at college。注意 college 前不加冠詞。

### 【譯例】

(a) "Have you been here before?" "Yes, I have been here once. That was 1974 when I was studying at the university. I came with a few schoolmates of mine."

(b) "Have you ever been here before?" "Yes, I came here once with a few schoolmates of mine in 1974, when I was still at college."

# 第21天

"喂, 我是約翰。庫柏先生在嗎?" "不, 他不在。我想他買東西去了。要叫他回個電話嗎?" "好的; 他知道我的電話號碼。"

### 【說明】

"我是約翰"在電話裏通常說 This is John here, This is John speaking, 或簡單說 John here, John speaking; 不可說 I'm John, 或 My name is John。

"不在": be not in; be out

"去買東西": go shopping

"回個電話": call back, ring back; "要叫他回個電話嗎?"

如以 you 作主語, 可說 Do you want him to call you back?; 如以 I 作主語, 則說 Shall I have him call you back?'Have some-one do something' 是 "叫某人做某事" 的意思, 如 I'll have my brother fix the bike for you。（我叫我的兄弟把你的自行車修好。）注意: have 後面的不定詞沒有 to。

"電話號碼": (tele)phone number, 只說 number 也可。

## 【譯例】

(a) "Hello. This is John here. Is Mr. Cooper in? " "No, he is out. I think he has gone shopping. Do you want him to call you back? "
"Yes, certainly. He knows my telephone number. "

(b) "Hello. John speaking. Is Mr. Cooper there? " "No, he is not in. He has gone shopping, I am afraid. Shall I have him call you back? "
"Yes, please. He knows my number. "

# 第22天

"喂, 我是約翰。我要同庫柏先生講話。""對不起, 庫柏先生要到下午才來。你在下午 2 點鐘再打電話來好嗎？""好的。"

## 【說明】

"我要同庫柏先生講話", 在電話裏通常說 Can（或 May） I speak to Mr. Cooper? 或 Could I talk to Mr. Cooper? 而不說 I want to speak to Mr. Cooper。

## 【譯例】

(a) "Hello. John here. Can I speak to Mr. Cooper?" "I'm sorry. Mr. Cooper won't be in till this afternoon. Will you call again at two?" "Ok."

(b) "Hello. John speaking. Could I talk to Mr. Cooper?" "Sorry, but Mr. Cooper won't be here until this afternoon. Ring again at two, will you?" "All right."

# 第23天

"請你在庫柏先生回來時告訴他打個電話給我好嗎? 我的電話號碼是583156, 轉接15號分機。""那麼你是誰?""我是約翰。"

## 【說明】

"你是誰?": 在電話裏問對方是誰通常說 Who is this speaking? 如非本人接聽也可說 Who shall I say is calling? 而不說 Who are you?

"分機": extension

## 【譯例】

(a) "Please ask Mr. Cooper to call me when he gets back. My phone number is 583156, extension 15." "Who shall I say is calling?" "John."

(b) "Will you please ask Mr. Cooper to give me a ring when he comes back? My number is 583156, extension 15." "Who shall I say is calling?" "John."

# 第24天

保羅要我打電話告訴你他很抱歉明天下午的招待會他不能來了。他身體有點不舒服。

**【說明】**

"招待會": reception

"身體不大好"可說 be not very well; not feel quite well 或 be not well disposed

**【譯例】**

(a) Paul asked me to call you up and tell you he is sorry he can't go to the reception tomorrow afternoon. He is not very well.

(b) Paul is sorry that he can't go to the reception tomorrow afternoon because he is not feeling quite well. He asked me to phone you about it.


# 第25天

請在5號前通知我下星期六你是否出席為我們前任校長舉行的歡送會。

**【說明】**

"下星期六": next Saturday 或 on Saturday next 都是指下一個星期六。如今天是星期四，下一個星期六就是後天；但如果是對話，大家都明白的話，也可以不加 next。如指下星期的星期六，則要說 On Saturday next week。當然，如果今天是星期六，則 next Saturday 是指下星期的星期六。

"是否出席": whether you will be present at (或 attend)…

"歡送會": farewell party; "爲…舉行的歡送會" 要說 give a farewell party in honour of…。

"請通知我": please let me know; please write to me; 或 kindly inform me

### 【譯例】

(a) Please let me know by the 5th whether you will be present at the farewell party which will be given next Saturday in honour of our former principal.

(b) Kindly inform me by the 5th whether you will attend the farewell party to be given on Saturday next in honour of our former principal.

(c) Will you please write to me by the 5th whether you will attend the farewell party which is to be given next Saturday in honour of our former principal.


# 第26天

你如有事找我，可打電話到我的辦公室。萬一是緊急的事情或在下班以後，請直接打到我家裏好了。

### 【說明】

"如有事找我": if you want me, 或 if I am wanted

"萬一是緊急的事情": in case of an emergency; in the event of an emergency, 注意：event 之前有冠詞 the。

"下班以後": after office hours

(a) If you want me, just call my office. In case of an emergency or after office hours, please call me at home.

(b) Just phone my office if I am wanted. In the event of an emergency or after office hours, you can phone me at my house.

# 第27天

你可能很忙，但也該隔一些時候寫封信給我。

## 【說明】

"可能很忙，但…"may be very busy, but …, 或 however busy you may be, …。

"隔一些時候" 可說 once in a while; every now and then。

"寫信給我"：除 write to me 之外，也可說 drop me a line。

## 【譯例】

(a) You may be very busy, but you might write to me once in a while.

(b) However busy you may be, can't you spare the time to write to me every now and then?

(c) I know you are a busy man, but you might drop me a line once in a while.

# 第28天

信上地址寫錯了，所以那封信沒寄到他手裏。

"信上地址寫錯"可說 the letter was wrongly addressed, 或 the letter was addressed to the wrong house。

"信未寄到他手裏" the letter didn't reach him, 或 the letter was not delivered to him

【譯例】

(a) Because the letter was wrongly addressed, it didn't reach him.

(b) The letter was not delivered to him because it was addressed to the wrong house.

# 第29天

"麻煩你，請你在回家途中替我寄這封信好不好？""好的。"

【說明】

"麻煩你"是請人家做些事情時說的一句客氣話，譯作 Will you kindly…?／May I ask you to…?／Would you mind…–ing…?／Be kind enough to…都可以。

"好的"是表示樂於這樣做的意思，可說 with pleasure 或 why not? 但如果問句是 Would（或 Do) you mind… –ing…? mind 在這裏作"反對"解，全句直譯作"你反對…嗎？"答句如表示願意，就該說 not at all, 或 Of course not。

(a) "Will you kindly post this letter for me on your way home? "

"With pleasure. "

(b) "Would you mind posting this letter for me on your way back? "

"Not at all. "

# 第30天

"祝你新年快樂順利。""多謝。也祝你快樂順利。"

【說明】

"祝你… ": I wish you…或 Allow me to wish you…

"新年快樂順利。":a happy and prosperous New Year

"也祝你"可說 The same to you! 或 you too! you 應重讀。

【譯例】

(a) "I wish you a happy and prosperous New Year! "

"Thanks. The same to you! "

(b) "Allow me to wish you a happy and prosperous New Year! "

"Thank you very much. The same to you! "

(c) "I hope the new year will bring you happiness and prosperity. "

"Thanks very much. You too! "

# Words and Expressions

| | |
|---|---|
| be away on holiday; spend one's holidays | 出去度假 |
| look well ( 或 fresh) | 面色好 |
| have a fever; run a temperature | 發燒 |
| be away on a journey | 出去旅行 |
| ask for advice; consult | 請教 |
| for the life of me ( 用於否定 ) | 怎麼也…( " 無論如何 "的意思 ) |
| call to mind | 想起 |
| come across | 偶然遇見 |
| a man of few words | 不大說話的人 |
| keep one's promises ( 或 word) | 守信 |
| a man of his word | 信守諾言的人 |
| rely upon | 信賴 |
| be acquainted with… | 與…相識 |
| from time to time; now and then | 常常；不時 |
| be very grateful for… | 不勝感激 |
| do a great favour; render a big help | 幫大忙 |
| go for a drive | 乘車兜風 |
| cinema | 電影院 |
| be not in the mood for… | 沒有心情… |

| | |
|---|---|
| can't afford the time | 抽不出時間 |
| There is no hurry about it. No hurry. | 別急 |
| say（或 bid）good-bye to someone | 向…告別 |
| see off | 送行 |
| have a good journey; bon voyage [bɔ̃:vwajˈɑːʒ] | 一路平安 |
| give one's best regards to… | 向…問好 |
| be not in; be out | 不在家 |
| go shopping | 買東西去 |
| call（或 ring）back | 回電話 |
| extension | 電話分機 |
| be not well disposed | 身體不適 |
| farewell party | 歡送會 |
| after office hours | 下班以後 |
| once in a while | 隔一些時候 |

# Exercise  3

Translate the following into English:

1. 甲：你好嗎？

乙：我很好，多謝。

甲：好久沒看到你，你工作忙（be busy with one's work），還是怎麼的？

乙：我出差（be away on business）去了，昨天才回來。（第

1, 2天）

2. 甲：他昨天沒有來上班，是不是病倒了？

   乙：是的，他發燒，但今天已經好些了。（第2天）

3. 上月他到日本去度假，直到上星期才回來。他的面色比我上次見
   到他時要好得多。（第2, 3天）

4. 前天我去看他，湊巧他不在家，我對他的家裏人說有空我會再去。
   （第4天）

5. 甲：他什麼時候來的？

   乙：他已經來了半小時。

   甲：噢，眞對不起，勞他久等了。（第5天）

6. 庫克先生，我可以把史密斯先生介紹給你嗎？史密斯先生對英國
   歷史很感興趣，他希望向你請教幾個問題。（第6天）

7. 甲：請你替我介紹一下你的朋友庫柏先生好不好？

   乙：我願意為你介紹，但他現在正忙着，請你等一會兒。（第7
   天）

8. 我找不到你昨天給我的那本書，我怎麼也記不起來放在哪裏。（第
   8天）

9. 前天在路上遇見中學的老師伯頓先生，我們已有十幾年不見了。
   （第9天）

10. 保羅是個信守諾言的人，他從不失信(break one's promises)，
    所以大家都信任他。（第10天）

11. 我們從小就住在一起，進同一間學校，現在又同在一間工廠工作。
    （第11天）

12. 通過朋友的介紹，我認識了那個圖書管理員（librarian）彼德，
    從此我們就成為好朋友。（第12天）

13. 自從到這裏以來，承蒙關注，不勝感激，我希望不久能再來貴地，
    那時我將再來看你。（第13天）

14. 我送了他一件禮物，表示感謝他的幫助。（第14天）

15. 如果你明天能和我一起到郊外去兜兜風，我將十分高興。（第15天）

16. 甲：你想到郊外去兜兜風嗎？

    乙：不，我不想去。我很忙，實在抽不出時間，但還是謝謝你的好意。（第15，16天）

17. 甲：噢，我們該走了。

    乙：你們不能再留一下嗎？

    甲：我們兩點鐘還想去看電影。

    乙：既然這樣，我就不留你們了。（第17天）

18. 我到她家裏去告別，恰巧她不在家。我告訴她家裏人我明早乘7點的火車走。（第4，18天）

19. 甲：你什麼時候動身？

    乙：我乘6：20的火車。

    甲：我到車站來送你。

    乙：這樣你太客氣了。

    甲：沒什麼，這是我起碼該做的事。

    乙：多謝你。（第18，19天）

20. 甲：約翰，祝你一路平安，希望你不久再來。

    乙：我也這樣希望，多謝你來給我送行。（第19天）

21. 甲：你到過澳門嗎？

    乙：是的，曾到過一次。

    甲：是什麼時候去的？

    乙：兩年前去過。（第20天）

22. 甲：喂，我是史密斯，我要同瓊斯先生講話。

    乙：對不起，瓊斯先生不在。

    甲：他什麼時候來？

乙：他說 3 點左右在這裏。

甲：那麼我在 3 點半再打吧。

乙：好的。（第21，22天）

23. 請你叫瓊斯先生在 4 點鐘打個電話給史密斯，我的電話號碼是
556843。（第23天）

24. 甲：保羅，請你打個電話給彼德，告訴他明天下午的招待會我不
能去了，因爲我身體有點不舒服。

乙：好的。（第24天）

25. 請你問一下瑪麗她是否出席下星期日爲幾位外國教師舉行的招待
會。（第25天）

26. 我到他家裏去過，他不在，後來我打電話到他的辦公室，答覆是
他已回家了，所以我沒有找到他。（第26天）

27. 萬一是緊急的事情，你可以打電話給他，他可能很忙，但我相信
他會幫助你的。（第26，27天）

28. 可能是信上的地址寫錯了，所以我沒有收到。（第28天）

29. 甲：你到圖書館去，請你把這幾本書替我還一下好嗎？

乙：好吧。（第29天）

30. 甲：我怕現在得走了。我乘的火車是5: 30開。

乙：那我不留你啦。到家時請向你父親問好。

甲：謝謝你，我一定轉告。再見！

乙：再見！（第17，18，19天）

# 第 4 月
# 健康、疾病、醫療

## 第 1 天

這裏天氣多變，時冷時熱，容易生病，望多多保重身體。

### 【說明】

"多變"：changeable; variable

"時冷時熱"可說 sometimes hot and sometimes cold，或 now hot, now cold。注意兩種說法的差別：前一種有連詞 and，後一種却沒有，但須用逗號分開。

"生病"在英國通常說 be ill，而在美國却說 be sick。be sick 在英國一般作"嘔吐"解，雖然 fall sick 或 be taken sick 也作"得病"解，這是英美兩國人民在用語方面的差別之一，不可不知。另外，作定語用時，不論在英國還是美國，一律用 sick 而不用 ill，如 sick baby（病嬰），sick leave（病假），sick bed（病床），不可說 ill baby, ill leave, 或 ill bed。

"多多保重身體"要說 take good care of your health（或 yourself），或單說 look after yourself 也可。注意："身體"不可譯作 body。

### 【譯例】

(a) The weather here is very changeable. It is sometimes hot and sometimes cold, so it's very easy for you to be ill. Please take good

86

care of your health.

(b) We have very variable weather here. It's now hot, now cold. You'd better look after yourself, or you might easily get ill.

# 第 2 天

他很注意運動，所以身體非常健康，終年不生病。

## 【說明】

"很注意"：pay（或 devote）much（或 great）attention to; care very much for

"運動"：exercise; sports

"身體非常健康"：be very healthy; be in excellent health; be keeping very well

"終年"：(all) the year round; throughout the year

"從不生病"：never get ill, be never laid up, 或 have never a day's sickness

## 【譯例】

(a) He pays much attention to exercise, so he is very healthy and never gets ill all the year round.

(b) He is in excellent health and is never laid up the year round because he cares very much for exercise.

(c) As he devotes great attention to sports, he is keeping very well and is never taken ill throughout the year.

# 第 3 天

早起對身體有好處，因此我把黎明即起作為一個守則。

"早起"除了 get up early 之外；也可用成語 be up with the sun 和 rise with the lark。（lark 是 "百靈鳥"，習慣早起。）

"對身體有好處"可說 be good for health, 或 be beneficial （或 conducive）to health。注意 good 之後用介詞 for, 而 beneficial 或 conducive 之後則用介詞 to。

"早起對身體有好處"：以 "早起"作主語用不定詞表達, 可說 To get up early is good for health, 或用形式主語 it 放在句首而把不定詞移置句末, 如 It is good for health to get up early。另外, 也可用動名詞表達說 Getting up early is good for health, 或 Early rising is good for health。

"守則"：rule；"我把早起（或黎明即起）作爲守則"要說 I make it a rule to get up early。注意這個句子裏動詞 make 的賓語是 to get up early, 而 it 是這個不定詞的形式賓語, 因爲在英語裏是不能說 I make to get up early a rule 的；此外也可用 "早起"作主語說 To get up early has become my rule, 或 It has become my rule to get up early。

**【譯例】**

(a) It is good for health to get up early, so I make it a rule to rise with the lark.

(b) Getting up early is beneficial to health, so it has become my rule to be up with the sun.

(c) I make it a rule to get up early, for early rising is conducive to health.

# 第4天

我認為成人每天睡8小時是重要的。要知道睡眠不足會影響健康。

## 【說明】

"成人": grown-up; adult

"睡8小時": sleep eight hours, 或改為名詞詞組說 eight-hour sleep。注意: hour 之後沒有 s

"我認為成人每天睡8小時是重要的"要說 I think it important for a grown-up to sleep eight hours a day, 這個句子裏的 it 是替代後面不定詞的形式賓語。注意: make, think, consider, believe 等動詞後面有個不定詞, 賓語再加一個補足語就需要用形式賓語 it 去替代不定詞而把這個不定詞移置於補足語之後, 如 I believe it good to get up early. He considers it a great honour to attend the meeting; 此外, 也可把這類簡單句改為複合句, 如 I believe that it is good to get up early. He considers that it is a great honour to attend the meeting. 這樣後面部分 that…就成為從句而 it 是後面不定詞的形式主語。

"睡眠不足"not get (或 have) enough sleep, 或改為名詞詞組說 lack of sufficient sleep。

"影響健康": affect one's health; tell on one's health

## 【譯例】

(a) I think it important for a grown-up to sleep eight hours a day. You must know that if you don't get enough sleep your health will be affected.

(b) I think (that) it is important for an adult to sleep eight hours a day. Lack of sufficient sleep will affect your health, you know.

(c) I consider that eight-hour sleep every day is important for an adult, as you know that lack of sufficient sleep will tell on your health.

# 第5天

爲了保持健康，生活要有規律，並注意體育鍛煉和適當的營養。

## 【說明】

"保持健康"：preserve one's health; keep fit

"生活要有規律"：have regular habits

"體育鍛煉"：physical training（或 exercise）

"營養"：nourishment; nutrition

## 【譯例】

(a) In order to preserve our health, we must have regular habits and pay attention to physical training and proper nutrition.

(b) If we wish to keep fit, we should have regular habits and pay attention to physical exercise and proper nourishment.

# 第6天

我的兒子漸漸地長肉了。看見他一天天地強壯起來，確使我感到欣慰。

【説明】

"長肉"：gain weight 或 put on weight

"看到…使我感到欣慰"可説 I am gratified to see…，或 It is gratifying for me to see…，gratified 與 gratifying 不可對調。

【譯例】

（a）My son is gaining weight, I'm really gratified to see him getting stronger day by day.

（b）My son is putting on weight. It's indeed gratifying for me to find him getting stronger day after day.

（c）My son is gaining weight. How gratified I am to see him getting stronger from day to day!


# 第7天

前幾年我常患失眠症，但現在幸好沒有這毛病了。

【説明】

"失眠症"：insomnia；"常患失眠症"是 used to have insomnia，或 used to be a victim to insomnia。used to 表示過去經常有的動作，如 At that time they used to meet every week。victim 是"受害者"或"犧牲者"；a victim to insomnia 是"失眠症患者"。

"沒有這毛病"是"病已痊癒"的意思，可説 have been（或 have got）over an illness。

【譯例】

(a) A few years ago I used to have insomnia; but I'm glad to have been over it now.

(b) I used to be a victim to insomnia several years ago; but happily I've got over the trouble now.

# 第8天

服用防止發胖藥並無用處。你所需要的只是運動。

### 【說明】

"防止發胖藥": anti-corpulence drugs

"並無用處" It's useless to…; It's no use…ing; 或用疑問句 What's the use of…? 也可。

### 【譯例】

(a) It's useless to take anti-corpulence drugs. What you need is exercise.

(b) It's no use taking anti-corpulence drugs. All you need is exercise.

(c) What's the use of taking anti-corpulence drugs? Exercise is all you need.

# 第9天

她很孱弱。像她這樣體質的女孩子很容易患肺結核病。

### 【說明】

"孱弱": weak; delicate

"體質": constitution

"肺結核病": tuberculosis, 或 TB; "容易患肺結核病"可說 be liable to be attacked by tuberculosis, 或 be an easy prey to TB; a prey to…是"成爲…的犧牲品"的意思。

## 【譯例】

(a) She is rather weak. A girl of her constitution is liable to be attacked by tuberculosis.

(b) She is so delicate. I believe a girl of her constitution is an easy prey to TB.

# 第 10 天

我的妹妹生來就體弱,但她很注意運動,所以現在身體好起來了。

## 【說明】

"生來體弱": be born weak; have (或 be of) delicate constitution

"身體好": be alive and well; get on well

## 【譯例】

(a) My younger sister was born weak; but as she pays great attention to exercise, she is getting on well now.

(b) Though my younger sister is of delicate constitution, she is alive and well now because she cares very much for sports.

# 第 11 天

注意健康當然是重要的，但過於害怕疾病也是不必要的。

## 【說明】

"當然"： of course; certainly; indeed 都可以。

"過於害怕疾病"： be too much afraid of illness（ 或 falling ill ）

"不必要的"： unnecessary

## 【譯例】

(a) Of course, it is very important to take care of one's health; but it is unnecessary to be too much afraid of illness.

(b) It is certainly of great importance to be careful about one's health. It is, however, unnecessary to be too much afraid of falling ill.

# 第 12 天

他似乎全然沒有意識到，輕度的感冒，不加注意，也很容易變成嚴重的疾病。

## 【說明】

"似乎"： seem; appear

"全然沒有"： not…at all

"意識到" be aware of; realize。 "似乎沒有意識到"如以 he 作主語，可說 He doesn't seem （ 或 appear ）to be aware…，或

It seems（或 appears）that he is not aware…; 也可說 It doesn't seem（或 appear）to have occurred to him that…。not occur to him 是 "他沒有想到" 的意思，這裏用完成時態表示 "未曾想到"。

"輕度感冒"：a mere cold; a slight cold

"不加注意" 有 "如果" 的意思，所以要說 if no care is taken, 或 if it is not taken care of。

"變成"：become; turn into; develop into

【譯例】

(a) He doesn't seem to realize at all how easy it is for a cold to become a bad illness if no care is taken.

(b) It seems that he is not aware at all that a mere cold may turn into something serious if it is not taken care of.

(c) It doesn't appear to have occurred to him at all that a serious illness may easily develop from a slight cold if no care is taken.


# 第 13 天

一個人往往在身體失去健康的時候才體會到健康的重要性。

【說明】

"一個人" 指任何人，可用 one, 也可用 we 或 people。但用了 one 之後，後面有關的代詞通常也要用 one, one's, oneself, 而不用 he, his, himself, 如：One usually eats what one likes. One must take care of one's health. One must take care of oneself。

"往往"：Often; more often than not; as often as not

"失去健康"可說 be broken in health, 或以 health 作主語說 one's health is wrecked。

"重要性": importance

## 【譯例】

(a) One often realizes the importance of health only when one is broken in health.

(b) It's often the case that one comes to appreciate the importance of health only when one's health is wrecked.

(c) More often than not, people don't realize the importance of health until their health is wrecked.

(d) As often as not, it's only when we are broken in health that we come to realize the importance of health.


# 第 14 天

"我現在苦於大便閉結, 你說該怎麼辦呢?" "每天多吃些蔬菜, 多做些運動, 我想這是最好的辦法。"

## 【說明】

"苦於"可說 suffer from 或 be troubled by。

"大便閉結": constipation

"怎麼辦?"是向對方徵求意見, 可說 What would you advise? 或 What do you think I shall do?

"蔬菜": vegetables

## 【譯例】

(a) "I'm suffering from constipation. What would you advise?" "Take more vegetables and more exercise every day. I think that's the best way."

(b) "I'm troubled by constipation. What do you think I should do?" "I think the best way is to take more vegetables and more exercise every day."

# 第 15 天

我的父親過去有心臟病,時時發作,但經過庫克醫生的細心治療,現在已經恢復健康。

## 【說明】

"心臟病": heart disease 或 heart trouble

"時時發作": be often subject to fits of attack; fits 指疾病的多次發作; be subject to…是 "常受" 的意思。

"醫生": doctor, 統指內外科醫生; 也可用於稱呼, 如 Dr. Cook。"內科醫生" 是 physician; "外科醫生" 是 surgeon。

"細心治療": careful ( 或 meticulous ) treatment

"恢復健康": recover ( 或 restore ) one's health

## 【譯例】

(a) My father used to have heart disease and was often subject to fits of attack. But now he has recovered his health after Dr. Cook's careful treatment.

(b) My father was suffering from heart trouble with frequent fits of attack, but now his health is recovered after the meticulous treatment of Dr. Cook.

# 第 16 天

天花是個可怕的病症，但我已替我的孩子種了牛痘，所以他就可以免疫。

## 【說明】

"天花"：smallpox

"種牛痘"：vaccinate，名詞是 vaccination。"我已替我的孩子種了牛痘"要說 I have got my child vaccinated。get（或 have）＋名詞＋過去分詞這個句型是常用的，如 I shall get my radio fixed（我要把我的收音機修好），He had a tooth pulled out（他把一隻牙齒拔掉了）。

"免疫"：be immune from; be proof against

## 【譯例】

(a) Smallpox is a terrible disease; but as I have got my child vaccinated, he is immune from it.

(b) As I have got my child vaccinated, he is proof against smallpox, which is a terrible disease.

# 第 17 天

"你喉痛，在服藥嗎？""是的，我去看過醫生。他開了個藥方，我服了藥已經好些。我想會好起來的。"

## 【說明】

"喉痛": sore throat

"服藥": take medicine

"藥方": prescription; 這個詞也可指所開的藥。

"好了些" 指服藥後病情減輕, 要說 relieve, 名詞是 relief。

"好起來": improve; be getting over an illness

## 【譯例】

(a) "Do you take any medicine for your sore throat?"
"Yes, I went to the doctor. He wrote me a prescription, which relieved me somewhat. I believe I'm improving."

(b) "Are you taking any medicine for your sore throat?"
"Yes, I went to the doctor and got a prescription. The medicine gave me some relief. I think I'm getting over it."

# 第 18 天

"我身體不適, 感到頭暈發冷。" "我來替你量量體溫看。39.2°。啊, 你在發高燒! "

## 【說明】

"頭暈": dizzy

"發冷": chilly; shivery

"量體溫": take one's temperature

## 【譯例】

(a) "I'm indisposed and feel dizzy and chilly."
"Let me take your temperature. Thirty-nine point two. Oh, you are

running a high temperature! "

(b) "I'm unwell, feeling dizzy and shivery. "
"I'll take your temperature. It's thirty-nine point two. Oh, my, you have got a high fever! "

# 第 19 天

"你有甚麼不舒服？""我頭痛得厲害，覺得要嘔吐。""我聽到很難過。你最好到醫院裏去看看有甚麼不妥。"

## 【說明】

"你有甚麼不舒服？": What's wrong with you?/ What ails you?

"我頭痛得厲害": My head aches violently, 或以 I 為主語說 I have got a splitting headache。(比較漢語 "頭痛欲裂")

"醫院": hospital

"去看看有甚麼不妥" 可說 to see what the trouble is, 或 to find out what is the matter。注意: what the trouble is 因為是從句，所以主謂語不倒裝，不說 what is the trouble; 但 what is the matter 作從句時却不可改作 what the matter is。

## 【譯例】

(a) "What's wrong with you? " "My head aches violently. I feel sick. " "I'm very sorry to hear that. You'd better go to the hospital to see what the trouble is. "

(b) "What ails you? " "I have got a splitting headache and feel sick. " "Very sorry to hear that. Better go to the hospital to find out what is the matter. "

100

# 第20天

我到診療所去看感冒，醫生說病情不嚴重，但必須臥床數天。

## 【說明】

"診療所"： clinic

"感冒"或"流行性感冒"： influenza; 也可用縮體詞 flu。

"臥床"： lie up; keep the bed

## 【譯例】

(a) I have been to the clinic for my influenza. The doctor says it's not serious, but I must lie up for a few days.

(b) I have been to the clinic to see the doctor about my flu. He says there is nothing serious, but I'll have to keep the bed for a couple of days.

# 第21天

他的兄弟昨晚進了醫院。醫生診斷是闌尾炎，決定在一二天內替他開刀。

## 【說明】

"進醫院"： be sent to the hospital; be hospitalized

"診斷"： diagnose, 名詞是 diagnosis。

"闌尾炎"： appendicitis

"開刀"： operate on (a patient for an illness)

101

(a) His brother was sent to the hospital last night. The doctor diagnosed his illness as appendicitis and decided to have him operated on in a day or two.

(b) His brother was hospitalized last night. The doctor found him through diagnosis to be ill with appendicitis, so he will be operated on in a couple of days.

# 第22天

"我牙痛得很厲害。""你為甚麼不去看牙醫呢? 我勸你愈早治療愈好。"

【說明】

"牙痛": toothache

"牙醫": dentist

"愈…愈…": The more…, the more…, 這兩個 the 叠用表示程度隨着條件的發展而發展。前面一句是條件句, 兩個 the 都是副詞, 前一個 the 並起連詞作用。主語和動詞都放在後面, 如: The more I read the book, the more I like it.

The more I study English, the better I can understand it.

The sooner we start, the earlier we shall get there.

在短句裏也可以沒有主語和動詞, 如:

The sooner you do something about it, the better.

"How much do you want?" "The more the better." (愈多愈好。)

"When shall we finish the work?" "The earlier the better."

（愈早愈好。）

【譯例】

(a) "I have a terrible toothache." "Why don't you go to see a dentist? I advise you to take care of it. The earlier the better."

(b) "My tooth aches terribly." "You'd better go and see a dentist. I would advise you to do something about it. The sooner the better."

# 第23天

從他的口臭和他舌上濃濁的舌苔看來，恐怕他的胃有毛病。

【說明】

"口臭"：foul breath; bad breath

"舌苔"：fur

"從…看來"：judge from…

"胃"：stomach；"他的胃有毛病"可說 He has stomach trouble, His stomach is out of order, 或 There is something the matter with his stomach。

【譯例】

(a) Judging from his foul breath and the thick fur on his tongue, I'm afraid there is something the matter with his stomach.

(b) I'm afraid he has stomach trouble as judged from his bad breath and thickly coated tongue.

# 第 24 天

她似乎染上了甚麼傳染病，已病了將近一個月了。

## 【說明】

"染上（某種疾病）"可說 catch, 或 contract。

"傳染病"： infectious disease 或 infection

"將近一個月"： for very nearly a month; for the best part of a month

## 【譯例】

(a) She seems to have caught some sort of infection and has been ill for very nearly a month.

(b) It seems that she has contracted some infectious disease and has been ill for the best part of a month.

# 第 25 天

每年全世界都有許多人死於癌症，其中不少是各方面傑出的人物，這是很可惜的。

## 【說明】

"癌症"： cancer; "死於癌症"要說 die of cancer, 或 succumb to cancer, 注意要用不同的介詞。

"傑出的人物"： eminent personage; great man

"可惜的"： deplorable

(a) It's quite deplorable that a large number of people in the world, many of whom are eminent personages from various circles, die of cancer every year.

(b) How deplorable it is that a large number of people in the world, including quite a few great men of various fields, should succumb to cancer every year!

# 第26天

到目前為止，癌症是危害人類生命最可怕的疾病之一。我們希望隨着醫學的發展，這種疾病將比較易於醫治。

## 【說明】

"到目前為止"：so far; up to the present
"危害人類生命"：endanger human life
"醫學"：medicine 或 medical science
"醫治"：cure

## 【譯例】

(a) Up to the present, cancer is one of the most terrible diseases endangering human life. We hope that with the development of medicine, this disease will become easier to be cured.

(b) As medical science advances, we hope that it will be easier to cure cancer, which is so far believed to be one of the most terrible diseases endangering human life.

# 第27天

他得了重病，但幸已痊癒，而且現在甚至比以前更健康了。有一個時期他病得很厲害，似乎沒有希望了。

## 【說明】

"得了重病"可說 be seriously ill, 或 be in a serious condition。

"幸而痊癒"：fortunately got well; was fortunate enough to get well

"比以前更健康"：be healthier than ever (before)

"似乎沒有希望"是"似乎沒有恢復的希望"的意思，所以要說 there seemed to be little hope of his recovery, 或 his life was nearly despaired of。

## 【譯例】

(a) He was seriously ill, but fortunately he got well and is now even healthier than ever. At one time he was so ill that there seemed to be little hope of his recovery.

(b) He was in a serious condition, but he was fortunate enough to recover and now he is even in better health than ever before. He was at one time in such a critical condition that his life was nearly despaired of.

# 第28天

"你想他有痊癒的希望嗎？""遺憾得很，這病是毫無指望了。

106

一切治療對他已屬無用。"

**【說明】**

"毫無指望": be beyond all hope; be a hopeless case
"治療": treat; 作爲名詞詞組可說 medical treatment。
"無用": be of no use; be of little avail

**【譯例】**

(a) "Do you think he will recover?" "I regret to say it is a hopeless case. No medical treatment is of any use to him."

(b) "Is there any hope of his recovery?" "I'm sorry to say it is beyond all hope. All medical treatments have already proved to be of little avail."


# 第29天

"你的腿怎麼啦?" "我踢足球時受傷了。你看要緊不要緊?" "不必擔憂, 這傷處容易癒合。"

**【說明】**

"你的腿怎麼啦?"除了說 "What's the matter with your leg?"之外, 還可說 "What have you done to your leg?"

"我踢足球時受傷": I got hurt while playing football, 或 I hurt it (in) playing football, it 指 my leg。

"不必擔憂": Don't worry; never mind.

"癒合": be (或 get) healed

(a) "What have you done to your leg?" "I hurt it playing football. Is it anything serious?" "Never mind. It will be healed without any difficulty."

(b) "What's the matter with your leg?" "I got hurt while playing football. I hope it won't be anything serious." "Don't worry. You will soon get healed."

# 第30天

我們最好隔一段時間到醫院裏去檢查一下身體，看看有沒有甚麼毛病。

## 【說明】

"隔一段時間"：once in a while

"檢查身體"：have a physical examination; have a medical check-up; have a health check

## 【譯例】

(a) We had better go to the hospital once in a while to have a physical examination to see whether there is anything the matter with our health.

(b) It is advisable for us to have a medical check-up once in a while at the hospital to see if there is anything wrong with our health.

# Words and Expressions

| | |
|---|---|
| sometimes hot and sometimes cold; now hot, now cold | 時冷時熱 |
| get ill; fall ill; be taken ill | 生病 |
| take good care of one's health | 保重身體 |
| pay ( 或 devote ) attention to exercise | 注意運動 |
| (all) the year round; throughout the year | 終年 |
| never get ill; be never laid up; have never a day's sickness | 從不生病 |
| be up with the sun; rise with the lark | 早起 |
| be good for health; be beneficial ( 或 conducive) to health | 對身體有好處 |
| affect one's health; tell on one's health | 影響健康 |
| preserve one's health; keep good health; keep fit | 保持健康 |
| physical training ( 或 exercise) | 體育鍛煉 |
| nutrition; nourishment [ˈnʌriʃmənt] | 營養 |
| gain weight; put on weight | 長肉 |
| insomnia [inˈsɔmniə] | 失眠症 |

| | |
|---|---|
| have been（或 got）over an illness | 病已痊癒 |
| anti-corpulence drug | 防止發胖藥 |
| constitution | 體質 |
| tuberculosis [tju(ː)bəːkjuˊlousis], TB | 肺結核病 |
| be born weak | 生來體弱 |
| get on well; be alive and well | 身體好 |
| be aware of | 意識到 |
| be broken in health | 失去健康 |
| constipation [ˌkɔnstiˊpeiʃən] | 大便閉結 |
| heart disease（或 trouble） | 心臟病 |
| treatment | 治療 |
| recover（或 restore）one's health | 恢復健康 |
| smallpox | 天花 |
| vaccinate [ˊvæksineit] | 種牛痘 |
| be immune from; be proof against | 免疫 |
| sore throat | 喉痛 |
| take medicine [ˊmedsin] | 服藥 |
| prescription [prisˊkripʃən] | 藥方 |
| relieve pain | 止痛 |
| take one's temperature | 量體溫 |
| hospital | 醫院 |
| clinic | 診療所 |
| influenza [ˌinfluˊenzə], flu | 流行性感冒 |

| | |
|---|---|
| lie up; keep the bed | （因病）臥床 |
| diagnosis [ˌdaiəgˊnousis] | 診斷 |
| appendicitis [əˌpendiˊsaitis] | 闌尾炎 |
| operate (on) | 開刀 |
| toothache | 牙痛 |
| dentist | 牙醫 |
| bad breath; foul breath | 口臭 |
| fur | 舌苔 |
| stomach [ˊstʌmək] | 胃 |
| infectious disease; infection | 傳染病 |
| cancer | 癌症 |
| die of; succumb [səˊkʌm] to | 死於 |
| eminent personage | 傑出人物 |
| so far; up to the present | 到目前為止 |
| medical science; medicine | 醫學 |
| cure | 治癒 |
| be seriously ill | 得了重病 |
| a hopeless case | 絕症 |
| be（或 get）healed | 癒合 |
| have a physical examination; have a medical check-up; have a health check | 檢查身體 |

# Exercise 4

Translate the following into English:

1. 這裏春天天氣多變，時冷時熱，身體差的人容易生病。(第 1 天)

2. 如果你注意運動，多多保重，身體一定會好起來的。（第 1，2
   天）

3. 我知道運動對身體有好處，因此我把每天運動作爲守則。（第 3
   天）

4. 甲：一個成年人每天該睡幾小時？
   乙：我想最好每天睡 8 小時。你要知道，睡眠不足會影響健康。
   （第 4 天）

5. 他生活很有規律，每天早起，並很注意運動和營養。（第 3,5 天）

6. 我相信生活有規律很重要。我的弟弟近來身體一天天地强壯起來，
   正因爲他有良好的習慣。（第 5，6 天）

7. 我的兒子以前身體很不好，現在幸好一天天地長肉了。（第 6，
   7 天）

8. 他經常患失眠症，由於睡眠不足，身體很不好。（第 4,7 天）

9. 甲：她很孱弱，服藥（medicine）又沒有用，你看怎麼辦？
   乙：我勸（advise）她多注意運動。（第 5,8,9 天）

10. 一個人有健全的體質就不易患肺結核病。（第 9 天）

11. 有些人生來體弱，但如能多注意運動，身體還是會結實起來的。
    （第 10 天）

12. 我們要知道，如果我們身體是好的，就不必過分害怕疾病。（第
    11，12 天）

13. 即使是輕度的感冒，也不可忽視(overlook)，因爲小病不注意，
    很容易釀成大病。（第 11，12 天）

14. 一個人往往在身體好的時候不大體會到健康的重要性。(第 13 天)

15. 我以前苦於大便閉結。醫生勸我每天多吃些蔬菜，多做些運動。
    現在幸好沒有這毛病了。（第 7，14 天）

16. 他有心臟病，時時發作。醫生勸他不要作劇烈的（strenuous）

112

運動。（第15天）

17. 天花很可怕，過去許多人死於（die of）這種病，但現在我們可用種痘的方法來預防（prevent）。（第16天）

18. 昨天我頭暈發冷。醫生開了個藥方，我服了藥以後已經覺得好了些。（第17，18天）

19. 我替他量體溫，發現他發高燒，我馬上把他送到醫院裏去看看是甚麼毛病。（第18，19天）

20. 他身體不適，頭痛得厲害。醫生說他患感冒,需要住院治療。（第18，19，20，21天）

21. 甲：你覺得有甚麼不妥？

乙：我頭暈，覺得要嘔吐。

甲：讓我替你量量體溫。你在發高燒，可能是患感冒。（第18，19，20天）

22. 醫生說他的病情不嚴重，休息幾天就會好的。（第20天）

23. 甲：醫生怎麼說？

乙：醫生說他患闌尾炎需要開刀。（第21天）

24. 昨天晚上她突然病倒了。醫生診斷是心臟病，決定讓她進醫院（admit her into the hospital）。（第1，21天）

25. 甲：我有胃病，有時痛得很厲害。

乙：那你為甚麼不去看醫生呢？這種病愈早治愈好。（第22，23天）

26. 甲：他已經病了將近一個月。

乙：生的是甚麼病？

甲：大概是染上了甚麼傳染病。（第24天）

27. 每年死於癌症的人真不少啊！我希望隨着醫學的發展能比較容易醫治這種可怕的疾病。（第25，26天）

28. 那個病人（patient）患了癌症。醫生說這病已毫無希望了，一切

治療方法對他都已無用。（第26，28天）

29. 即使我們不覺得有甚麼不妥，但最好能隔一段時間到醫院裏去檢查一下，看看有沒有甚麼毛病。（第30天）

30. 他有一個時期病得很厲害，似乎沒有痊癒的希望了。幸而經瓊斯醫生細心治療，身體一天比一天好起來，現在甚至比以前更健康了。（第15，27天）

# 第 5 月
# 生活、衛生、公害

## 第 1 天

我們的公寓在五樓，前面俯覽一座漂亮的花園，花園裏有各種樹木和許多美麗的花。

### 【說明】

"公寓"：flat; apartment

"五樓"：fourth floor; 按照英國習慣，一樓稱 ground floor, 二樓稱 first floor, 三樓稱 second floor, 餘類推；而按照美國習慣，一樓稱 first floor, 二樓稱 second floor, 三樓稱 third floor, 餘類推。這裏是按照英國習慣。

"俯覽"：overlook; command

### 【譯例】

(a) Our flat is on the fourth floor. It overlooks a fine garden where there are different kinds of trees and plenty of beautiful flowers.

(b) Our apartment is on the fourth floor, commanding a fine garden with various kinds of trees and lots of beautiful flowers.

## 第 2 天

"這房間在第十三層樓，俯覽景色極佳。順便問一下，這裏電梯是不是日夜服務？""是的。"

## 【說明】

"俯覽景色極佳"要說 overlook a fine view, 或 command a magnificent view。

"順便問一下"：by the way, incidentally, 是插入語。

"電梯"：lift, elevator, 前者是英語，後者是美語。"電梯是不是日夜服務？"可以說 "Does the lift run day and night?" 或以 you 爲主語說 "Do you have a round-the-clock lift service?" round-the-clock 是"晝夜不停"的意思。

## 【譯例】

(a) "This room is on the twelfth floor and overlooks a fine view. By the way, does the lift here run day and night?" "Yes, it does."

(b) "This 12th-floor room commands a very fine view. Incidentally, do you have a round-the-clock lift service?" "Yes, we do."

# 第 3 天

你會看到我們門前種了幾棵夾竹桃，因此你不會找不到。有便請光臨。

## 【說明】

"夾竹桃"：oleander

"門前"：in front of one's house; 如果前面已經提到房子則

116

單用 in front 就可以了。

"不會找不到": You can't miss it, 或 You can easily find it

"有便" 這是說 "你如果到這一帶來的話" If you happen to be hereabouts, 或 When you are around here。

## 【譯例】

(a) You will find several oleanders planted in front of our house, so you can't miss it. Please drop in when you are around here.

(b) If you happen to be hereabouts, please drop in at our house. As a number of oleanders are planted in front, you can easily find it.

# 第4天

"你們新公寓裏各種現代設備都有嗎?" "是的, 水、電、煤氣都有, 還有收音機、電視機、冰箱等, 一應俱全。"

## 【說明】

"現代設備" 指水電等設備, modern conveniences。

"水" 指 "自來水", 要說 running water。

"電": electricity

"煤氣": gas

"收音機": radio set

"電視機": TV set

"冰箱": refrigerator

"一應俱全" 指一切東西, all things, everything。

"你們…都有嗎？"可用一般疑問句，如"Do you have…？"也可用附加疑問句（tag question），如"You have…, haven't you?"注意這類句子，如果前面是肯定的，後面附加疑問要用否定的；反之，前面是否定的，後面附加疑問要用肯定的，如"You are not late, are you?"另外，前後時態也要一致，如 You will…, won't you?/He wasn't…, was he?/ They can't…, can they? 等。

**【譯例】**

(a) "Have you got all modern conveniences in your new flat?" "Yes, we have running water, electricity and gas. We also have a radio set, a TV set, a refrigerator; in fact everything."

(b) "You have all modern conveniences in your new flat, haven't you?" "Yes, we have a radio set, a TV set, a refrigerator and all other things in addition to running water, electricity and gas."

# 第 5 天

我的母親過去經常住在鄉下。那裏空氣新鮮，環境安靜，所以現在她不大習慣城市生活。

**【說明】**

"過去經常"可照前例用 used to。注意 used 後面用不定詞，如 used to live in the country; used 沒有時態變化。

"不習慣"：be not used to，這裏 to 是介詞，如 be not used to city life。注意：be used to 不可與 used to 相混，She used to live in the country 是"她過去經常住在鄉下"；而 She is used to living in the country 是"她習慣住在鄉下"；兩者意義是不同

的。此外也可用 accustom 這個詞，如 be not accustomed to city life，或 not accustom oneself to city life。

"環境"：surroundings; environment

## 【譯例】

(a) My mother used to live in the country, where the air is fresh and the surroundings are peaceful, so she is not quite used to city life.

(b) My mother finds it difficult to accustom herself to city life, because she used to live in the country, where she could enjoy fresh air and peaceful surroundings.

# 第6天

當今城市裏空氣很髒，郊區也如此。現在在這裏附近我們已經難得聽到野禽的叫聲了。

## 【說明】

"當今"：nowadays; at present; these days

"城市裏空氣很髒，郊區也如此"可譯作 The air in the city is very dirty, so is it in the suburbs。so is it…是 "…也如此" 的意思。注意前面必須是肯定句，否定句就不可以這樣說。另外，so 後面的主謂語要倒裝，如：My brother is a pupil. So is my sister；前面如為表意動詞（notional verb），則後面要用助動詞，如：He swims well. So does she/ I can speak English. So can my brother/ I've passed the examination. So has he。上列句子也可譯作 The air is very dirty, not only in the city, but also in the

119

suburbs。not only…but also…是連詞"不但…而且…"。此外，還可譯作 The air is very dirty in the suburbs as well as in the city。這裏 suburbs 與 city 不能對調，對調了就要作" 空氣不但在郊區很髒而且城市裏也如此 "解釋，意思就會不對。

"野禽的叫聲"：the songs of wild birds

"附近"：in the neighbourhood

### 【譯例】

(a) Nowadays the air in the city is very dirty. So is it in the suburbs. We can no longer hear the songs of wild birds in our neighbourhood.

(b) At present the air is foul in the suburbs as well as in the city. Even in our neighbourhood the songs of wild birds can no longer be heard.

(c) The songs of wild birds can no longer be heard in our neighbourhood because the air is now very dirty not only in the city but also in the suburbs.

# 第7天

城市的灰塵是很不衛生的。據説全帶病菌。因此，遇到灰塵多的日子，我回來時總要用高錳酸鉀溶液漱漱口。

### 【説明】

"城市的灰塵"：the dust in the city; 也可簡單地説 city dust.

"不衞生"：unhealthy

"病菌"：disease germs; "全帶病菌"：be full of disease

germs

    "高錳酸鉀溶液"：solution of potassium permanganate

    "漱口"：gargle

## 【譯例】

    (a) The dust in the city is very unhealthy. They say it is full of disease germs, so I always gargle with a solution of potassium permanganate after coming in on a dusty day.

    (b) It is said that city dust is full of disease germs and is very unhealthy, so I always gargle with a solution of potassium permanganate when I get back on a dusty day.


# 第8天

    住在郊外住宅區的人們深夜回家的苦惱是末班汽車已經開了，而出租汽車又不易找到。

## 【說明】

    "住宅區"：residential quarters（或 district）

    "深夜"：late at night

    "苦惱"：trouble 可作動詞；也可作名詞。"住在郊外…的苦惱"可譯作 The trouble with the people…is…, 或 What troubles those…is…。

    "出租汽車"：taxi

## 【譯例】

    (a) The trouble with the people who go back home late at

121

night to the residential quarters in the suburbs is that the last bus has already gone and a taxi is not easy to get.

(b) What troubles those who get back home late at night to the residential district in the suburbs is that the last bus has already left and there is great difficulty in getting a taxi.

# 第9天

他的房子原定再過一個月就可以完成，但由於人手不足，佑計到建築完成還要好些日子。

## 【說明】

"再過一個月"：in another month，或 in one more month。"原定再過一個月可以完成"：was scheduled（或 expected）to be completed in another month

"由於人手不足"：owing to manpower shortage，或 for want of manpower

"到建築完成"：before the completion of the construction，或單說 before completion 也可以。

"好些日子" 除了可以把 it 作主語說 It will take a good many days to⋯之外；也可用 a good many days 作主語說 a good many days will be needed。

## 【譯例】

(a) His house was scheduled to be completed in another month, but owing to manpower shortage, a good many days will be needed before it is completed.

122

(b) His house, which was expected to be completed in one more month, will need many more days before its completion owing to the shortage of manpower.

(c) His house was expected to be completed in one more month, but for want of manpower it will take a good many days to complete the work.

# 第 10 天

100 年前文明世界爲了獲得乾淨的食水而盡力，但現在全世界却渴望得到清潔的空氣。

## 【說明】

"文明世界"：civilized world

"乾淨的食水"：pure drinking water, 或 pure water to drink

"爲了…而盡力"：make great efforts to…, 或 take great pains in…

"渴望得到清潔的空氣"：be anxious to get pure air, 或 be anxious about pure air

## 【譯例】

(a) A hundred years ago, the civilized world took great pains in obtaining pure drinking water. But now all the world is anxious about pure air.

(b) A century ago, the civilized world made great efforts to obtain pure water to drink. Today, however, the whole world is anxious to get pure air.

# 第 11 天

　　工廠有毒的廢液污染了海水。如果不採取適當的措施，水產必將日益減少。

## 【說明】

　　"有毒的廢液"：poisonous waste liquid

　　"污染"：pollute (with); 名詞可用 pollution。

　　"適當的措施"：due（或 suitable）measures

　　"水產"：aquatic product; 產在海裏也可說 sea（或 marine）product。

## 【譯例】

　　(a) The poisonous liquid from the factories has caused the pollution of the sea water. If no suitable measures are taken, it is certain that aquatic products will decrease day by day.

　　(b) As the sea water has been polluted with the poisonous waste liquid from the factories, sea products will surely decrease day by day unless due measures are adopted.

# 第 12 天

　　由於大城市有噪音污染，如果有現代設備的話，愈來愈多的人寧願住在郊野。

## 【說明】

　　"噪音污染"：noise pollution

124

"愈來愈多": more and more

"寧願": would rather; would prefer

"如果"除了 if 之外，還可用 provided (that), on condition that, 但這些說法多用於書面。

## 【譯例】

(a) Owing to the noise pollution in large cities, more and more people would rather make their abodes in the country if they are supplied with modern conveniences.

(b) With the noise pollution in large cities, more and more people would prefer to live in the country provided there are modern conveniences.

# 第 13 天

現代社會環境有許多因素在威脅着我們的健康。古代沒有這些因素。就這點來說，我們甚至要羨慕原始社會了。

## 【說明】

"現代社會環境": modern social environment

"因素": factor; cause

"古代"作狀語可說 in ancient times，或 in early times。

"羨慕": envy

"原始社會": primitive society

## 【譯例】

(a) Our modern social environment has many causes that threaten to damage our health. We almost envy primitive society because there were very few, if any, of those causes in early times.

(b) Our modern social environment contains many factors endangering our health. In point of the scarcity of those factors in ancient times, we almost envy primitive society.


# 第 14 天

許多人對幼年時代住過的地方往往終生難忘。在這點上你是否也如此?

## 【說明】

"幼年時代": childhood

"終生": all one's life; 改為從句也可說 as long as one lives。

"難忘"作形容詞用要說 unforgettable 或 memorable。

## 【譯例】

(a) People usually can't forget the place where they have passed their childhood as long as they live. Is it also the case with you?

(b) For many people, the place where their childhood was spent is unforgettable all their lives. Is it also the same with you?


# 第 15 天

去年夏天她住在海濱,每天洗海水浴或沿着海濱作長時間的散步。她相信這是她一生中最難忘的一段時間。

126

"洗海水浴"：bathe in the sea

"一生中"：in one's life；也可說 all one's life。

【譯例】

(a) Last summer she stayed at the seaside bathing in the sea or taking long walks along the shore every day. She believes that is the most unforgettable time in her life.

(b) She believes that the summer she spent last year at the seaside bathing in the sea or taking long walks along the beach every day is the most memorable time in her life.

# 第 16 天

有人説洗了個熱水浴之後，酣睡在一張舒服的床上是人生最好的享受。你以爲如何？

【說明】

"有人說"：someone has said；it is said 也可。

"熱水浴"：hot bath

"酣睡"：sleep soundly；改爲名詞是 a sound sleep。

"舒服的"：comfortable

"享受"：enjoy；名詞是 enjoyment。

"你以爲如何？"："What do you think of it?" 或 "Do you think so?"

【譯例】

(a) Someone has said that a sound sleep in a comfortable bed after a hot bath is the best thing one can enjoy in life. What do you think of it?

(b) It is said that the best enjoyment in life is to sleep soundly in a comfortable bed after a hot bath. Do you think so?

# 第 17 天

"你不留在這裏吃便飯嗎?""你真客氣,但我必須走了。""真可惜!"

## 【說明】

"便飯": simple meal; potluck

"你真客氣": It's very kind of you. 或 You are very kind indeed.

"真可惜": 除了 What a pity 之外,還可說 What a shame。注意這裏 shame 不作"恥辱"解。

## 【譯例】

(a) "Wouldn't you like to stay here for a simple meal?" "That's very kind of you, but I must go away now." "What a pity!"

(b) "Won't you stay and share potluck with us?" "You are very kind indeed, but I really think it's about time I left." "Oh, dear! What a shame!"

# 第 18 天

一般地說來，北方人喜歡吃麵粉或其他穀類做的饅頭、烙餅或麵條，而南方人却喜歡以飯爲主食。

## 【說明】

"一般地說來"：generally speaking, generally, 或 as a rule
"北（南）方人"：people from the north (south), 或 northerners (southerners)
"穀類"：cereals；"麵粉或其他穀類做的"：made from flour or other cereals。
"饅頭"：(steamed) bun; steamed bread
"烙餅"：(baked) pancake
"麵條"：noodles
"主食"：Staple food；"副食"是 non-staple food。

## 【譯例】

(a) People from the north generally prefer buns, pancakes or noodles made from flour or other cereals, while those from the south like rice as their staple food.

(b) Generally speaking, the northerners like to take buns, pancakes or noodles made from flour or other cereals, whereas the southerners will have rice as their staple food.

# 第 19 天

"請抽支烟。""不，謝謝。我正打算戒烟哩。報上說抽烟是得肺癌的主要原因之一。"

"請抽支烟"可說 Have a cigarette, 如請人自己取吸可說 Help yourself to a cigarette。

"戒烟"：give up smoking 或 drop smoking

"報上說"：The newspaper says that…, 或 The newspaper has it that…

"肺癌"：lung cancer

## 【譯例】

(a) "Have a cigarette." "No, thanks. I'm trying to give up (smoking). The newspaper says smoking is one of the chief causes of lung cancer."

(b) "Help yourself to a cigarette." "No, thanks very much. The newspaper has it that smoking is one of the chief causes of lung cancer, so I'm trying to drop it."

# 第20天

"我還沒見過像你穿着的那樣漂亮的短上衣。""那是父親去年買給我的。從那時起我已經把它送到洗衣店去洗過三次了。"

## 【說明】

"漂亮的"除了 nice, pretty 之外；也可說 swell, smart。

"短上衣"：jacket。"像你穿着的那樣漂亮的短上衣"要說 such a nice jacket as the one are wearing, such 之後的關係代詞通常用 as, 如 such a book as the one you are reading。注意冠

130

詞a要放在 such 之後。

"洗衣店": laundry; 動詞是 launder, 作 "洗燙" 解。

"從那時起": since then。 "從那時起我已經把它送到洗衣店去洗過三次了" 可說 I've sent it to the laundry three times since then, 或 I've had it laundered three times since then。

## 【譯例】

(a) "I've never seen such a nice jacket as the one you are wearing." "Father bought it for me last year. I've sent it to the laundry three times since then."

(b) "What a swell jacket you are wearing!" "Oh, this? Daddy's present last year. I've had it laundered three times since then."

# 第21天

"你認為我的新裙子怎麼樣?" "看上去好極了, 而且你的圍巾也配得很好。"

## 【說明】

"你認為…怎麼樣?": "What do you think of…?" 或 "How do you like…?"

"裙子": skirt

"好極": 口語可用 marvellous, 或 wonderful。

"圍巾": scarf

"配得好": go well with, 或 match well。match 可作動詞或名詞。

【譯例】

(a) "What do you think of my new skirt?" "It looks wonderful, it also matches your scarf well."

(b) "How do you like my new skirt?" "It suits you marvellously and goes well with your scarf, too."

(c) "Do you think this skirt suits me?" "Of course it does. Your scarf is a good match, too."


# 第22天

"你隔多久去理一次髮？""大約兩星期一次，但我自己每天刮臉。"

【說明】

"隔多久…？"：How often…?

"去理一次髮"：go for a haircut; have one's hair cut; 也可理解爲 "到理髮店去" 而說 go to the barbershop。

"兩星期一次"：once every two weeks, once a fortnight 或 twice a month 都可以。

"刮臉"：shave; have a shave

【譯例】

(a) "How often do you go for a haircut?" "Once every two weeks or so, but I shave myself every day."

(b) "How often do you go to the barbershop?" "About twice a month, but I have a shave every day."

132

# 第23天

"我想和校長約個時間。明天9點鐘行嗎？""恐怕不行。他明天整天有事。"

## 【說明】

"約個時間"： make（或 fix）an appointment（with）

"行"是"辦得到"的意思，可說 be all right, will do 或 be convenient; convenient 是"方便"的意思。

"整天有事"除了 be fully engaged 之外；也可說 get a full day。

## 【譯例】

(a) "I'd like to make an appointment with the principal. Would nine tomorrow be all right?" "I'm afraid not. He's fully engaged tomorrow."

(b) "I wonder if I could fix an appointment with the principal. Would it be convenient to see him at nine tomorrow?" "I don't think that will do. He's got rather a full day tomorrow."

# 第24天

不問人家是否方便而突然到訪是不好的。特別像伯頓先生那種情況，因為他是位忙人，這樣做會使他感到麻煩。

## 【說明】

"不問人家是否方便"： without asking one's convenience

"突然到訪": pay a surprise visit to a person; call on a person unexpectedly

"像…那種情況": in the case of…; 注意 case 前面有冠詞 the。

"忙人": busy man

"感到麻煩": be annoyed（或 troubled）; be put to trouble; be put out

## 【譯例】

(a) It's not good to pay a surprise visit to a person without asking his convenience. Especially in the case of Mr. Burton, he will be annoyed because he is a busy man.

(b) It's not good manners paying a surprise visit to a person without caring for his convenience. This is especially the case with Mr. Burton. As he is a busy man, he will be put to trouble.

# 第25天

世上有許多不愉快的事情，但最不愉快的莫過於叫人苦苦等候。

## 【說明】

"世上": in the world

"最不愉快的(事)莫過於…" 可說 The most unpleasant thing is…，或 Nothing is more unpleasant than…; 也可說 Of all things the most unpleasant is…。

## 【譯例】

(a) There are many unpleasant things in the world, but nothing is more unpleasant than to be kept waiting.

(b) Of all things in the world, the most unpleasant thing is to be kept waiting.

(c) The most unpleasant thing in the world is to be kept waiting.


# 第26天

他堅持要讓他在中飯後去游泳，但他的父親勸他不要去，因為飽肚游泳對身體是有害的。

## 【說明】

"堅持"：insist，這個動詞後面要跟介詞 on，如 He insisted on going to swim；如果後面跟 that 引起的賓語從句，則為虛擬語氣，要用 should+動詞原形式，但不加 should 也可，如 He insisted that he (should) be allowed to go swimming。

"勸"：advise。"勸他不要去"：advise him not to, to 後省了 go swimming；也可說 dissuade him from doing so, dissuade 是"勸阻"的意思，注意後面要跟介詞 from。

"飽肚"作狀語可說 with one's stomach fully loaded；改為從句可說 when one's stomach is full。

"有害"：harmful (to); detrimental (to)

## 【譯例】

(a) He insisted that he be allowed to go swimming after lunch. But his father advised him not to, because it would be harmful to his health to swim with his stomach fully loaded.

(b) He insisted on going to swim after lunch. His father, however, dissuaded him from doing so, as it would be detrimental to
his health to go swimming when his stomach was full.

# 第27天

那裏的水很深,孩子踩不到底; 如沒有人照料他,別讓他去游泳。

## 【說明】

"水很深…踩不到底"可用 so deep…that 或 too deep for…句
型翻譯。

"照料": take care of

## 【譯例】

(a) The water there is so deep that the boy can't touch the bottom.
Don't let him go there to swim if there is no one to take care of him.
(b) The water there is too deep for the boy to touch the
bottom, so he should not be allowed to swim there if he is not
taken care of.

# 第28天

登山是很好的運動, 這當然是毫無疑問的; 但因爲有很大危險,
所以去的時候要十分小心。

## 【說明】

"登山": climb up a mountain, scale a mountain; 名詞是 mountain-climbing 和 mountaineering, 可作"登山運動"解。

"當然是毫無問題的": to be sure, indeed, certainly, 或用 It is true that…也可。

"有": involve; be accompanied by

"危險": risk

"十分小心": be very careful (in), take every possible care (in), 或 can't be too careful (in); 後一種說法是"小心不嫌過份", 也即"愈小心愈好"的意思。

## 【譯例】

(a) Mountain-climbing is a fine sport, to be sure, but it involves many risks, so you must be very careful when you go climbing.

(b) It's true that mountaineering is a good form of exercise; but it is accompanied by many risks, so you must take every possible care in scaling a mountain.

(c) You can't be too careful in climbing a mountain, since it is accompanied by various risks. However, it is a fine form of exercise.

# 第29天

遠離家鄉, 大概沒有比收到父母、兄弟、姐妹等的來信更為高興的事了。

## 【說明】

"遠離家鄉": be far away from home, 這裏有"當…的時候"

的意思，所以要用連詞 when 或 while。

"大概"： probably 或 it is probable that…

## 【譯例】

(a) When we are far away from home, probably few things are more pleasant than a letter from our parents, brothers or sisters.

(b) A letter from our parents, brothers or sisters is probably the most delightful thing when we are far away from home.

(c) It is probable that nothing is more pleasant than a letter from our parents, brothers or sisters while we are far away from home.


# 第30天

你難道不知道人有時也需要輕鬆一下的嗎？要是一直很緊張的話，就會活不下去。

## 【說明】

"輕鬆"： relax

"人"： man, 指人類，前面不用冠詞；也可譯作 human beings。

"人有時需要輕鬆一下"可用 man 作主語，說 Man must sometimes relax；也可說 It is sometimes necessary for human beings to relax。

"一直很緊張"是"經常在緊張狀態下"的意思，可譯作 under constant strain。

## 【譯例】

(a) Don't you know that man must sometimes relax? He can't live if he is put under constant strain.

(b) Are you not aware that it is sometimes necessary for human beings to relax? They can't live under constant strain.

# Words and Expressions

| | |
|---|---|
| flat; apartment | 公寓 |
| overlook ( 或 command ) a fine view | 俯覽景色極佳 |
| lift; elevator ['eliveitə] | 電梯 |
| round-the-clock service | 日夜服務 |
| by the way; incidentally [ˌinsi'dentəli] | 順便問一下 |
| oleander [ˌouli'ændə] | 夾竹桃 |
| modern conveniences | 現代設備(如水電等) |
| electricity [ilek'trisiti] | 電 |
| gas | 煤氣 |
| radio set | 收音機 |
| TV set | 電視機 |
| refrigerator [ri'fridʒəreitə] | 冰箱 |
| be used ( 或 accustomed) to | 慣於 |
| surroundings; environment [in'vaiərənmənt] | 環境 |
| nowadays | 當今 |
| in the neighbourhood | 附近 |
| unhealthy | 不衛生的 |

| | |
|---|---|
| disease germs | 病菌 |
| gargle | 漱口 |
| residential [ˌreziˈdenʃəl] quarters ( 或 district ) | 住宅區 |
| late at night | 深夜 |
| taxi | 出租汽車 |
| manpower shortage | 人手不足 |
| civilized world | 文明世界 |
| make great efforts (to do); take great pains (in) | 爲…而盡力 |
| pollution; noise pollution | 污染；噪音污染 |
| aquatic [əˈkwætik] product | 水產 |
| all one's life; in one's life | 終生 |
| bathe in the sea | 洗海水浴 |
| comfortable [ˈkʌmfətəbl] | 舒服的 |
| a sound sleep | 酣睡 |
| enjoyment | 享受 |
| simple meal; potluck | 便飯 |
| (steamed) bun; steamed bread | 饅頭 |
| (baked) pancake | 烙餅 |
| noodles | 麵條 |
| staple food; non-staple food | 主食；副食 |
| give up ( 或 drop ) smoking | 戒烟 |
| lung cancer | 肺癌 |
| jacket | 短上衣 |
| laundry | 洗衣店 |
| skirt | 裙子 |

| | |
|---|---|
| scarf | 圍巾 |
| wonderful; marvellous (口) | 好極 |
| have a haircut | 理一次髮 |
| shave; have a shave | 刮臉 |
| make（或 fix）an appointment | 定一次約會 |
| harmful (to); detrimental [ˌdetriˈmentl] (to) | 有害(於) |
| mountaineering [ˌmauntiˈniəriŋ] | 登山運動 |

# Exercise 5

Translate the following into English:

1. 我們的房間在六樓，馬路對面是個公園。我們能看到公園裏的各種花木。（第1，2天）

2. 我們登臨山頂，俯覽周圍的鄉村，景色極佳。（第2天）

3. 我家正在公園對面，門前種了幾棵櫻桃樹，所以你不會找不到。（第3天）

4. 甲：你們有電視機嗎？
   乙：有的，我們有電視機，收音機，冰箱等，一應俱全。（第4天）

5. 雖然郊野空氣新鮮，環境安靜，但由於缺乏現代設備，有些人不大習慣郊野生活。（第4，5天）

6. 他的兄弟過去經常在鄉村工作，所以習慣鄉村的生活。（第5天）

7. 他會講英語，他的姐妹也會講，但他的哥哥不但會講英語而且會講日語（用 as well as）。（第6天）

8. 城市裏空氣很髒,灰塵全帶病菌,所以很容易得傳染病。（第6，7天）

9. 我的一個朋友過去一向在郊外住宅區居住，但現在已搬到我們附近的一個新公寓裏了。（第5，6，8天）

10. 這個計劃原定再過一個月可以完成，但由於人手不足，估計要到年底才能完成。（第9天）

11. 工廠的廢液和廢氣污染了水和空氣，如果不採取適當的措施，人們的健康定會受到嚴重的危害。（第11天）

12. 愈來愈多人感到大城市裏空氣很髒，因此他們渴望搬到空氣新鮮的地方去住。（第10，12天）

13. 如果有現代設備的話，可以肯定許多人寧願住在鄉村，因為那裏的空氣要比城市裏好得多。（第12天）

14. 我們應該竭力保護環境，防止污染。（第10.11，13天）

15. 原始社會裏的生活自然是艱苦的，但威脅人們健康的因素似不多，就這點來看，我們甚至要羨慕原始社會了。（第13天）

16. 去年夏天她在夏威夷（Hawaii）住了整整一個星期，幾乎天天去游泳，她說這是她一生中最愉快的一段時間。（第15天）

17. 你認為洗了熱水浴之後在一張舒適的床上酣睡一夜是享受嗎？（第16天）

18. 甲：如果你願意和我們一道吃便飯的話，我們將非常高興。

    乙：多謝，你真客氣，但上午還有事，所以我得走了。（第17天）

19. 南方人通常以飯為主食，但為了換換口味（for a change of taste），有時也吃些麵粉做的饅頭、麵條或其他東西。（第18天）

20. 甲：請吸支烟。

    乙：不，謝謝。我已經戒掉了。

    甲：你為甚麼要戒烟呢？

    乙：報上說抽烟是害肺癌的主要原因之一。（第19天）

21. 甲：你看我這件新的短上衣怎麼樣？看上去好嗎？

    乙：好的，而且和你的褲子（trousers）也配得很好。（第20，

21天）

22. 我通常每隔兩星期去理一次髮。有些人一個月理一次。但多數人大約三星期左右上一次理髮店。（第22天）

23. 甲：校長在嗎？

乙：在，你想找他嗎？

甲：是的，我想和他談談。

乙：今天怕不行，他現在正在開會。（第23天）

24. 如果你的朋友很忙，你最好不要突然去探訪他，因爲這樣做會使他感到麻煩。（第24天）

25. 昨天我去看一個朋友。他讓我等了整整一個小時，這眞是最不愉快的事了。（第25天）

26. 他堅持要冒雨外出，但他的母親勸他不要去，因爲給雨淋濕了對身體有害。（第26天）

27. 她的兒子堅持要讓他到河裏去游泳。她不讓他去，因爲那裏水很深，沒有人照料可能會有生命危險。（be in danger of losing one's life）。（第27天）

28. 游泳是很好的運動，這是大家都同意的；但初學的人(beginners)要十分小心，以免發生危險。（第28天）

29. 他出國留學已經兩年，因爲遠離家鄉，所以每次接到家裏人的來信都感到非常高興。（第29天）

30. 如果我們經常處於緊張狀態，我們的健康就會受影響，因此我們有時需要輕鬆一下。（第30天）

# 第 6 月
# 愛好、娛樂、習慣

## 第 1 天

他最喜歡攝影，出外時總帶着照相機，但他還算不上是個攝影家。

### 【說明】

"喜歡"除了 like, love 等詞外；還可說 be fond of, be keen on。注意用不同的介詞。

"攝影"：take pictures（或 photos）

"照相機"：camera

"攝影家" photographer。"算不上是個攝影家"可說 be not much of a photographer, can't be counted as a photographer, 或 be no photographer。

### 【譯例】

(a) He loves to take pictures and always carries a camera with him when he goes out. But he is not much of a photographer yet.

(b) He is very fond of taking photos, so he always goes out with a camera. But he can't be counted as a photographer yet.

(c) Being keen on taking photos, he never fails to carry a camera with him when he goes out. But he is no photographer.

# 第 2 天

"你的愛好是甚麼?" "我最喜歡看電影,每星期最少要看一次電影,偶然也有多至一星期5次的。" "你真是個影迷!"

## 【說明】

"愛好": hobby。"你的愛好是甚麼?": "What's your hobby?"也可說 "What are you interested in?" 注意 interested 之後要用介詞 in。

"愛看電影" 可說 like movies, like to go to the movies, be interested in movies, take great interest in movies, 或 like to go to the cinema。

"偶然": occasionally 是狀語; 如改成句子, 可以說 there are occasions when…; occasion 是 "場合" 的意思。

"影迷": film ( 或 movie ) fan

## 【譯例】

(a) "What's your hobby?" "I like movies very much. I go to the cinema at least once a week. Occasionally, I go there as often as five times a week." "You are really a film fan."

(b) "What are you interested in?" "I'm very much interested in movies. I never fail to see a movie at least once a week. There are even occasions when I go to the cinema as often as five times a week." "What a movie fan you are!"

# 第 3 天

不知道爲甚麼他不喜歡看電影; 相反地, 他對京劇却非常感興趣,

145

每月總要去看一次。

【說明】

"不知爲甚麼"：somehow 或 for some reason or other

"他不喜歡看電影"除了可照前例譯作 He does not like movies. 之外；也可以 movies 作主語說 The movies don't appeal to him; appeal to 是 "受…所歡迎"的意思。

"相反地"在這裏是 "在另一方面"的意思，要說 on the other hand。

"京劇"：Peking opera

【譯例】

(a) Somehow he doesn't like movies. On the other hand, he takes great interest in Peking opera, and never fails to see it at least once a month.

(b) For some reason or other, the movies don't appeal to him. On the other hand, he is greatly interested in Peking opera and makes it a rule to see it at least once a month.

# 第4天

"你父親空閒的時候做些甚麼？""他多半看看電視，但他對下棋也很有興趣。

【說明】

"空閒的時候"作狀語要說 in one's spare time。

"多半"是 "大部分時間"的意思，要說 most of the time。

146

"看電視": watch TV

"下棋": play chess

## 【譯例】

(a) "What does your father do in his spare time?" "He just watches TV most of the time, but he is also interested in playing chess."

(b) "How does your father spend his spare time?" "He spends most of the time watching TV, though he is also fond of playing chess."


# 第5天

"你開始下圍棋到現在多久了？""剛好3年；但是毫無進步。"

## 【說明】

"圍棋": go, 這是名詞。"下圍棋" play go。

"進步": make progress。"毫無進步": make no progress, 或 make little progress。注意這裏 little 是 "極小" 或 "幾乎沒有" 的意思, 表示否定語氣, 用在不可數名詞之前, 如 He makes little progress in English （他學英語幾乎沒有甚麼進步）; There is little water in the bottle（瓶裏幾乎沒有水）。如用 a little 則表示肯定語氣, 如 He makes a little progress in English（他學英語有點進步）, There is a little water in the bottle（瓶裏有點水）。little 和 a little 的這種區別也適用於 few 和 a few, 但 few 和 a few 要用在可數名詞之前, 如 He has few friends（他幾乎沒有朋友）, He has a few relatives（他有幾個親戚）。little, few 既有否定意義，所以往往也可用 no 去替代它，但其語氣沒有像 no 那樣強。

## 【譯例】

(a) " How long is it since you began to play go? " " Just three years. But I have made little progress. "
(b) " How long have you been playing go? " " Just for three years. But I'm still a poor player. "

# 第 6 天

我的愛好是看書。我想看些新的美國小說。你認為最近出的美國小說中哪本最有趣？

## 【說明】

" 小說 "： novel

" 最近出的 "： latest

" 有趣的 "： interesting；如果是娛樂方面，有趣的可用 entertaining。注意 interesting 與 interested 的區別： interesting 是 " 有趣的 "，如 interesting novel, interesting story, interesting book 等； interested 是 " 感興趣的 "，如 I am（或 feel）interested in the novel, in the story, in the study of English 等。

## 【譯例】

(a) My hobby is reading. I want to read some new American novels. What do you think is the most interesting of the latest ones?
(b) Reading is my hobby. I should like to read some new

American novels. What do you consider to be the most entertaining of the latest ones?

# 第7天

學習英語是我的一項業餘愛好。我經常在空閒時間收聽電台的英語節目。

## 【說明】

"業餘愛好": avocation

"收聽": listen in to; listen to

"節目": programme

## 【譯例】

(a) Learning English is my avocation. I always listen in to the English programmes over the radio in my spare time.

(b) My avocation is to learn English. I make it a rule to listen in my spare time to the English programmes over the radio.

# 第8天

當他埋頭看小説時，不叫他兩三遍是不會來吃晚飯的。

## 【說明】

"埋頭": be absorbed in…; be engrossed in…

"晚飯"這裏譯作 dinner。按照英美人習慣，dinner 是較爲正

149

式的一頓膳食，通常在晚上吃；但也有在中午吃 dinner 的，那晚飯就叫做 supper。

"不叫他兩三遍他不會來吃晚飯的" 可譯作 He will have to be called two or three times before he comes to dinner，或 He will not come to dinner unless he is called two or three times。

## 【譯例】

(a) When he is absorbed in reading a novel, he will have to be called two or three times before he comes to dinner.

(b) When he is engrossed in reading a novel, he will not come to dinner unless he is called two or three times.

# 第 9 天

他像是個 " 書迷 "，一有空就讀這讀那。

## 【說明】

" 像是 "： as it were; so to speak，是 " 可以這麼說 " 的意思。

" 書迷 "： bookworm；這個詞也可作 " 書蟲 " 解，但在英語裏 bookworm 是指 " 極愛讀書的人 "，並無 " 書蟲 " 或 " 書獸 " 等語所含的貶義，所以當面稱人為 bookworm 並不是侮辱或恥笑他。

" 一有空 "： whenever he finds time，或 as often as he finds time; as often as 是 " 每當 " 的意思。

" 讀這讀那 "： read some book or other

## 【譯例】

(a) He is, as it were, a "bookworm", and is always reading some book or other whenever he finds time.

(b) As often as he finds time, he reads some book or other. He is, so to speak, a "bookworm"

# 第 10 天

我既不是學者，也不是作家。我只是喜愛搜羅珍本書籍。我在找尋書的時候覺得時間比我在呷咖啡時還過得快。

## 【說明】

"既不是…也不是… "：neither…nor…。注意：neither, nor 連接句子時主謂語要倒裝，如 I'm not a scholar, nor am I a writer. You don't know his name, neither do I。

"學者"：scholar

"作家"：writer

"搜羅"：collect

"珍本書籍"：rare books

"找尋"：look for; hunt for

"呷"：sip

## 【譯例】

(a) I'm neither a scholar nor a writer. I'm simply fond of collecting rare books. When I'm looking for books, it seems to me that time passes more quickly than when I'm sipping coffee.

(b) I'm not a scholar, nor am I a writer. Only I'm interested in collecting rare books. Time seems to me to pass more quickly while I'm hunting for books than when I'm having a cup of coffee.

# 第 11 天

我的姪兒太愛打撲克了。如果繼續這樣打下去的話，入學考試怕
會不及格。

## 【說明】

"太愛"除了 be too much absorbed in, be too fond of 之外；
對於某些習慣如烟、酒、賭博之類，也可說 indulge too much in。

"撲克"：poker。"打撲克"通常說 play cards。

"入學考試"：entrance examination。"考試及格"可說 pass
the examination, 或 succeed in the examination。"考試不及格"：
fail (in) the examination。

## 【譯例】

(a) My nephew is too much absorbed in playing cards. If he
goes on like that, I'm afraid he will not be able to pass the entrance examination.

(b) My nephew indulges too much in playing cards. I'm afraid
he will fail in the entrance examination if he doesn't break off this
evil habit.


# 第 12 天

"如果到無人島去居住的話，你帶甚麼書去呢？""帶《魯濱遜
漂流記》去。"

## 【說明】

"如果⋯，你帶⋯？"這句話純屬假設，實際上不會有這種事，所以要用虛擬語氣。假設如爲現在的，動詞要用過去時，如 If I had time, I would certainly go。在條件句中動詞用到 be 的，不論人稱，一律用 were, 如 If he were here, he would help us。假設如爲未來的事，條件句中動詞用 were to（或 should）＋動詞原形，如 If he were to（或 should）do it, he would not fail; 也可不用 if, 而把 were 放在句首，如 Were he to do it, he would not fail。

"無人島"：a desert island, 或 an uninhabited island; uninhabited 是 "無人居住的"的意思。

"帶去"：take, 後面要跟 with you。

"魯濱遜漂流記"：書名 Robinson Crusoe

【譯例】

(a) "If you were to live on a desert island, what book would you take with you?" "I would like 'Robinson Crusoe'"

(b) "Suppose you were to go and live on some uninhabited island, what book would you choose to carry?" "Robinson Crusoe."


# 第 13 天

那個女演員唱得多好啊! 如果能演得更好些，一定會成爲第一流的演員。

【說明】

"女演員"：actress。"男演員"是 actor; performer 則男女通用。

153

" 演 " ： act; play; perform

" 第一流的 " ： first-class

## 【譯例】

(a) How marvellously that actress sings! If she could act a little better, she would certainly be one of the best performers.

(b) What a wonderful singer that actress is! She would surely be rated (as) a first-class actress if she could perform better.


# 第 14 天

" 你踢足球還是打籃球？ " " 我兩種都玩。我很喜愛球類活動，但遺憾的是我既不是足球運動員，也不是籃球運動員。 "

## 【說明】

" 足球 " ： football。 " 足球運動員 " ： footballer, football player

" 籃球 " ： basketball。 " 籃球運動員 " ： basketballer; basketball player

" 球類活動 " ： ball games

## 【譯例】

(a) " Which do you play, football or basketball? " " I play both of them. I like ball games very much; but sorry to say, I'm neither a footballer nor a basketballer. "

(b) " Which game do you play, football or basketball? " " Both of them. I like to play ball; but to my regret, I'm neither a football player nor a basketball player. "

# 第 15 天

　　雖然他現在已經上了年紀，但在今天的足球比賽中，他踢得十分出色。據說年輕時他是個足球健將。

## 【說明】

　　"足球比賽"：football match
　　"踢得十分出色"：play admirably（或 extraordinarily）well
　　"足球健將"：top-notch footballer（或 football player）

## 【譯例】

　　(a) Although he is getting on in years, he played admirably well in today's football match. In his youth, he was a top-notch footballer, they say.

　　(b) He is getting old, but in today's football match he played extraordinarily well. It is said that he was a top-notch football player when he was a young man.


# 第 16 天

　　他問我："今天下午你想不想去看網球比賽？如果想去的話，我開車來接你。"

## 【說明】

　　"今天下午你想不想去看網球比賽？…"這是直接引語，可照字譯；也可把這段話改爲間接引語。在間接引語裏的代詞、時間狀語和動詞的時態都要作相應的改變, 如 "今天下午" 要改爲 "那天下午"；

155

"你"要改爲"我"；"我"要改爲"他"；動詞要改爲過去時。

"網球比賽"：tennis match

"開車來接"：call for someone in a car, 或照前例用 pick someone up。

## 【譯例】

(a) He said to me, "Would you like to go to the tennis match this afternoon? If so, I'll call for you in my car."

(b) He asked me if I would like to go to the tennis match this afternoon. If so, he would pick me up.

# 第 17 天

*她不擅長體育活動，但因爲少年時代是在沿海地區度過的關係，所以對游泳還是滿有把握的。*

## 【說明】

"體育活動"：sports

"擅長"：be good（或 skilful）at。"不擅長體育活動"：be not good at sports; 也可說 be not a clever athlete; athlete 是 "運動員"。

"少年時代" 因爲這裏所指的是個女孩子，所以要說 girlhood。 "度過少年時代"：spend her girlhood。

"沿海地區"：coastal areas

"有把握" have confidence in 或 be confident in, 注意要用介詞 in。

(a) She is not good at sports, but as she spent her girlhood in the coastal areas, at least she has confidence in her swimming.

(b) Though (she is) not a clever athlete, she is confident in her swimming at least, as she spent her girlhood in the coastal areas.

# 第 18 天

年輕的時候我本來頗擅長游泳，但現在由於身體不好，所以要我游 3 哩是相當困難的。

【說明】

"本來" 在英語裏可以不譯，只用動詞過去時就可以了。

"身體（不）好"：be in (out of) condition; be in good (poor 或 bad) health

"相當"：rather, pretty。"要我游 3 哩是相當困難的" 可用 it is…for me to… 這個句型。

【譯例】

(a) I was a pretty good swimmer when I was young. But now I'm out of condition, so it is rather hard for me to swim three miles.

(b) I was pretty good at swimming in my youth, but as I'm in poor health now, it is hard for me to swim three miles.

# 第 19 天

羽毛球好像漸漸變得流行了。我真想能學一下。

## 【說明】

"羽毛球"： badminton

"變得流行"： become popular; win popularity

"真想"： wish，這個動詞後面的從句要用虛擬語氣，如 I wish I were a student。如所想的事是過去的，則動詞要用過去完成時，如 I wish I had studied English better at school。

## 【譯例】

(a) It seems that badminton is gradually winning popularity. I wish I could learn how to play it.

(b) Badminton seems to be becoming more and more popular. How I wish I could learn to play it!

# 第 20 天

溜冰季節就要到了。我開始溜冰到現在已經 5 年，但還遠遠說不上高明。

## 【說明】

"溜冰季節"： the skating season, 或 the season for skating

"就要到了"： be near at hand, 或 be drawing near

"高明"是"成為一個溜冰能手"的意思，要說 be a good skater。

"還遠遠說不上高明"就是說"要成為一個溜冰能手還有一段很長的

時間 ", 可譯爲 It will be a long time before I'm a good skater, 或意譯爲 I find it pretty hard to make great progress in a short time。

## 【譯例】

(a) The skating season is near at hand. It's already five years since I first learned to skate, but it will be a long time before I'm a good skater.

(b) The season for skating is drawing near. Five years have already passed since I started to learn skating, but I find it pretty hard to make any great progress in a short time.

# 第21天

在所有冬季體育運動中, 就它們對我們的健康和娛樂來說, 把溜冰算作最好是不會言之過甚的。

## 【說明】

"冬季體育運動 ": winter sports

"就…來說 ": as ( 或 so ) far as…is (are) concerned

"最好 ": best

"不會言之過甚 ": It is not too much to say that…, It is not going too far to say that…, 或 It is no exaggeration to say that…; exaggeration 是 " 誇張 "。

## 【譯例】

(a) It is not too much to say that, of all winter sports, skating is the best as far as our health and enjoyment are concerned.

(b) It is no exaggeration to say that skating is the best of all winter sports, so far as our health and enjoyment are concerned.

# 第 22 天

我的妹妹善於拉小提琴。上星期在音樂會上參加演出博得全場喝彩。

## 【說明】

"拉小提琴": play the violin。注意: 玩某種樂器, 在樂器名詞之前要有冠詞 the, 如 play the piano ( 彈鋼琴 ), play the accordion ( 拉手風琴 ), play the flute ( 吹長笛 ); 但如作某種遊戲如打球、下棋之類則名詞之前不加冠詞, 如 play football, play basketball, play chess。

"參加": take part in; participate in, 注意要用介詞 in。

"音樂會": concert

"演出": performance

"博得全場喝彩": draw loud applause from the audience, 或 bring down the house

## 【譯例】

(a) My younger sister is very good at playing the violin. Last week she took part in the performance at the concert and drew loud applause from the audience.

(b) My younger sister, who is now very skilful at playing the violin, brought down the house last week when she participated in the performance at the concert.

160

# 第23天

"從你的説話來判斷，你一定是位音樂家。""不，差遠哩。我只是個業餘愛好者，不過我非常喜歡音樂，特別是貝多芬的作品。"

## 【説明】

"從…來判斷"：Judging from…，或 To judge from…

"説話"：remarks。"從你的説話來判斷"可説 Judging from your remarks；也可説 Judging from what you say。

"一定"除了 surely, certainly 等副詞外；也可用情態動詞must 表示推斷，如 You must be a musician。

"差遠哩"：far from it；也可説 not in the least。

"業餘愛好者"：amateur

"貝多芬"：Beethoven

## 【譯例】

(a) "Judging from your remarks, you are surely a musician." "No, far from it. I'm only an amateur. But I like music very much, particularly the music by Beethoven."

(b) "To judge from what you say, you must be a musician." "No, not in the least. I'm nothing more than an amateur. But I'm really very keen on music, especially that by Beethoven."

# 第24天

他説他不懂音樂。彈鋼琴是完全不行的。

"不懂音樂" 要說 have no musical sense, 或 have no ear for music。

"彈鋼琴完全不行" 是 "絕對不會彈鋼琴" 的意思, 可譯作 can't play the piano at all; 或用比喻的說法 can no more play the piano than a pig can fly.

【譯例】

(a) He says he has no musical sense and can't play the piano at all.

(b) He confesses that he has no ear for music and can no more play the piano than a pig can fly.

# 第 25 天

我的父親原來期望我的妹妹當內科醫生, 但她却喜歡繪畫, 把每天的時間都化在繪畫上, 所以最後他讓步了, 讓她去當畫家。

【說明】

"期望": desire, 這個動詞後面可接賓語和不定詞, 如 My father desired my younger sister to be a physician; 也可接以 that 引起的賓語從句, 那從句裏的動詞通常用 should 或動詞原形, 如 My father desired that my younger sister (should) be a physician。

"繪畫": paint; 名詞是 painting。 "畫家" 是 painter。

"讓步": give in

(a) My father desired that my younger sister be a physician, but as she was so fond of painting tnat she spent every day with her brush, he finally gave in and permitted her to become a painter.

(b) Though my father desired my younger sister to be a physician, she was so fond of painting as to paint every day, so at last he gave in and permitted her to become a painter.

# 第 26 天

多出色的雕塑啊！這是我所看到的最好的一件藝術品。我想你也沒有看到過這樣的傑作吧。

【說明】

"雕塑": sculpture

"藝術品": work of art

"傑作": masterpiece。"你也沒有看到過這樣的傑作": You too have never seen such a masterpiece。注意 too 不可放在否定詞之後，如可以說 I don't know German, and he too doesn't know it, 但不可說 he doesn't know it too, 這裏的 too 該改作 either。

【譯例】

(a) What a fine piece of sculpture this is! I have never seen such a splendid work of art. Perhaps you too have never seen one like it.

(b) What a fine piece of sculpture! It's the finest work of art I have ever seen. I suppose you have never seen such a masterpiece either.

# 第27天

昨天天氣很好，又沒有甚麼特殊的事情；因此下午我和我的兄弟出去釣魚，但很可惜，一條也沒捕到。

## 【說明】

"沒有甚麼特殊的事情":have nothing particular to do; particular 要放在 nothing 之後。同樣, something, anything 等代詞, 有形容詞時也要放在後面, 如 There is something new. Is there anything wrong?

"去釣魚": go fishing

"捕到": catch

## 【譯例】

(a) Yesterday it was very fine and I had nothing particular to do, so I went fishing with my brother, but unluckily we couldn't catch a fish.

(b) As it was fine and I was free yesterday, I went fishing with my brother, but sorry to say, we didn't catch a single fish.

# 第28天

"下星期今天想和朋友去露營。""那好啊!但是山上天氣多變, 要作周密的準備才好。"

## 【說明】

"下星期今天": this day week, 或 today week, 這種說法也可

164

指上星期今天，因此是指上星期或下星期就要看句子裏的動詞了，如 He got back this day week（上星期今天他回來了），He will get back this day week（下星期今天他會回來）；同樣的用法還有 this day（或 today）month, this day（或 today）year。

"露營"：camp 是動詞。"去露營"可仿照 go fishing 的結構說 go camping; 類似的例子有 go skating, go skiing, go hunting, go shopping, go boating 等。

"那好啊！"：That's fine, 或 That's a good idea.

"作周密的準備"：make careful preparations

## 【譯例】

(a) "I'm planning to go camping with my friends this day week." "That's fine! But you'd better make careful preparations. The weather in the mountains is very changeable."

(b) "I'll go camping with my friends today week." "That's a good idea. But I advise you to make careful preparations as the weather is so changeable in the mountains."

# 第 29 天

"請你同我跳舞好不好？""怕不行，我從來沒學過。""那麼我來教你吧。我帶舞是很不錯的，來吧！"

## 【說明】

"怕不行"是"恐怕我跳不來"的意思，要說 I'm afraid I can't, 或 Sorry, I can't.

"那麼"：then

"帶舞不錯": be a good pilot; pilot 是指一個技巧熟練的舞伴 (dancing partner 或 partner)。

"來吧": Come on, 或 Let's go.

## 【譯例】

(a) "Won't you dance with me?" "I'm afraid I can't. — I've never learned." "I'll teach you then. I'm a good pilot. Come on!"

(b) "Excuse me, but let's have a dance." "Sorry, I can't. — I've never learned." "Then, I'll teach you. A good pilot, I am. Let's go."


# 第30天

倘若早上沒看報就去學校, 你是否會覺得好像遺忘了甚麼東西?

## 【說明】

"沒有看報": without reading the newspaper

"去學校": leave home for school, 或 set out for school

"覺得好像": feel as if…; as if 之後要用虛擬語氣。

"遺忘了甚麼東西": leave something behind

## 【譯例】

(a) When you leave home for school in the morning without reading the newspaper, don't you feel as if you had left something behind?

(b) We feel as if we had left something behind if we set out for school in the morning without reading the newspaper, don't we?

# Words and Expressions

| | |
|---|---|
| be interested in; be keen on | 喜愛 |
| take pictures ( 或 photos ) | 攝影 |
| camera | 照相機 |
| photographer [fə'tɔgrəfə] | 攝影家 |
| hobby | 愛好 |
| avocation [ˌævou'keiʃən] | 業餘愛好 |
| occasionally | 偶然 |
| movie ( 或 film ) fan | 影迷 |
| Peking opera | 京劇 |
| in one's spare time | 在空閑的時候 |
| watch TV | 看電視 |
| play chess (go) | 下棋 ( 圍棋 ) |
| make progress ['prougres] | 進步 |
| novel ['nɔvəl] | 小說 |
| listen in to; listen to | 收聽 |
| programme ['prougræm] | 節目 |
| be absorbed in; be engrossed [in'groust] in | 埋頭於 |
| scholar | 學者 |
| writer | 作家 |
| play cards | 打牌 |
| entrance examination | 入學考試 |

| | |
|---|---|
| pass the examination; succeed in the examination | 考試及格 |
| fail (in) the examination | 考試不及格 |
| actor（男）; actress（女）; performer | 演員 |
| football | 足球 |
| basketball | 籃球 |
| tennis | 網球 |
| badminton [ˈbædmintən] | 羽毛球 |
| ball games | 球類活動 |
| match | 比賽 |
| be good at; be skilful at | 善於（擅長） |
| have confidence in; be confident in | 有把握 |
| be near at hand; be drawing near | 就要到來 |
| as（或 so）far as…is (are) concerned | 就…來說 |
| concert [ˈkɔnsət] | 音樂會 |
| performance | 演出 |
| take part in; participate in [pɑːˈtisipeit] | 參加 |
| draw loud applause from the audience; bring down the house | 博得全場喝彩 |
| amateur [ˈæmətəː] | 業餘愛好者 |
| have no ear for music | 不懂音樂 |
| painting; painter | 繪畫; 畫家 |
| sculpture [ˈskʌlptʃə] | 雕塑 |

work of art                    藝術品

masterpiece                    傑作

go fishing                     去釣魚


# Exercise  6

Translate the following into English:

1. 我的侄兒很喜歡畫畫，每天總要畫上一二小時，但他還不能畫得很好。（第1天）

2. 他很喜歡看電影。他說每星期至少要看一次電影。（第2天）

3. 不知道爲甚麼他不喜歡學數學，相反對音樂却非常感興趣，每天至少要拉一小時小提琴。（第3天）

4. 甲：你每逢星期天做些甚麼？
   乙：通常同家裏人一道去看看電影，有時也同朋友下下棋。（第4天）

5. 我拉小提琴已經5年，但可惜我還不是個音樂家。（第1,5天）

6. 我的業餘愛好是學習英語。我想買一本英語語法書。你認爲哪一本最好？（第6,7天）

7. 在空閑的時候我經常看看小說。有時我也看英文小說。但由於我的英語水平差（poor knowledge of English）要完全看懂還有困難。（第6,7天）

8. 看小說確是非常有趣的，有時別人不提醒（remind）我，我甚至會忘記吃飯。（第8天）

9. 他像是個影迷，一有空就去看電影。有些電影他甚至看上兩三遍。（第2,9天）

10. 他既不吸烟也不飲酒，只是愛喝咖啡。他覺得每餐之後喝上一杯

咖啡是個享受。（第10天）

11. 他的兒子既不念書也不工作，但專愛打撲克。我怕他對家裏會全無用處。（第10，11天）

12. 如果你懂英語，就能看原版（original）的《魯濱遜漂流記了》。（第12天）

13. 要是我能進大學，我要學醫學。（第12，13天）

14. 要是這本小說能譯成英文的話，那麼懂英文的人一定會對它感到興趣。（第13天）

15. 甲：你是足球運動員還是籃球運動員？

乙：我既不是足球運動員，也不是籃球運動員，但我對這兩種運動（games）都喜歡。（第14天）

16. 雖然他的父親現在已經上了年紀，但走起路來還像個年輕人。據說40年前他還是個運動健將哩。（第15天）

17. 他對我說："明天有一場籃球比賽。如果你想去看的話，我可以替你去買票。"（第16天）

18. 他告訴我他年輕時擅長體育活動，一口氣（at a stretch）游5哩全不在乎（it was nothing for him to…）。（第16，17，18天）

19. 近年來乒乓球（table tennis）變得愈來愈流行了。許多年輕人都擅長打乒乓球。我的弟弟也很希望能學一下。（第17，19天）

20. 甲：你喜歡溜冰嗎？

乙：是的，我已經學了4年。

甲：那麼你一定溜得很好了吧？

乙：差得遠呢！（第20，23天）

21. 就其有用來說，英語是世界上最重要的語言之一，這大概不會是言之過甚的。（第21天）

22. 他的哥哥擅長下圍棋，上星期參加比賽贏得了第一名（come out

first）。（第22天）

23. 甲：從你的英語水平（level）來判斷，你一定是個留學生。

乙：不,我不曾到過外國,不過我非常喜歡學英語, 說我英語好,
其實還差得遠呢。（第23天）

24. 從她的說話來判斷, 她似乎不懂音樂, 我猜想她不會拉小提琴。
（第23, 24天）

25. 我原來期望我的兒子當工程師, 但他却要學物理, 作爲一個物理
學家, 他並不出色。（第25天）

26. 多麼美麗的詩（poem）啊! 我認爲這是他所寫的最好的一首詩,
你看過這樣的傑作嗎? （第26天）

27. 昨天晚上因爲沒有甚麼重要的事情, 我的朋友詹妮邀我去參加音
樂會,但遺憾得很, 我是不懂音樂的, 所以並不感到有甚麼樂趣。
（第27天）

28. 上星期今天, 我同幾個同學一道去露營。山中氣候多變, 幸虧事
前（in advance）作了周密的準備, 所以我們過得很愉快。（第
28天）

29. 甲：你會跳舞嗎?

乙：我從來沒學過。

甲：那麼我來教你吧。只要你肯嘗試,我相信一定會跳得很不錯。
（第29天）

30. 甲：你的愛好是甚麼?

乙：我最喜歡音樂。

甲：那你一定是個音樂家。

乙：差遠哩。我只是個業餘愛好者。

甲：你會玩甚麼樂器嗎? （musical instrument）

乙：我偶然拉拉手風琴, 對小提琴也有興趣, 但可惜兩者我都拉
得不好。（第2, 10, 23天）

# 第7月
# 旅行、遊覽、參觀

## 第1天

只要有足夠的錢,旅行真是件樂事。我只要一儲蓄了足夠的旅費,馬上就去旅行。

### 【說明】

"只要"除了 as long as, so long as 之外;也可說 If only。

"旅行": travelling; 動詞是 travel。"旅行者"是 traveller。"去旅行"可說 go to travel, go travelling, go on a journey, 或 set out on a journey; journey 是"旅程"的意思。

"真是件樂事"可照字譯說 be really a pleasure;但也可說 be the pleasantest thing there is; there is 前面省去了關係代詞 that, 是定語從句, 意思是"現有的", 如 This is the fastest train there is to Shatin (這是到沙田的最快一班車); I must make full use of the time there is to study English well (我必須充分利用現有的時間學好英語)。

"儲蓄": save up money

"旅費": travelling expenses

"一…馬上就…"除了 as soon as 之外;也可用 whenever, 是"每當…"的意思, 如 Please come here whenever you have time。

### 【譯例】

(a) So long as one has enough money, travelling is the pleasantest

172

thing there is. I always make it a rule to go on a journey whenever I have saved up money enough to meet my travelling expenses.

(b) If we can only secure enough money, travelling is really a pleasure. As soon as I have saved up money sufficient to pay the travelling expenses, I never fail to set out on a journey.

# 第 2 天

過去旅行者常常要步行，如今因爲有各種快速的交通工具，所以在世界上任何地方我們都能自由地享受這種方便。

## 【說明】

“過去”這裏指古代，所以要說 in olden times, 或 in former days; times, days 都要用複數。

“常常要步行”是指過去經常性的動作，可按前例說 used to go on foot, 或 very often had to go on foot; 如理解爲過去人們習慣於這樣做，也可說 were used（或 accustomed）to going on foot.

“快速的交通工具”：quick（或 fast）communication facilities; facilities 這個詞涵義很廣。它的基本意義是“方便”，如 facilities for travellers 是“對旅行者的各種方便”，引伸就指設備或工具，所以 communication facilities 就作“交通工具”解。

## 【譯例】

(a) In former days, travellers used to go on foot, but nowadays we have various means of fast communication and can freely enjoy the benefits of those facilities in every part of the world.

(b) In olden times, travellers were accustomed to going on foot, but today we can avail ourselves of various quick communication facilities everywhere in the world.

# 第3天

你一踏上外國的國土就會感到奇怪，好比突然從自己的國家進入了一個新的世界。

## 【說明】

"你"這裏籠統地指任何人，所以可譯作 you；也可用 one。

"踏上"：land

"外國"：foreign country

"突然進入" suddenly go into；也可說 jump into。

## 【譯例】

(a) You will feel strange as soon as you land in a foreign country. It is like jumping from your own country into a new world.

(b) How strange one feels after just landing in a foreign country, which is like a new world one has jumped into from one's own country!

# 第4天

"你準備怎樣旅行，是乘車、乘船還是乘飛機？""我還未決定哩。我要到旅行社去詢問一下。""是一次遊覽旅行吧？""不，是出差去的。"

**【說明】**

"乘車、乘船還是乘飛機": by train, by ship or by plane; 也可說 by land, by sea ( 或 water ) or by air, 是 "由陸路、水路還是航空" 的意思。注意名詞前都不用冠詞。

"還未決定": haven't made up one's mind; 也可簡單地說 can't say。

"旅行社": travel bureau; travel service

"詢問": make inquiries。"到旅行社去詢問" 可說 make inquiries at the travel bureau; 也可說 go to the travel service for some information.

"遊覽旅行": sightseeing trip, pleasure trip, 或 a trip for pleasure

"出差": go on business; be away on official business

**【譯例】**

(a) "How will you travel—by train, by ship or by plane?" "I haven't made up my mind yet. I'm going to make inquiries at the travel bureau." "Will it be a sightseeing trip?" "No, I'm going on business."

(b) "Are you going to travel by land, by sea or by air?" "Well, I can't say. I'll go to the travel service for some information." "Is it a pleasure trip?" "No, I'll be away on official business."

# 第5天

"聽說你寒假去新加坡旅行，是嗎？" "是的，但不是去遊覽，是去探望住在醫院裏的伯父。"

"旅行"作動詞, 除了 travel 之外; 也可說 take a trip, 或 make a trip。

"伯父": uncle

【譯例】

(a) "I hear you took a trip to Singapore during the winter vacation." "Yes, I did, but it was not for sightseeing. I went to visit my uncle who was in the hospital."

(b) "Somebody told me you went to Singapore during the winter vacation." "Yes, but not for pleasure, I only went there to see my uncle in the hospital."

# 第 6 天

一聲汽笛火車開行了, 旅客向他們送行的朋友和親戚揮手告別。

【説明】

"汽笛": whistle

"旅客": passenger

"親戚": relative

"揮手": wave one's hand, 或 wave。"揮手告別" wave good-bye to somebody。

【譯例】

(a) A whistle was heard and the train started. The passengers waved their last good-bye to the friends and relatives who had come to wish them bon voyage.

(b) The train started after the whistle and the passengers waved their hands to the friends and relatives who had come to see them off.

# 第7天

我盡可能避免乘飛機旅行。從飛機上俯視天空、雲彩以及遙遙在下的地面很快就感到厭倦。

## 【說明】

"盡可能"：if (it is) possible; if I can help it

"避免乘飛機旅行"：try not to travel by air，或 avoid travelling by air。注意動詞 avoid 後面要用動名詞，不可用不定詞，如不可說 avoid to travel by air。

"俯視"：look down, 後面接 at 及 upon, 如 look down at the sky, or clouds, or upon the surface of the earth。

"遙遙在下的地面"：the surface of the earth far below; 簡單地譯作 beneath me 也可。

"感到厭倦"：get tired（或 weary）of

## 【譯例】

(a) I have been trying not to travel by air if possible. I soon get tired of looking down from the plane at the sky, or clouds, or upon the surface of the earth far below.

(b) I always avoid travelling by air if I can help it, because I soon get weary of looking down from the plane at the sky or clouds, or upon the world beneath me.

# 第8天

"我怕乘飛機旅行要比乘火車貴得多。這票價我負担不起。""飛機票的價錢肯定要比火車票貴些, 但你到達目的地却要快得多。"

## 【說明】

"貴": expensive; costly; dear。"貴得多"much more expensive; 同樣, "快得多"可以說 much quicker。

"票價": fare

"負担不起": can't afford, 是"買不起"的意思, 如 This car is dear. I can't afford to buy it; 也可說 I can't afford the car。

"價錢": price

"火車票": railway ticket。"飛機票"是 airline ticket。

## 【譯例】

(a) "I'm afraid travelling by air is much more expensive than by land. I can't afford the fare." "Surely, the price is higher than a railway ticket, but you'll reach your destination much quicker."

(b) "Travelling by air may be much more expensive than by land. I can't afford to buy the ticket, I'm afraid." "Of course, an airline ticket is more expensive, but think how much quicker you can reach your destination."

# 第9天

對那些要節省時間的人來說, 乘飛機旅行是最好的辦法; 但對那些有充裕時間的人來說, 乘火車旅行似乎更好, 因爲乘車旅行可以在路上觀賞景色。

178

"節省時間": save time。"對那些要節省時間的人來說": for those who want to save time

"充裕的時間": plenty of time; much time

"在路上觀賞景色": enjoy sightseeing on one's way; see the sights on one's way

【譯例】

(a) Travelling by air is the best way for those who want to save time. But for those who have plenty of time, it seems better to travel by land. By doing so, they can enjoy sightseeing on their way.

(b) Those who want to save time had better travel by air, while those who have much time will find it better to travel by land because they can see the sights on their way.

# 第 10 天

如今旅行者只求盡快到達目的地,對路上的風景幾乎不大關心了。

【說明】

"只求": think only of

"盡快": as soon as possible

"風景": scenery; views。"路上的風景": the scenery（或 views）on the way。

"不關心": be indifferent to; 如以 scenery 或 views 作主語 也可以說 The views on the way matter little to them。

179

## 【譯例】

(a) Nowadays, travellers think only of reaching their destination as soon as possible, they are almost indifferent to the scenery on the way.

(b) Today, travellers only think of reaching their destination as soon as possible. The views on the way matter comparatively little to them.

# 第 11 天

"飛機甚麼時候起飛？""在午夜。""我們怎麼去機場呢？""從市中心到飛機場有公共汽車，但如果你願意的話，也可叫出租汽車。"

## 【說明】

"起飛"：take off

"從…到…有公共汽車"可以說 There is a bus service from…to…; 或以 we 爲主語說 We can take the bus from…to…。

"市中心"：the centre of the city, 或 city centre

"飛機場"：airport; airfield

"如果你願意的話"：if you like; if you wish

"叫出租汽車"take a taxi; 也可以 taxi 作主語說 a taxi is available; available 是"可以叫得到"的意思。

## 【譯例】

(a) "When does the plane take off?" "At midnight." "How shall we go to the airport?" "There is a bus service from the centre of the city to the airport. But we can take a taxi if you wish."

(b) "What time is the plane going to take off?" "At midnight."

"How shall we get to the airport?" "We can take the bus from the city centre to the airport. A taxi is also available if you want to have one."

# 第 12 天

"現在是適合飛行的天氣嗎？天空陰暗，我怕會取消飛行。" "誰說這不是飛行天氣？既無霧又無風暴，不會阻礙飛行的。"

## 【說明】

"適合飛行的天氣"：flying weather

"陰暗"：overcast

"取消飛行"：cancel the flights

"霧"：fog；（薄的）mist

"阻礙"：prevent

## 【譯例】

(a) "Is it flying weather just now? The sky is so overcast that they might cancel the flights, I'm afraid."
"Who says it is not flying weather? There is no fog, no storm, nothing to prevent the flight."

(b) "I doubt whether it is flying weather just now. It is overcast, so I think the flights might be cancelled."
"Has anybody told you it is not flying weather? You see there is neither mist nor storm to prevent the flight."

# 第 13 天

去年夏天我乘船到日本去，海上風浪很大，船顛簸搖擺，有些旅客暈船暈得十分屬害。

## 【說明】

"海上風浪很大"：可譯作 The sea was very rough; rough 是 "不平靜"的意思；也可用 choppy 這個詞。

"顛簸搖擺"：toss; 也可用 pitch and roll 這兩個詞。pitch 是 "前後顛簸"，roll 是"左右搖擺"。

"暈船"：seasick; 名詞是 seasickness。

## 【譯例】

(a) Last summer I went to Japan by water. As the sea was very rough and the ship tossed terribly, some passengers were quite seasick.

(b) When I went to Japan by water last summer, the sea was very choppy. The ship pitched and rolled so terribly that some passengers were completely seasick.

# 第 14 天

天氣好，海上旅行總是件愉快的事；但海上風浪大的時候，那是最不舒服的，特別是易於暈船的話。

## 【說明】

"天氣好"是"在天氣好的時候"的意思，所以要說 when the weather is fine, 或改成短語說 in fine weather 也可。

"海上旅行"：sea trip

"容易暈船": 除了 get seasick easily 之外; 也可說 be not a good sailor。注意: be a good sailor 是 "不會暈船的人"; 反之 be a bad sailor 就是 "會暈船的人", 這裏不可照字面解釋。

## 【譯例】

(a) A sea trip is always enjoyable in fine weather, but it is most uncomfortable when the sea is rough, especially if one gets seasick easily.

(b) It is always delightful to take a sea trip when the weather is fine. But if the sea is choppy, it is most uncomfortable, especially for those who are not good sailors.

# 第 15 天

"你想海面會平靜嗎?""是的, 按照天氣預報, 海面可能是平靜的。你在担憂暈船, 是不是?""是的, 我是會暈船的。"

## 【說明】

"平靜": calm; smooth。"海面會平靜的" The sea will be calm; 也可用 we 作主語, 說 we shall have a calm sea。

"可能": likely

"担憂": worry about

"我是會暈船的" 可按照前例說 I'm a poor sailor, 或 I'm not much of a sailor。

## 【譯例】

(a) "Do you think we shall have a calm sea?" "Yes, according to the weather forecast the sea is likely to be calm. Why, you are worrying about seasickness, aren't you?" "Yes, rather. I'm a poor sailor."

(b) "Do you believe the sea will be smooth?" "Yes, the weather forecast promises us a smooth sea. Are you afraid of being seasick?" "Yes, I'm not much of a sailor."


# 第 16 天

港口雖然只是船隻進進出出的場所，但却有某些不可思議的魅力。

## 【說明】

"港口"：harbour

"只是船隻進進出出的場所"：be only a place where ships are coming in and going out

"有某些不可思議的魅力"：has a strange fascination; 或把 fascination 改成形容詞 fascinating，說 there is something peculiarly（或 strangely）fascinating about it 也可。

## 【譯例】

(a) A harbour is only a place where ships are coming in and going out, but there is something peculiarly fascinating about it.

(b) A harbour is no better than a place where ships go in and out, but it has a strange fascination of its own.


# 第 17 天

"輪船不在碼頭停泊嗎？""是的，我想它會在港口拋錨。""我們怎樣上岸呢，乘汽艇還是小船？""大概是汽艇吧。"

【說明】

"停泊"：moor

"碼頭"：wharf; quay; pier。"輪船不在碼頭停泊嗎？"：Doesn't the steamer moor at the wharf? 這是否定的疑問句，在答句裏如果同意對方的話不可用 yes 而要用 no。這是英語在用語習慣上與漢語不同的地方，因爲漢語在這種場合要用"是的"，如"Don't you know him?"（你不認識他嗎？）"No, I don't."（是的，我不認識他。）Yes, I do.（不，我認識他。）這裏的一個規律是答句如爲否定的要用 no；如爲肯定的要用 Yes。

"拋錨"：cast anchor; drop anchor; anchor。"它在港口拋錨"：She anchors in the harbour, 指船可以用代詞 she。

"上岸"：get ashore; go on shore

"汽艇"：(steam) launch

"小船"：boat

【譯例】

(a) "Doesn't the steamer moor at the wharf?" " No, she anchors in the harbour, I believe." "How do we get ashore, by steam launch or by boat?" " By steam launch, I think."

(b) " The steamer doesn't moor at the pier, does she?" " No, she will cast anchor in the harbour, I think." " How shall we go on shore, by launch or by boat?" " Probably by launch."

# 第18天

我曾一度由陸路在美洲大陸各地旅行。我可以說，如果你眞想看看一個國家的話，那就一定要乘汽車和火車旅行。

## 【說明】

"美洲大陸"： American continent。"在美洲大陸各地旅行"：travel around the American continent

"如果你真想看看一個國家"： if you really want to see a country, 或 to see how a country is

"一定"： by all means

## 【譯例】

(a) I've travelled around the American continent by land once and I can say that if you really want to see a country, you will have to make a bus-and-train tour by all means.

(b) According to my experience of travelling around the continent of America by land, I would like to advise you to try by all means to travel by bus and train if you really want to see how a country is.

# 第 19 天

"我想乘船而不乘飛機到美國去。""但那是一種奢侈，除了有充裕時間的人之外，誰也不能享受。"

## 【說明】

"想乘船而不乘飛機到美國去"：除了可譯作 go over to America not by plane but by ship 之外； 也可說 go over to America on board a ship instead of a plane; instead of 是 "而不…" 的意思; 此外, 還可說 prefer a voyage to flying when I go over to America。

"有充裕時間的人": those who have much time to spare, 或簡單地說 leisured people 也可；leisured 是 "空閑的" 的意思。

"奢侈": luxury

## 【譯例】

(a) "I'd like to go over to America on board a ship instead of a plane." "But it is a luxury which can't be enjoyed by anybody except those who have much time to spare."

(b) "I prefer a voyage to flying when I go over to America." "But it is a luxury which only leisured people can enjoy."

# 第 20 天

"你到過美國嗎？" "沒有。有一次差點兒就要去了。預定同一個代表團一起去的，但到最後計劃取消了。"

## 【說明】

"差一點兒就要去了": I very nearly went once.

"預定…去": be to go; be ＋不定詞可表示預定的動作，如 I am to go to the movies this evening; 表示過去預定要做某事則要用 was (were)＋不定詞。

"代表團": delegation

"到最後" 是 "在最後時刻" 的意思，要說 at the last moment。

"取消計劃": cancel ( 或 call off ) the plan

## 【譯例】

(a) " Have you ever been in America?" " No. I very nearly went once. I was to go with a delegation, but the plan was cancelled at the last moment. ”

(b) “ Ever been to the United States? ” “ No. On one occasion I was almost going with a delegation, but they called off the plan at the last moment. ”

# 第 21 天

“ 我要到歐洲去。由於我不懂歐洲的風俗習慣，我希望你給我提些建議。” “ 抱歉得很，我並不比你懂得更多。”

## 【說明】

“ 歐洲 ”：Europe；形容詞是 European。

“ 風俗習慣 ”：customs

“ 建議 ”：suggestion

“ 我並不比你懂得更多 ” 可照字譯說 I know no more than you (do)；也可意譯為 I'm in the same box ( 或 boat )，是 “ 處在同樣困境 ” 的意思。

## 【譯例】

(a) “ I'm leaving for Europe. As I know nothing of European customs, I hope you'll give me some suggestions. ” “ I'm very sorry. I know no more than you do. ”

(b) “ I'll be leaving for Europe. As I know nothing of European customs, may I ask you to give me some suggestions? ” “ Sorry, I'm in the same box. ”

# 第22天

　　一個寒冷的晚上，經過長途跋涉我們來到了一個鄉村小鎮，在鎮上唯一的一家旅店住宿了一夜。

## 【說明】

　　"一個寒冷的晚上"：one cold night，作狀語用；如果改成一個句子要說 It was a cold night。

　　"經過長途跋涉"是"在長途旅行之後"的意思，可譯作 after a long journey。

　　"鄉村小鎮"：country town

　　"旅店"：inn; tavern

　　"住宿一夜"：put up for the night; pass the night

## 【譯例】

　　(a) It was a cold night. After a long journey we arrived at a small country town and put up at the only inn there.

　　(b) One cold night we came to a small country town after a long journey and passed the night at a tavern, the only one in the town.

# 第23天

　　我們在湖邊一家旅館過夜。第二天攀登附近的一座小山。從山頂遠望，景緻之佳非筆墨所能形容。

## 【說明】

"旅館": hotel

"第二天": on the following day

"攀登": climb (up)

"附近": a nearby hill, 或 a hill nearby

"非筆墨所能形容"是"難以形容"的意思，可說 indescribable, 或 beyond description。"景緻之佳非筆墨所能形容": The view was indescribably beautiful（或 magnificent），或 The view was beyond description; 也可說 The view defied my pen。defy 有"使無能爲力"的意思，所以 defy my pen 就是"筆難盡述"，也即"非筆墨所能形容"的意思。

【譯例】

(a) We passed the night at a hotel by the lake. On the following day, we climbed a nearby hill. The view from the summit of the hill was beyond description.

(b) After we had spent the night at a lakeside hotel, we climbed up a nearby hill on the following day. The view from the top was indescribably beautiful.

(c) We spent the night at a hotel by the lake. On the following day, we climbed up a hill nearby. The magnificent view from the top defied my pen.

# 第24天

在湖上划船，環顧四週的風景，確是件很大的樂事。我們直至日落以後才回到旅館。

【說明】

"划船": row

"日落以後" after sunset。"直至日落以後才回到旅館"可用
not…until…這個句型，說 We didn't return to the hotel until after
sunset; 也可說 It was only after sunset that we returned to the hotel, 或 It was not until after sunset that we returned to the hotel。

## 【譯例】

(a) It was really a great pleasure to row on the lake and enjoy the
beautiful scenery all round. It was only after sunset that we returned to
the hotel.

(b) Rowing on the lake was really a great pleasure. We enjoyed the
beautiful scenery all round and did not return to the hotel until after
sunset.


# 第25天

從旅館的窗口凝視藍色的海洋時，他隱隱地聽到遠處海面上輪船
的汽笛聲，那大概是開往美國的船吧。

## 【說明】

"凝視": gaze out over; gaze at; look intently out over
"隱隱地聽到輪船的汽笛聲": hear the faint whistle of a steamer
"遠處海面上": in the offing
"開往": go to; be bound for

## 【譯例】

(a) As he was gazing out over the blue sea from the window of his hotel room, he heard the faint whistle of a steamer in the offing. Perhaps she was bound for America.

(b) From the window of his hotel room he was looking intently out over the blue sea. He heard the faint whistle of a steamer in the offing. Maybe she was going to America.

# 第 26 天

"我想參觀市容，你願意幫忙嗎？""當然啦，我很願意。今天我全天休息，我可以陪你去參觀。"

## 【說明】

"市容"：the sights of the city。"參觀市容"可說 see the sights of the city, go sightseeing in the city, 或 have a look around ( 或 round ) the city; around 和 round 作介詞或副詞時其意義基本相同, around 多用於美國, round 多用於英國。

"全天休息"：have the whole day off

"陪你去參觀"： show ( 或 take ) you around

## 【譯例】

(a) " I'd like to see the sights of the city. Will you help me? " " Of course, I will. I have the whole day off today, so I'll show you around here. "

(b) " Will you please help me have a look around the city? " "Yes, with pleasure. I'm free today. Let me take you around here. "

# 第 27 天

"街上好多人呀! 他們似乎在漫步。這裏的人有這麼多的空閒時間嗎? ""今天是星期天, 他們在享受他們的假日。"

**【說明】**

"街上好多人呀! ": What a lot of people on the street! 或 What a crowd of people there is on the street!

"假曰"指工作休息的一天, 要說 an off day, 或 a day off。

**【譯例】**

(a) "What a lot of people on the street! They seem to be just strolling around. Do the people here have so much free time?" "Why, today is Sunday. They are enjoying their day off."

(b) "What a crowd of people there is on the street! It seems that they have much time to spare to stroll around." "Well, today is Sunday, you know. They are spending their off day here."

# 第 28 天

我們今天參觀了動物園。最能引起孩子們興趣的是猴子。它們一直爬啊, 跳啊, 鬧着玩啊, 樣子挺有趣。

**【說明】**

"動物園": zoological garden; zoo

"最能引起孩子們興趣的是猴子"可以說 What interested the children most were the monkeys, 或 The most interesting to the

193

children were the monkeys; 也可以 children 爲主語說 The children were most interested in the monkeys。

"鬧着玩": frolic。注意過去時要寫作 frolicked。

## 【譯例】

(a) We visited the zoological garden today. The most interesting to the children were the monkeys. They climbed and jumped and frolicked all the while and their manner was extremely amusing.

(b) Today we made a visit to the zoo. The children were most interested in the monkeys which climbed and jumped and frolicked all the while. Their manner was quite amusing.

# 第 29 天

一個管理員帶我們參觀了博物館。他對我們作了一切必要的解釋。參觀是很成功的，我們學到了許多東西。

## 【說明】

"管理員": curator

"博物館": museum

"一切必要的解釋": all the necessary explanations

"成功": success; 形容詞是 successful。"參觀是很成功的" The visit proved quite successful; 也可說 The visit was a great success。

## 【譯例】

(a) A curator showed us around the museum and gave us all the necessary explanations. The visit was a great success. We learned a great deal.

(b) In the museum we were shown around by a curator, who gave us all the necessary explanations. We learned a lot, so the visit proved quite successful.

# 第30天

"你到這裏以來遊覽了不少地方吧？""是的，看了不少。""你對這裏的印象怎樣？""要不是天氣，我是喜歡這個地方的。"

## 【說明】

"遊覽了不少地方"：除了 have visited many places 之外，也可說 have done much sightseeing。

"印象"：impression

"要不是天氣"：but for the weather; 改成句子也可說 if it were not for the weather。

## 【譯例】

(a) "Have you visited many places since you got here?" "Yes, quite a lot." "What are your impressions of this city?" "Well, but for the weather, I'd like it."

(b) "Have you done much sightseeing since you came here?" "Yes, quite a bit." "What do you think of this city?" "I think I'd like it if it were not for the weather."

# Words and Expressions

| | |
|---|---|
| save up some money | 儲蓄 |
| travelling expenses | 旅費 |
| in olden times; in former days | 古代 |
| communication facilities | 交通工具 |
| travel by train (ship, plane) | 乘火車(船,飛機)旅行 |
| make up one's mind | 下決心 |
| travel bureau [bjuə'rou]; travel service | 旅行社 |
| sightseeing trip; pleasure trip | 遊覽旅行 |
| go on business; be away on official business ['biznis] | 出差 |
| whistle ['hwisl] | 汽笛 |
| passenger | 旅客 |
| wave good-bye to… | 向…揮手告別 |
| expensive; costly; dear | 貴 |
| fare | 票價 |
| can't afford (to buy) something | 買不起甚麼東西 |
| price | 價錢 |
| railway ticket | 火車票 |
| airline ticket | 飛機票 |
| scenery; view | 風景 |
| take off | 起飛 |

196

| | |
|---|---|
| city centre | 市中心 |
| airport; airfield | 飛機場 |
| flying weather | 適合飛行的天氣 |
| overcast | (天空) 陰暗 |
| toss | 顛簸, 搖擺 |
| seasick | 暈船 |
| sea trip | 海上旅行 |
| be a bad (good) sailor | (不) 會暈船的人 |
| worry about | 担憂 |
| harbour | 港口 |
| moor | 停泊 |
| wharf; quay [ki:]; pier | 碼頭 |
| cast anchor; drop anchor; anchor [ˈæŋkə] | 拋錨 |
| get ashore | 上岸 |
| steam launch | 汽艇 |
| by all means | 一定要 |
| delegation | 代表團 |
| be in the same box; be in the same boat | 處在同樣的困境 |
| inn; tavern [ˈtævə(:)n] | 旅店 |
| pass the night; put up for the night | 住宿一夜 |
| hotel | 旅館 |
| indescribable; beyond description | 非筆墨所能形容 |
| row | 划船 |
| after sunset | 日落以後 |

| | |
|---|---|
| be bound for | 開往 |
| show somebody around | 帶領某人參觀 |
| off day | 休假日 |
| zoological [zouə´lɔdʒikəl] garden; zoo | 動物園 |
| museum [mju(:)´ziəm] | 博物館 |
| impression | 印象 |
| but for…; if it were not for… | 要不是… |

# Exercise 7

Translate the following into English:

1. 旅行是件樂事。我勸你有足夠錢的時候就去旅行。（第 1 天）

2. 過去由於沒有好的交通工具，旅行是件苦事。人們常常要步行，所以到一個遠的地方去是很費時間的。（第 2 天）

3. 如今我們已經有了各種快速的交通工具，如火車和飛機，你到世界上任何地方去都會感到很方便。（第 2 天）

4. 甲：你以前到過這裏嗎？

   乙：不，這是我第一次到貴國訪問。

   甲：你的印象怎樣？

   乙：我覺得一切都很新奇，正像突然從自己的國家進入了一個新的世界。（第 3 天）

5. 最近我要出差到北京去。是乘車去還是乘飛機去我還未決定。（第 4 天）

6. 上星期遇到彼德，他告訴我他剛從英國回來。他是探親去的。（第 5 天）

7. 昨天下午我到機場去為庫克先生送行。他是到倫敦去出差的。（第

4，6天）

8. 乘飛機旅行要比坐火車快得多，這是肯定的；但從飛機上俯視只見天空、雲彩和遙遙在下的地面，你一定會感到厭倦。（第7，8天）

9. 我不想乘飛機旅行而想乘火車。火車雖比飛機慢，但沿途可以瀏覽風景。（第7，9天）

10. 我要盡快到達目的地。所以我想最好是乘飛機去。（第9，10天）

11. 我們登上了飛機。不久飛機起飛了。幾分鐘以後我們就在雲層上。有時在雲間可以看到遙遙在下的地面。（第7，11天）

12. 從這裏到飛機場沒有直達的公共汽車，所以我想我們還是叫一輛出租汽車較好。（第11天）

13. 甲：今天天空陰暗，你看是適合飛行的天氣嗎？
　　乙：只要沒有霧或風暴，我想他們不會取消飛行的。（第12天）

14. 我們的船正在高速行駛（sail at a high speed）。海上風浪漸大，船開始顛簸搖擺，有些旅客易於暈船，但其他旅客却不怕風浪，他們仍在甲板（deck）上來往走動。（第13，14天）

15. 我是會暈船的。去年我到日本去，海上風浪很大，我感到很不舒服。（第13，14天）

16. 今天海面平靜，船一點不顛簸搖擺，我感到海上旅行是件愉快的事。（第13，14，15天）

17. 這裏每天有許多船隻進進出出。有的在碼頭停泊，也有的在港口拋錨，旅客須乘汽艇或小船上岸。（第16，17天）

18. 甲：你沒有在美洲大陸旅行過嗎？
　　乙：是的，我從來沒有去過。我真盼望能有機會去看看。（第17，18天）

19. 我沒有充裕的時間，所以只好乘飛機旅行。要是乘汽車和火車的話，在路上就可瀏覽美麗的風景。（第9，18，19天）

20. 上月我預定作為代表團成員之一到日本去，但最後計劃改變了，我沒有去。（第20天）

21. 我沒有到過歐洲，所以不懂那裏的風俗習慣。我想去請教詹妮，她可能可以提些建議。（第20，21天）

22. 一個黑暗的晚上他們登上了小船，渡過了河，來到一個鄉村小鎮，在那裏住宿一夜。（第22天）

23. 經過了長途跋涉，我們來到了一座傍湖的小山。此處風景之美非筆墨所能形容。（第22，23天）

24. 湖上有許多人在划船，有些人在唱歌，有的在拉手風琴或其他樂器，看樣子他們都很快樂。（第24天）

25. 我們登上了小山，那時太陽正在下去，凝視江上遠處的帆影，景緻之美確是難以形容。（第23，24，25天）

26. 近來我有個朋友初次到香港。他想參觀市容，我答應他待我有空就陪他去參觀。（第26天）

27. 星期天總有許多人在街上漫步享受他們的假日，也有些人從其他地方來參觀市容或購買東西，所以街上要比平日擁擠。（第26，27天）

28. 甲：在動物園裏你最愛看甚麼動物？

乙：那些猴子。無論老幼見了猴子都覺得挺有趣。（第28天）

29. 這是我第一次到這裏訪問。我遊覽了不少地方，對這裏美麗的風景有深刻的印象。（第30天）

30. 不久前有一天我去參觀博物館。我是同一羣朋友一起去的——這是一次遊覽 （excursion）。這地方以前我是去過的，但還有許多東西我想再看看。一個管理員帶我們參觀。他對我們作了一切必要的解釋。參觀很成功，我們學到了許多東西，而且感到很愉快。（第29天）

200

# 第 8 月
# 交通、問訊、問路

## 第 1 天

這條公路通過市中心。它總是擁塞的，在上下班時候更糟。

### 【說明】

"公路": highway

"通過": pass through; run through

"擁塞的": congested; jammed

"上下班的時候": rush hours

### 【譯例】

(a) This is the highway running through the city centre. It is always congested. It is even worse in the rush hours.

(b) This highway passes through the heart of the city. It is always jammed, especially during the rush hours.

## 第 2 天

公共汽車擠滿了遊客，所以我一直站到終點站。

### 【說明】

"擠滿": be crowded with; be packed with; be full of

"遊客": 這裏指假日出遊的人，可用 holiday makers; excursionists, 或 picnickers; 後者指自帶食物的郊遊者。

"一直"是"一路"的意思，可說 all the way; the whole way。

"終點站": terminal station, terminal, terminus

## 【譯例】

(a) As the bus was crowded with holiday makers, I had to keep standing all the way to the terminal station.

(b) The bus was so packed with excursionists that I was obliged to keep standing the whole way to the terminal.

(c) The bus being full of picnickers, I was kept standing as far as the terminus.

# 第3天

"我想橫過馬路也許需要化些時間。""不會太多。但你得小心，只能在綠燈亮的時候過去，否則會被車子撞倒的。"

## 【說明】

"橫過": cross。"橫過馬路也許需要化些時間"可說 Crossing the street may take some time, 或 It may take (me) some time to cross the street.

"綠燈": green light。"只能在綠燈亮的時候過去": cross the street only under the green light, 或 cross the street only when the green light is on。

"撞倒": knock down

【譯例】

(a) " I suppose crossing the street may take some time. " " Not very much. But be careful! Mind you cross the street only under the green light. Otherwise you may be knocked down by a car. "

(b) " Will it take me much time to cross the street? " " No, not much. But you must be careful. You can cross the street only when the green light is on, or you may be knocked down by a car. "

# 第4天

我要從城裏這一頭到那一頭去，可是却沒有直達公共汽車，所以我想還是叫一輛出租汽車吧。

【說明】

"從城裏這一頭到那一頭 " : from one end of the city to the other

"直達公共汽車 " : direct bus; direct bus service

"叫一輛出租汽車 " : call a taxi, hail a taxi; hail 是 "招呼 "的意思。"還是叫一輛出租汽車 "可以說 It is better for me to call a taxi; 也可說 I had better hail a taxi。注意: had better 是習語，必須用 had, 不可用 have, 後面要跟沒有 to 的不定詞。

【譯例】

(a) I want to go from one end of the city to the other. Unfortunately there is no direct bus service. So I think I had better hail a taxi.

(b) I would like to go to the other end of the city. But as there is no direct bus going there, I think it is better for me to call a taxi.

# 第5天

"啊! 我們要乘的車來了。我們趕快上車吧。""這車擁擠不堪, 我們擠不進去, 等下一輛車吧。"

【説明】

"我們要乘的車": our car

"這車擁擠不堪": The car is filled to capacity, The car is packed like sardines, 或簡單地說 The car is full。sardines 是"沙丁魚", 裝在罐子裏滿滿的, 形容十分擁擠。

"擠不進去": can't crowd in; can't squeeze in; 也可說 can't get in。

【譯例】

(a) "Oh! there is our car. Let's hurry and catch it." "The car is filled to capacity; we can't squeeze in. Let's wait for the next one."

(b) "Here comes our car. Be quick. Let's catch it." "The car is full. How can we get in? We'll have to wait for the next one."

# 第6天

我上了公共汽車。售票員説: "請大家買票啦。"我告訴他我要去的地方, 買了票。我一直望着窗外, 路上交通十分擁擠。

**【說明】**

"上了公共汽車": get in a bus; board a bus; board 這裏是動詞, 作 "登上" 解。

"售票員" 指公共車輛上的售票員, 要說 conductor。

"交通" 指街上來往行人及車輛, 要說 traffic。"路上交通十分擁擠" 可說 There is a lot of traffic in the streets, 或 The street traffic is very heavy。

**【譯例】**

(a) I got in a bus. The conductor said: " All fares, please." I told him where I wanted to go and paid for a ticket. All the time I looked out of the window. There was a lot of traffic in the streets.

(b) When I boarded a bus, the conductor asked all the passengers to pay fares. I mentioned the place where I wanted to go and got a ticket. All the while I looked out of the window. How heavy the traffic in the streets was!

# 第7天

"快點坐上來, 追上他們。" "好! 快走吧。"

**【說明】**

"快點坐上來" 是催人家上車的話, 可照前例譯作 Get in quickly, 或 Step in at the double。at (或 on) the double 是 "用快步" 的意思; 如要加強催促的語氣, 動詞前可加個 do, 如 Do get in quickly。do 在這裏要重讀。

"追上": catch up with

"快走吧"：Go ahead, 或 Step on the gas; 後一句是 "踩油門" 的意思，可作 "加速前進" 解。

## 【譯例】

(a) "Do get in quickly, and let's catch up with them." " OK, now go ahead. "

(b) " Step in at the double and let's catch up with them!" " Oh, sure. Step on the gas. "


# 第8天

因時間忽促，乘上了一輛在路上兜客的出租汽車。但是由於交通阻塞不能動彈，遲到了20分鐘。

## 【說明】

"時間忽促" 照字譯可說 Time pressed; 但也可說 I was pressed for time, 或 I was in a hurry, I was in great haste。

"一輛在路上兜客的出租汽車"：a taxi that was cruising along, 或 a cruising taxi; cruise 是 "在路上徘徊兜客" 的意思。

"交通阻塞"：traffic jam; traffic block

"不能動彈" 照字譯是 couldn't move at all, 但不如說 was held up 或 was detained 較好。

## 【譯例】

(a) As I was pressed for time, I took a taxi that was cruising along. But it was held up in a traffic jam, and I was twenty minutes late.

(b) I took a taxi that came cruising along because I was in great haste. But I was detained in a traffic block and was late by twenty minutes.

# 第 9 天

"從車站回來時，我不得不和別人同乘一輛出租汽車。""是呀，叫車是相當困難的。"

## 【說明】

"別人"這裏是指一個不相識的人，要說 stranger。"和別人同乘一輛出租汽車"照字譯是 ride with a stranger in the same taxi; 但較好的說法是 share the taxi with a stranger, 用了動詞 share 就可取得文字簡潔的效果。

"不得不": have to; cannot help but

"…是相當困難的"可以說 it is difficult（或 a hard job）to…; 也可說 there is great difficulty in…。

## 【譯例】

(a) "I had to share the taxi with a stranger from the station." "Yes. There was great difficulty in getting one."

(b) "From the station I couldn't help but share the taxi with a stranger." "Right you are. It was a hard job to get a taxi."

# 第 10 天

這是特別快車，所以小站不停; 但大站或樞紐站旅客要換車是停的。

## 【說明】

"特別快車": express train, express。"快車"是 fast train。
"慢車"是 slow train。

"小站": (little) way station

"樞紐站": junction station, junction

"換車": change trains (buses)

## 【譯例】

(a) It is an express train. It doesn't stop at little way stations; but at big stations and junctions, it makes stops because some passengers change trains there.

(b) It is an express and so it doesn't stop at way stations. However, it stops at big stations and junctions where some passengers change trains.

# 第 11 天

火車應該早已到了，但由於嚴重的風雪而誤點。這樣大的風雪就是在這個地區也是少見的。

## 【說明】

"應該早已到了": ought to be in already；也可說 ought to have arrived already。ought to 之後用完成時不定式,表示應該做但未曾實現的事，如 You ought to have done it long ago（這事你早就應該做了〔可是你不曾做〕）；如用否定則表示不應該做而做了的事，如 You ought not to have asked him to come（你本不應該叫他來〔可是你已

經叫他來了〕）。

"誤點"：be behind time; be overdue

"由於"：owing to, because of, on account of。"由於嚴重的風雪而誤點了"：be behind time owing to a severe snowstorm(或 blizzard )；也可以說 be delayed by a severe snowstorm。

"地區"：locality。"這個地區"this locality, 或 this part of the country。

## 【譯例】

(a) The train ought to be in already, but it has been delayed by a severe snowstorm. Even in this locality such a terrific snowstorm can rarely be met with.

(b) The train, which ought to have arrived already, is behind time owing to a heavy blizzard. Such a terrific blizzard is quite uncommon even in this part of the country.

(c) The train is long overdue because of a severe snowstorm. Even in this part of the country we rarely have such a terrific one as this.

# 第 12 天

最近鐵路事故實在太多，出外旅行時的確很担憂。

## 【說明】

"最近"作狀語, 可說 recently, lately, 或 of late。

"鐵路事故"：railway accidents; railway trouble。"鐵路事故實在太多"以 railway accidents 為主語要說 Railway accidents have happened quite frequently, 或 There have been frequent railway accidents; 也可用 we 作主語說 We have had too much railway trouble。

"担憂" 除了 worry 之外; 也可說 be（或 feel）uneasy。"的確很担憂" can't help but worry, can't help worrying, 或 can't but worry, can't help but, can't help…ing, 或 can't but 都作 "不得不" 或 "不禁" 解。

## 【譯例】

(a) Railway accidents have happened quite frequently of late. We really feel uneasy when we go on a journey.

(b) We have had too many railway troubles lately, so we can't help worrying when we start on a journey.

(c) How frequently railway accidents happen nowadays! We can't but be uneasy when we have to make a trip.

# 第 13 天

近幾年來由於汽車數量激增，所以幾乎每天都有車禍發生。

## 【說明】

"近年來"：in recent years

"激增"：increase sharply, increase so much; 改成名詞詞組是 sharp increase 或 frightful increase。"由於汽車數量激增"：owing to the sharp increase in the number of motorcars; 譯成句子可說 as the number of motorcars has increased so much。

"幾乎每天發生" happen almost every day, 也可譯成 be an everyday occurrence, 或 be of daily occurrence。occurrence 是 "發

生的事情"。

"車禍"：car accident; traffic accident; road accident

## 【譯例】

(a) As the number of motorcars has increased so much in recent years, car accidents happen almost every day.

(b) Owing to the sharp increase in the number of motorcars in recent years, traffic accidents are of daily occurrence.

(c) Just think of the frightful increase in the number of motorcars in recent years! It is only natural that road accidents should happen almost every day.

# 第 14 天

渡船應該早已到了。不要出了甚麼事情吧。

## 【說明】

"渡船"：ferry-boat

"不要出了甚麼事情吧"：I wonder if something has happened, 或 I'm afraid something has gone wrong.

## 【譯例】

(a) The ferry-boat is long overdue. I wonder if something has happened.

(b) I'm afraid something has gone wrong with the ferry-boat, because it has not arrived yet.

(c) The ferry-boat ought to have arrived by now. What is the matter with it, I wonder?

# 第 15 天

這地方靠近商業中心。為了加寬馬路, 許多房屋要拆毀。

## 【說明】

"商業中心": commercial centre; shopping centre

"加寬": widen; broaden。"為了加寬馬路": in order to widen the streets, 或 owing to road-broadening project; project 是 "規劃" 的意思。

"拆毀": pull down; demolish

## 【譯例】

(a) As this place is near the commercial centre, a considerable number of houses will be pulled down owing to the road-broadening project.

(b) In order to widen the streets near the shopping centre, a large number of houses in this locality will be demolished.

# 第 16 天

很幸運, 在郊區找到了一個住房, 可是到大學裏去却要多花一倍的時間。

## 【說明】

"住房": lodgings, 要用複數; 也可用 room。

"比以前多花一倍的時間" take twice as much time as before, 是 "花了兩倍時間" 的意思。

212

(a) Luckily I have found lodgings in the suburbs here, but at the same time it will take twice as much time as before to get to my university.

(b) I was fortunate enough to have found rooms in the suburbs here. The trouble, however, is that it takes me twice as much time as before to go to my university.

# 第17天

我們乘的船雖然遭到了颱風, 但還能平安無事地入港, 所以我們鬆了一口氣。

## 【說明】

"我們乘的船" 可譯成 our ship, 或 our steamer。

"遭到了颱風": be caught in a typhoon, 或 encountered a typhoon; encounter 是 "遭到", "遇到" 的意思。

"平安無事地": safely, 或 in safety; 也可說 safe and sound。

"入港": enter port; arrive in port; come into port。port 前不用冠詞。

"鬆了一口氣" 可譯作 be (或 feel) relieved, 或 heave a sigh of relief; 但也可改成詞組說 to our relief。

## 【譯例】

(a) Our ship was caught in a typhoon, but she could safely enter port, so we felt relieved.

(b) Our ship encountered a typhoon, but to our great relief she could come into port in safety.

(c) Unfortunately our steamer was caught in a typhoon; so when we could arrive in port safe and sound, we heaved a sigh of relief.

# 第 18 天

"對不起，先生。請問你可知道那邊是不是有一位名叫史密斯的人？""對不起，不能告訴你。這裏我也不熟。"

## 【說明】

"你可知道…？"當然可譯作"Do you know…？"但如說"Do you happen to know…？"則更好。happen 在這裏是"碰巧"的意思。問話人不敢肯定對方是否知道，只是作一次試探，所以語氣比較婉轉。

"一位名叫史密斯的人"：a gentleman named Smith，或 a gentleman by（或 of, under）the name of Smith; gentleman 指有身份的人，比用 man 有禮貌。

"這裏不熟"：be strange here; 也可說 be a stranger here。stranger 是"生客"或"過客"。

## 【譯例】

(a) "Pardon me, sir. Do you happen to know a gentleman by the name of Smith down there?" "Sorry, I can't tell you. I'm strange here myself."

(b) "Excuse me, sir. I'm trying to find a gentleman by the name of Smith. Do you happen to know him?" "I'm sorry, but I don't. I'm a stranger here myself."

214

# 第 19 天

"對不起，好像在哪兒見過您，很面熟。""噯，不是上個月一起坐飛機的嗎？"

## 【說明】

"在哪兒見過？"可用 we 作主語說 we have met somewhere, haven't we?

"很面熟"意思是"我記得見過您"，可譯作 I remember seeing you once。注意 remember 這個動詞後面可跟不定詞或動名詞，但兩者意義不同，如 Remember to post this letter tomorrow morning（記着明天早上必須把這封信寄出）；to post 指未來的動作。I remember posting the letter last week（我記得上星期已寄了這信）；posting 指過去的動作，這句話與 I remember having posted the letter last week 相當，但不可說 I remember to have posted the letter last week。

## 【譯例】

(a) "Excuse me, but we have met somewhere, haven't we? I remember seeing you once." "Why, we happened to be in the same plane last month."

(b) "Pardon me, but this is not the first time we have met, is it? I believe I saw you once." "That's right. We happened to be travelling in the same plane last month."

# 第20天

"我可以訂一張十號星期五去倫敦的飛機票嗎？""我替你查一下時間表。"

【說明】

"訂一張飛機票"：book a flight; book a ticket, book an airline ticket

"十號星期五"：Friday the tenth

"時間表"：timetable；"查一下時間表"：see the timetable, 或 have a look in the timetable

【譯例】

(a) "Can I book a flight to London for Friday the tenth?" "I'll see the timetable."

(b) "I wonder if I could book a ticket to London for Friday the tenth." "I'll have a look in the timetable for you."

# 第21天

"你認為能在半小時內把我送到飛機場嗎？""如果一路是綠燈的話，那應該是可以的。"

【說明】

"半小時內"：in half an hour; within half an hour

"如果一路是綠燈的話"：if the lights are green；也可說 if the lights are with us, 或 unless the lights are against us; 後一句話是

216

"老是碰到紅燈"的意思。

　　"可以的"除了 can arrive there, can get there 之外; 也可說 can make it。make 在這裏作"到達"解; 另外還可說 be all right, be OK, all right, 或 OK 是"行"或"可以", 就是"可以到達"的意思。

### 【譯例】

　　(a) "Do you think you can get me to the airport in half an hour?" "We should make it if the lights are green."

　　(b) "Is it possible for you to get me to the airport within half an hour?" "We should be OK if the lights are with us."

## 第22天

　　"請你告訴我到火車站去怎麼走最方便?" "最便當的路是在這裏乘無軌電車到市中心。在那裏再乘直達火車站的公共汽車。"

### 【說明】

　　"最方便"這裏是"最好"的意思, 可以譯作 the best way。
　　"無軌電車": trolley bus

### 【譯例】

　　(a) "Will you tell me the best way to the railway station?" "Well, the simplest way is for you to take the trolley bus here down to the city centre, where you can catch a bus direct to the station."

　　(b) "Excuse me, but can you show me the best way to the railway station?" "Yes, you can take the trolley bus from here down to the city centre, where you will find a direct bus to the station. I think this is the simplest way."

# 第23天

"你看我在40分鐘內能趕到火車站嗎？我要乘的火車再過50分鐘就要開了，我必須趕上它。""你25分鐘一定能趕到火車站，所以不用着急。"

## 【說明】

"再過50分鐘就要開"：be leaving in fifty minutes，或 leave fifty minutes from now.

"必須趕上它"：have got to catch it; have got to 多用在口語裏，表示極端需要，這個詞組形式上是現在完成時，但實際上是表示未來的動作，如 I have got to finish my work before six this afternoon; 有時也可把 have 省去而只用 got。

"不用着急"：you don't have to hurry，或 There is no need to hurry

## 【譯例】

(a) "Do you think I can get to the station in forty minutes? My train is leaving fifty minutes from now and I have got to catch it." "You'll sure reach the station in twenty-five minutes. There is no need to worry."

(b) "Will I have time to reach the station in forty minutes? You see I have got to catch my train which leaves fifty minutes from now." "Certainly, you'll arrive at the station in some twenty-five minutes. So you don't have to worry."

# 第24天

"這是到市政廳去的公共汽車嗎？""不，你該乘12路。到橋頭就下車，在那兒改乘12路吧。"

**【說明】**

"市政廳"：Town Hall

"該乘 12 路"：should have caught a No. 12 bus（或 a 12）；should 的意義與 ought to 差不多；像 ought to 一樣，後面如跟完成體不定式也表示該做而未做的動作。

"下車"：get off；也可用 jump out 表示"趕快下去"的意思。

**【譯例】**

(a) "Is this the right bus for the Town Hall?" "No, you should have caught a No. 12 bus. Jump out at the bridge and get one there."

(b) "Does this bus go to the Town Hall?" "No, you should have gone by a 12. Get off at the bridge and catch one there."

# 第25天

"請問到郵局去怎麼走啊？""過了橋後在第二條馬路向左拐彎，右邊奶油色的建築物就是郵局。"

**【說明】**

"到…怎麼走啊？"："Will you kindly tell me the way to…？"或 "May I ask you the way to…？"

"過橋"：cross the bridge。"過了橋，在第二條馬路向左拐彎"：cross the bridge and turn down the second street on the left, 或 take the second turning to the left after crossing the bridge.

219

"奶油色的"： cream-coloured

"建築物"： building

【譯例】

(a) "Will you kindly tell me the way to the post office?" "Cross the bridge and turn down the second street on the left, and you will see a cream-coloured building on the right. That is the post office."

(b) "May I ask you the way to the post office?" "Take the second turning to the left after crossing the bridge and you will find a cream-coloured building on the right. That is the post office."

# 第26天

"這裏離公共圖書館遠嗎？""是的，相當遠。""請你告訴我怎麼走，好嗎？""一直下去，到了交叉路可再問。"

【說明】

"請你告訴我…好嗎？"： "Will you be so kind as to tell me…?"或"Will you be kind enough to tell me…?"這樣說比較客氣。

"交叉路"： crossroad

【譯例】

(a) "Is it far from here to the public library?" "Yes, it is some distance." "Will you be so kind as to tell me how I can get there?" "Just walk down the street, and when you come to the crossroad, ask again."

(b) "How far is it from here to the public library?" "Well, it's

220

quite a way yet." "Will you be kind enough to tell me how to go there?" "Go on until you come to the crossroad and then ask again."

# 第27天

"對不起，請你指引我到體育場去的路好嗎？""路遠哩，你不能步行去。你得乘15路公共汽車去。""到甚麼地方下車呢？""售票員會告訴你的。"

## 【說明】

"指引我到…好嗎？"："Could you direct me to…？"或"Can you show me the way to…？"

"體育場"：stadium

"路遠哩，你不能步行"：It's far; you can't walk，或 It's too far to walk

## 【譯例】

(a) "Excuse me, please. Could you direct me to the stadium?" "It's far; you can't walk. I think you'll have to take the No. 15 bus." "How far shall I go?" "The conductor will tell you."

(b) "Pardon me, sir. Can you show me the way to the stadium?" "It's too far to walk. You'll have to go by the 15 bus." "Where shall I get off?" "Ask the conductor and he will tell you."

# 第28天

"先生，這是到電報局去的路嗎？""不，你走錯了。請隨我來，你就不會迷路。"

"電報局": telegraph office

"這是到…的路嗎？": "Is it the right way to…?"或"Does this street lead to…?"

"走錯路": go（或 come）the wrong way

【譯例】

(a) "Is this the right way to the telegraph office, sir?" "No, you are going the wrong way. Come along with me and you won't get lost."

(b) "May I ask if this street leads to the telegraph office, sir?" "Oh, no! You have come the wrong way. Follow me please, and you won't lose your way."

# 第 29 天

"你想乘公共汽車還是步行？假如你想乘公共汽車的話，車站就在那邊。""路不遠可以走到的話，我想還是步行去吧。"

【說明】

"公共汽車站": bus-stop

"路不遠可以走到的話": if it is within walking distance, 或 if it is no distance

(a) " Would you like to take a bus or walk? The bus-stop is over there if you want to go by bus. " " Well, I'd like to walk if it's within walking distance. "

(b) Would you like to go by bus or on foot? If you want to take a bus, the stop is just over there. " " I think I'd rather walk if it is no distance. "

# 第30天

幾天前我想到動物園去。我向一位過路人問路,但他回答說他也不熟那地方,要我去問警察,說警察可能會幫助我。

【說明】

"幾天前": the other day

"過路人": passer-by

"警察": policeman

【譯例】

(a) The other day I wanted to go to the zoo. I asked a passer-by if he knew the way. But he said he was a stranger there and advised me to ask the policeman, who might be able to help me.

(b) The other day I intended to visit the zoo. I asked a passer-by how I could get there, but he answered, " I'm sorry, but I can't tell. I'm a stranger here myself. You may ask the policeman. He will be able to help you. "

# Words and Expressions

highway                                    公路

congested; jammed                  擁塞的

rush hours                            上下班時間

crowded; packed                    擠滿

all the way; the whole way    一路上

terminal station; terminus     終點站

green light                           綠燈

knock down                         撞倒

direct bus; direct bus service   直達公共汽車

be filled to capacity; be packed   擁擠不堪
   like sardines [sɑːˊdiːnz]

conductor                           售票員

All fares!                            請買票啦!

catch up with                     追上

be pressed for time          時間緊

traffic jam; traffic block      交通阻塞

can't (help) but+動詞原形; can't   不得不; 不禁
   help+動名詞

express train; express        特別快車

way station                       小站

junction station; junction     樞紐站

change trains (buses)         換火車 ( 公共汽車 )

| | |
|---|---|
| be behind time; be overdue | 誤點；脫班 |
| owing to; because of; on account of | 由於 |
| in recent years | 近年來 |
| car accident; traffic accident; road accident | 車禍 |
| ferry-boat | 渡船 |
| commercial centre; shopping centre | 商業中心 |
| pull down; demolish | 拆毀 |
| lodgings | 住房 |
| safe and sound | 平安無事地 |
| feel relieved; heave a sigh of relief | 鬆一口氣 |
| book (v.) | （動詞）預定（車票、船票、戲票等） |
| timetable | 時間表 |
| trolley bus | 無軌電車 |
| get in (off) a car | 上（下）車 |
| crossroad | 交叉路 |
| stadium [ˊsteidjəm] | 體育場，運動場 |
| telegraph [ˊteligrɑːf] office | 電報局 |
| bus-stop | 公共汽車站 |
| the other day | 幾天前 |
| passer-by | 過路人 |
| policeman | 警察 |

# Exercise  8

Translate the following into English:

1. 這條路通到（lead to）商業中心，所以總是擁塞的，在星期日更糟。（第1天）

2. 公共汽車擠滿了到海濱去遊覽的遊客，車上沒有座位，我只好一直站到終點站。（第2天）

3. 馬路上有許多車，你必須十分小心，要在綠燈亮時才過去，否則會被車子輾過的（run over）。（第3天）

4. 我想從城裏這一頭到那一頭需要花些時間，因爲沒有直達車輛，我得在途中換車。（第3，4天）

5. 這是到郊區去的公共汽車，車子這樣擁擠，已無法擠進去。我們還是等下一班車吧。（第4，5天）

6. 我乘上了一輛無軌電車，坐在一個後排的位子上。我告訴售票員我要去的地方，買了一張票。不久我到了目的地。（第6天）

7. 路上交通十分擁擠，特別在上下班時間，所以過馬路時要十分小心。（第1，3，6天）

8. 快點坐上來，現在已經遲了，如果路上交通阻塞，我怕我們不能準時到達。（第7，8天）

9. 我從學校回來時，因爲公共汽車擁擠不堪，只得和別人同乘一輛出租汽車。（第5，9天）

10. 這是慢車，沿途車站都停，所以到目的地要比特別快車慢得多。（第10天）

11. 多數旅客在大站或樞紐站換車或下車，要在小站下車的就得乘慢

車，因爲快車在那裏是不停的。（第10天）

12. 甲：火車應該早已到了，不知道爲甚麼誤點。

   乙：大概受阻於風暴，不然是不會遲到的。（第11天）

13. 近年來隨着汽車數量的增加，交通事故不斷發生，我們外出時確實爲自己的安全而擔憂。（第12，13天）

14. 據說飛機因天氣不好而受阻。我希望不要出甚麼事故。（第11，14天）

15. 靠近商業中心有許多房屋已被拆毀，所以那一帶的馬路就可以加寬。（第15天）

16. 我很幸運地在我們工廠附近找到了一個住房。雖然以後上班很方便，但要多花一倍的房租。（第16天）

17. 由於天氣不好，飛機遲到2小時，但還能平安無事地降落，所以我們鬆了一口氣。（第17天）

18. 我問一個過路人（passer-by）是否認得名叫史密斯的人，他說他不能告訴我，因爲他那裏也不熟。（第18天）

19. 請記得收到這封信以後，打個電話給我的伯父告訴他我已平安抵達香港。（第17，19天）

20. 甲：我要在1號或1號左右飛日內瓦。

   乙：我替你查一下有甚麼班機。

   甲：順便提一下，我不要夜航班機（night flight）。

   乙：好的，先生。（第20天）

21. 甲：我要趕上11點15分那班火車。

   乙：假如路上沒有耽擱（hold-ups）是可以趕得到的。（第21天）

22. 甲：請你告訴我到火車站去該怎麼走？

   乙：你最好從這裏乘18路無軌電車到市政廳，在那裏換乘5路公共汽車到火車站。（第22天）

23. 甲：我乘的飛機再過1小時就要起飛了，我必須趕上它。

乙：我相信你大約在40分鐘內就可到達飛機場，所以不用着急。
（第23天）

24. 甲：21路公共汽車到郵政總局去嗎？

乙：郵政總局嗎？不，21路只到橋頭！你得乘12路。（第24天）

25. 甲：你能指引我到電報局去的路嗎？

乙：過了那條橋後一直走，到了路的盡頭向左轉，再於第二個轉
彎處向右拐。（第25天）

26. 甲：請問南大街在哪裏？

乙：到了第二條馬路向左拐，然後再問一下。

甲：遠嗎？

乙：不遠，只要走5分鐘就到了。（第25，26天）

27. 甲：勞駕，請你告訴我到動物園去的路好嗎？

乙：從這裏去相當遠，你可乘18路公共汽車去。

甲：甚麼地方下車呢？

乙：你問售票員好了，他會告訴你的。（第27天）

28. 甲：這是到海濱去的路嗎？

乙：不，你走錯了。回頭走，到了紅綠燈向左拐。（第28天）

29. 甲：我到公共圖書館去，要乘公共汽車嗎？

乙：不，路不遠，可以走到的。

甲：多謝你。

乙：沒關係。（第29天）

30. 甲：對不起，先生。你能告訴我體育場在哪裏嗎？

乙：抱歉，可是我無能為力。這裏我也不熟。不過我看到街道拐角
上站着一位警員，他將能夠幫你的忙。

甲：那麼我問他好了。謝謝你，再見。

乙：再見。（第30天）

# 第9月
# 旅館、商店、郵局

## 第1天

　　我要求旅館的辦事員給我一間附有浴室的朝南房間。我問了租金，把護照交給了他，填了來客登記表，領到了房間的鑰匙。

### 【說明】

　　"辦事員"：clerk

　　"浴室"：bathroom。"附有浴室的" with a bathroom attached；attached 是"附屬"的意思。

　　"朝南"：face south, face the south, face to the south 都可以說；"朝南的房間" a room facing south，或 a room on the sunny side; sunny side 是"向陽的一面"。

　　"護照"：passport

　　"來客登記簿"：arrival form

### 【譯例】

　　(a) I requested the clerk of the hotel to give me a room facing south with a bathroom attached. I asked about the price of the room, handed in my passport, filled in an arrival form and got the key of my room.

　　(b) At my request the clerk of the hotel gave me a room on the sunny side with a bathroom attached. He also informed me of the price of the room. I gave him my passport together with the arrival form which I had filled in, and got the key of my room.

# 第2天

　　我在旅館詢問能否爲我安排住宿。辦事員答稱還有幾個房間空着。我定了一間在三樓的。接着旅館的搬運工人把我的行李送到房間裏去。這房間十分舒適，我很喜歡它。

## 【說明】

　　"安排住宿"除了前面見過的 put up for the night 之外；也可說 give accommodation; accommodation 是"住宿的設備"。The hotel has accommodation(s) for 1000 guests 是"這旅館能接納一千名旅客"的意思。

　　"空着"：free; vacant; disengaged

　　"搬運工人"：porter

　　"行李"：luggage; baggage。在英國一般用 luggage, 在美國則多用 baggage。注意: luggage 和 baggage 前面都不可加 a; 也不可用複數。一件行李要說 a piece of luggage, 或 an article of luggage 而不可說 a luggage; 許多行李要說 a large amount of luggage 而不可說 many luggages。

## 【譯例】

　　(a) I made inquiries at the hotel if they could put me up for the night. The clerk said there were still several rooms left. I took one on the second floor. Then the hotel porter carried my luggage to the room. It was quite comfortable. I liked it very much.

　　(b) When I asked at the hotel if they could give me any accommodation, the clerk answered they still had several rooms free. I booked one that was on the second floor. Next I asked the hotel porter to carry my luggage to the room. I found the room quite comfortable, so I liked it very much.

# 第3天

我在旅館裏定了一間單人房間。房間是很清潔的，但不太通風。 不過我還是很喜歡這房間，因為離鬧市較遠。

## 【說明】

"單人房間"：single room

"很清潔"照字譯當然可以說 very clean；但也可說 nice and clean。這裏 nice and…作"因為…所以好"解，就是說"很…"，如 The wind is nice and cool（這陣風很涼快），The car is going nice and fast（這汽車跑得很快）；有時不用 and 而單用 nice 也可以，如 The room is nice clean。

"通風"：ventilate; be airy。"不大通風"be not very well ventilated; be not very airy。

"不過…還是…"：nevertheless; all the same

"鬧市"：noisy street。"離鬧市較遠"：be far from the noisy street；也可說 be away from the noise of the traffic。

## 【譯例】

(a) I booked a single room at a hotel. It looked very clean, but it was not well ventilated. All the same I liked my room, because it was far from the noisy street.

231

(b) The single room I booked at the hotel was nice and clean, but it was not very airy. Nevertheless I was pleased with my room as it was away from the noise of the traffic.

# 第4天

一個晚上我在小車站附近一家旅店住宿。也許是不大通風的關係，我發覺床舖有點霉氣。這旅店很舊，我猜想不大有人光顧。

## 【說明】

"一個晚上" 是狀語，可照 one cold night 的前例說 one night。

"有霉氣"：musty; mouldy。"床舖有霉氣" 照字譯是 The bed has a musty smell; 但也可說 The bed smells musty。這裏 smell 作 "發出…的氣味" 解，後面要用形容詞，不可用副詞。

"光顧"：patronize。"不大有人光顧" be not too well patronized, 或 have not many guests, have very few guests 也可以。

## 【譯例】

(a) One night I was put up at an inn near a small station. Probably owing to the bad ventilation of the room, the bed was found to have a musty smell. I guessed they didn't have many guests as the inn was rather old.

(b) I stopped at an inn near a way station one night. The bed smelt a bit musty. Probably they didn't air the room enough. I imagined the inn was rather old, and not too well patronized.

# 第5天

“請問今晚有空房間嗎？”“有的，二樓還有一間。”“我可以看看房間嗎？”“當然可以。”

## 【說明】

“空房間”：disengaged room, vacant room, 或 vacancy

“二樓還有一間”可以有幾種說法：There is still one room on the first floor, We still have one room left on the first floor, 或 We can still offer you one room on the first floor。

## 【譯例】

(a) “I wonder if you have any vacancies for tonight.” “Yes, we still have one left on the first floor.” “May I have a look at the room?” “Yes, certainly.”

(b) “Have you any rooms disengaged tonight?” “Yes, we can still offer you one on the first floo.” “Can I see it, please?” “Certainly, sir.”

# 第6天

“有可住兩夜的單人房間嗎？”“有的，不過只有頂層的房間。”“房租多少？”“每夜××元，侍應費在外。”“價錢倒是公道的，但我想先看看房間。”“當然可以。這邊來吧。”

## 【說明】

“頂層”：top floor

“侍應費”就是“服務費”service charge。“侍應費在外”：not counting the service, excluding service charge, 或 service charge excluded。

"公道"是"公平合理"的意思，可說 fair, 或 reasonable。

"這邊來吧"是為別人引路的話，可說 come this way, 或 would you please come this way?

## 【譯例】

(a) " Have you a single room for two nights? " " Yes, but only on the top floor. " " What price is it? " " ×× dollars a night, not counting the service. " " Fair enough. But I'll see it first. " " Yes, you can. Come this way, please. "

(b) " Would you please let me have a single room for two nights? " " Yes, you can have one; but it is on the top floor. " " How much do you charge? " " ×× dollars per night, service charge excluded. " " The price is reasonable; but let me see it first. " " All right. Would you please come this way? "

# 第7天

保羅·瓊斯在打長途電話給公園旅館，他想定個房間。"我想預定一個雙人房間。我將在下星期一、14號到達。我的名字叫保羅·瓊斯。""雙人房間，14號要用，是不是？""對。""請你把名字再說一遍，好嗎？""保羅·瓊斯。"

## 【說明】

"長途電話": trunk call, 主要用在英國; 在美國通常說 long-distance call。"打長途電話" make a trunk call。

"預定"除了 book 之外; 也可說 reserve, 或 make a reservation for。

"雙人房間": double room

"我的名字叫保羅·瓊斯"可以說 My name is Paul Jones, 或 I'm called Paul Jones。但不可照漢語說法, 譯作 My name is called Paul Jones; name 和 called 不可同時並用。

## 【譯例】

(a) Paul Jones is making a trunk call to book a room at the Park Hotel.

"I'd like to make a reservation for a double room. I'll be arriving next Monday, the 14th. My name is Paul Jones." "A double room for the 14th?" "Yes, that's right." "Would you mind repeating your name?" "Paul Jones."

(b) Paul Jones is asking the Park Hotel to reserve a room for him over the trunk call.

"I'm called Paul Jones. I'll be at your place next Monday, the 14th. Can you let me have a double room?" "Yes, sir. A double room for the 14th, is it?" "Right." "Would you please repeat your name?" "Paul Jones."

# 第8天

"你介紹我到甚麼旅館去住呢?" "公園旅館。" "這旅館價錢貴嗎?" "不, 不像多數旅館那樣貴。如果我沒有記錯的話, 單人房間是×元一天。" "×元一天, 是嗎? 那倒是適合我的經濟能力的。"

## 【說明】

"介紹": recommend

"價錢" 除了 price 之外; 也可說 rate。 "這旅館價錢貴嗎?"

照字譯可說 "Is the price very high at this hotel？" 注意 "價錢貴" 要說 The price is high, 一般不說 The price is dear; 如不照字譯, 也可說 "Is it an expensive place？" 或 "Will it be too expensive for me？"

"不像多數旅館那樣貴" not so expensive as most hotels, 或 not as most hotels go; 也可解釋爲 "比多數旅館便宜" cheaper than most hotels。

"如果沒有記錯的話" 可說 If I remember right(ly), 或 If my memory doesn't fail me。

"×元一天，是嗎？" 可簡單說 "× dollars a day？" 或 "A ×-dollar-a-day room, is it？" 注意在連字號中的 dollar 不用複數。

"適合我的經濟能力"：suit my purse; purse 在這裏作 "財力" 解，如 It's beyond my purse to buy this car（購置這輛汽車非我財力所及）。

## 【譯例】

(a) "What hotel would you recommend me to stop at？" "The Park Hotel." "Is it an expensive place？" "No, not as most hotels go. The rate for a single room is × dollars a day, if I remember right." "A ×-dollar-a-day room, is it？ That will suit my purse."

(b) "What hotel do you think you will recommend me？" "I would recommend the Park Hotel." "Will it be too expensive for me？" "No, it's cheaper than most hotels. The price is × dollars per day for a single room, if my memory doesn't fail me." "× dollars a day？ That will suit me all right."

# 第9天

"你的房間朝甚麼方向？""是朝南的，但面向一條小巷，甚麼景緻也沒有。你的房間怎樣？""我的房間面向大街，因此吵得很。"

## 【說明】

"你的房間朝甚麼方向？"："Which way does your room face?"或 "How does your room face?"

"面向"：look out on; look out over, 或 overlook

"小巷"：small alley; narrow lane

"甚麼景緻也沒有"：without any view, 或 with no view whatever; 改成句子可說 There is no view at all。

## 【譯例】

(a) "Which way does your room face?" "It faces south, I think; but it looks out on a small alley. There is no view at all. How is yours?" "Mine faces the main street. That's why it's so noisy."

(b) "How does your room face?" "It faces to the south, but it looks out over a narrow lane with no view whatever. How is your room?" "My room overlooks the main street. Perhaps that's why there is so much noise."

# 第 10 天

因為即將離開旅館，我告訴辦事員開好帳單，同時請他代叫一輛出租汽車。結帳以後，我同他告別，然後繼續我的旅程。

## 【說明】

"帳單" bill。"開好帳單" make out the bill, 或 get the bill

237

ready。

　　"結帳"是"付清帳目"的意思，可說 pay the bill。"結帳以後，我同他告別"：After having paid my bill, I said good-bye to him。after 後面的動名詞 having paid 用完成體，表示結帳的動作早於告別的動作。如果這個詞組改爲從句，就要說 After I had paid my bill, I said good-bye to him。

　　"繼續我的旅程"：set out again on my journey；也可說 resume my journey; resume 是"重新開始"的意思。

## 【譯例】

　　(a) As I was leaving the hotel, I told the clerk to make out my bill. At the same time I asked him to call a taxi for me. After having paid my bill, I said good-bye to him and set out again on my journey.

　　(b) I was going to leave the hotel, so I asked the clerk to get my bill ready and call a taxi for me. After I had paid my bill, I bid him good-bye and resumed my journey.


# 第 11 天

　　有一天我的朋友想買些東西。我帶他到一家百貨商店去。這裏出售各種消費品，如食品、文具、雜貨、家庭用具、衣服、鞋、帽、皮貨等等。

## 【說明】

　　"有一天"按照 one night 的前例可說 one day。

　　"買些東西"當然可以說 buy something；但也可說 do some shopping。不過兩者之間也不是沒有區別的，後者是指到店裏去買東西。

"百貨商店": department store

"消費品": consumer goods

"食品": provisions, articles of food 或 food

"文具": stationery

"雜貨": grocery

"家庭用具": household utensils

"鞋類": shoes; 也可說 footwear.

"皮貨": furs

"等等": and so on; and what not

## 【譯例】

(a) One day my friend wanted to do some shopping. I took him to a department store which sells all kinds of consumer goods: provisions, stationery, grocery, household utensils, clothes, footwear, hats, furs and so on.

(b) One day I went to a department store with a friend who wanted to buy something. Here we can get all kinds of consumer goods: provisions, stationery, grocery, household utensils, clothes, shoes, hats, furs and what not.

# 第 12 天

"有人在招呼你嗎?" "沒有。我打算買一件42號海軍藍雨衣。" "我們最大的只有40號的。" "你能否為我弄到一件呢?" "當然可以。如果你留下地址,我會通知你的。"

## 【說明】

"有人在招呼你嗎？"：這是售貨員對顧客說的話，可譯作 "Are you being served?" "Are you being attended（或 seen）to?" 或 "Is anybody looking after you?"

"海軍藍"：navy blue

"我們最大的…"：The biggest we have is…，或 The best we can do is…

## 【譯例】

(a) "Are you being served?" "No, I'm trying to find a navy blue raincoat, size 42." "The best we can do is a 40." "Do you think you could get one for me?" "Yes, of course. If you leave your address, I'll let you know."

(b) "Is anybody looking after you?" "No. I'm after a size 42 navy blue raincoat." "Sorry, but size 40 is the biggest we have." "Could you get one for me?" "I should imagine so, yes. I'll inform you if you leave your address."

# 第13天

"今天你有空幫我一道去買些東西嗎？""好的，你要買甚麼呢？""我想買件大衣。""噢，我們到商業區去吧。那裏甚麼東西都有。如果現成的不合適，可以定做一件。他們有很好的裁縫。""那好。你想我們到那裏要花許多時間嗎？""不會的，我們就走吧。"

## 【說明】

"幫我買些東西"：help me do some shopping。注意動詞 help 後面如用不定詞，那個 to 往往省去，這種省略在美國比在英國普遍。

240

這句話也可譯成 help me with some shopping; shopping 之前要用介詞 with。

"商業區": business district（或 quarter）; commercial district; downtown。downtown 是美國用語，可作名詞、形容詞或副詞用。在用作副詞時往往寫作 down town 兩個詞，如 go down town。

"大衣": overcoat

"現成的": ready-made

"定做": have something made to order; have something custom-made

"裁縫": tailor

### 【譯例】

(a) " Have you any time to spare today? I'd like you to help me do some shopping. " " I'd be glad to. What are you going to buy? " " I want to buy an overcoat. " " Well, let's go down town. You can get practically everything there. If the ready-made coats don't fit you, you can have one made to order. They have got excellent tailors. " " All right. But do you think it will take us long? " " No, I don't think so. Come along. "

(b) " Could you find time to help me with some shopping today?" " Yes. What do you want to buy? " " I'm going to buy an overcoat. " " Oh, I see. We'd better go to the business district where you can get whatever you need. If you don't like the ready-made coats, you can order one from them, because they have got very good tailors. " " That's good. But would it take us long to go there? " " Not at all. Let's go. "

# 第 14 天

"我想看看大衣。""好的。甚麼尺寸？是你自己穿的嗎？""是

241

的。我要一件中號的。""請試穿這一件，好嗎？這料子很經穿，而且皮領很暖和。""甚麼價錢？""××元。""我沒有打算買這麼貴的。有沒有便宜些的？""很抱歉，便宜些的都已售完。"

## 【說明】

"尺寸"：size

"中號的"：medium size, 或 medium-sized

"試穿"：try on

"料子"：material

"經穿"：wear well

"皮領"：fur collar

"我沒有打算買這麼貴的"照字譯可說 I didn't expect to buy one so expensive; 也可說 It's more than I was thinking of paying, 或 It's more expensive than I cared to go; 這裏 go 作"花費"解。這兩句直譯是"這個價錢比我原來打算花的要多些"。注意：was thinking, cared 動詞都用過去時，因為指原來的想法。

## 【譯例】

(a) " I'd like to see some overcoats, please. " " What is the size? Is it for yourself? " " Yes. Let me have a medium size one. " " Please try this one on. The material is very good and the fur collar will keep you nice and warm. " " How much is it? " " ×× dollars. " " It's more than I was thinking of paying. Do you have any cheaper ones? " " Sorry, the cheaper ones are all sold out. "

(b) " Can I see some overcoats, please ? " " Yes, certainly. What size? Is it for yourself? " " Yes. I think I'll take a medium-sized one. " " Would you please try this one on? You see, the material will wear well and the fur collar is nice and warm. " " What's the price? " " ×× dollars. " " That's more expensive than I cared to go. Haven't you got

242

anything cheaper?" " I'm sorry we have nothing cheaper in stock at present."

# 第 15 天

"對不起，皮鞋部在哪裏？""在四樓，太太。你可乘自動樓梯上去。皮鞋部就在自動樓梯對面。""謝謝你。""別客氣，太太。"

## 【說明】

"太太"：ma'am，是 madam 的縮略，用於口語。

"自動樓梯"：escalator

"正在…對面"：just（或 right）opposite…

## 【譯例】

(a) " Excuse me. Where can I find the shoe department? " " It's on the third floor, ma'am. You may go up the escalator. The shoe department is right opposite it. " " Thank you very much. " " You are welcome, ma'am. "

(b) " Excuse me, please. Where is the shoe department? " " On the third floor, ma'am. Go up the escalator and you will find the shoe department just opposite it. " " Thanks. " " Not at all. "

# 第 16 天

"早安，我想看看高跟鞋。""太太，你穿甚麼尺碼？""九號半。""這裏有一雙你穿的號碼。""讓我來試穿一下。噢，這雙有點緊，夾腳的。請再拿一雙來，好嗎？""好的。這雙怎樣？""這雙正合我的尺寸。我就買這雙吧。"

**【說明】**

"高跟鞋": high-heeled shoes

"這裏有一雙你穿的號碼": Here is a pair in your size, 或
Here is the size you want

"夾脚": pinch

"正合我的尺寸"可說 They are just my size, 或 They suit me
perfectly。

**【譯例】**

(a) "Good morning. I'd like to see some high-heeled shoes."
"What's your size, ma'am?" "Nine and a half." "Here is a pair in
your size." "Let me try them on. Oh, they are a little tight. They pinch
me. Will you please bring me another pair?" "All right. How about
this pair?" "Yes, I think they are just my size. I'll buy them."

(b) "Good morning. Will you please let me see some high-heeled
shoes?" "Certainly, ma'am. What is the size?" "Nine and a half."
"Here you are." "I'll try them on. Well, they are somewhat too small
and pinch me at the toe. Show me another pair, please." "All right.
How do you like this pair?" "Yes, this pair suits me perfectly. I'll take
them."

# 第 17 天

"今天早上我要買點東西，請你陪我一起去，好嗎？""好的，
我很願意。到哪裏去呢？""我想先到藥房去看看。""如果我沒有
記錯的話，過去轉角上有一家。""是的，那裏有。"

"陪同": accompany

"藥房": dispensary; pharmacy; chemist's (shop)

"我願意去"照字譯可說 I'm willing to go; 但也可說 I don't care if I go。注意動詞 care 的用法，I don't care 作"我不放在心上"或"我不以爲意"解；但後面接不定詞就作"不肯"或"不願意"解，如 I don't care to go 是"我不願意去"；但 I don't care if I go 卻又作"我願意去"解，這句直譯是"即使我去，我也不以爲意"也就是說"我可以去"。

【譯例】

(a) "I'll have to do a little shopping this morning. Would you please accompany me?" "Yes, I don't care if I go. Where have you to go?" "I want to call at a dispensary first." "There is one on the next corner if I remember right." "Yes, I believe there is."

(b) "I'm going to do some shopping this morning. Would you mind accompanying me?" "No, of course. Where will you go?" "First, I'd like to visit a pharmacy." "I remember there is one on the next corner." "Yes, there is."

# 第 18 天

"你能替我配這張藥方嗎?""我馬上給你配。""順便問一聲，便祕你說用甚麼藥好呢?""服些瀉劑就可以了。"

【說明】

"配藥方": fill（或 make up）a prescription

"馬上"除了 at once 之外；也可說 right away, straight away。

"你說用甚麼藥好呢？"是徵求別人意見的話，可譯作 " What ( medicine ) would you suggest for …? "或"What do you say is good for …? "

"瀉劑"： purgative; cathartic

## 【譯例】

(a) " Could you make up this prescription for me, please? " " I'll do it for you right away. " " By the way, what would you suggest for constipation? " " A purgative is all you need. "

(b) " Will you please fill this prescription for me? " " Yes, I'll have it ready for you in a few minutes. " " Incidentally, what do you say is good for constipation? " " A cathartic should give you relief. "

# 第 19 天

下星期六父親要過生日了。我打算買些書籍之類的東西給他。我到書店裏去了一下，但沒有甚麼有趣的東西。後來我在文具店挑了一枝精美的自來水筆，並刻上了名字。我想父親會喜愛這枝筆的。

## 【說明】

"過生日"： have one's birthday; celebrate one's birthday

"買些書籍之類的東西"： buy something in the way of books。in the way of 是 "…之類;關於… "的意思;也可簡單說 buy some books。

"書店"： bookstore; bookseller's (shop)

"自來水筆"： fountain pen

"文具店"： stationery shop; stationer's

"刻": engrave

**【譯例】**

(a) My father is having his birthday next Saturday. I thought to buy him something in the way of books. I went to the bookstore, but didn't find anything of interest. At last I bought at a stationer's a nice fountain pen with his name engraved on it. I think my father would like it very much.

(b) As next Saturday will be my father's birthday, I'd like to buy him some books. I tried to get something interesting at the bookseller's, but I was not successful. Finally, at the stationery shop I picked up a beautiful fountain pen and got his name engraved on it. My father would be very pleased with the present.

# 第20天

"請你把那枝自來水筆給我看看，好嗎？""你指的是這一枝嗎？""對了,謝謝你。我要買一枝,但我想在上面刻個名字,行嗎？""行。""筆和刻字一共多少錢？""××元×角。""這裏是××元。""謝謝你這是找頭和發票。"

**【說明】**

"指"是"意指",要說 mean。

"一共多少錢？": "How much does it come to?" "How much is it in all?"或"How much shall I pay altogether?"

"找頭": change

"發票": receipt; invoice

(a) "Will you kindly show me that fountain pen?" "Is it this one you mean?" "Yes, thank you. I think I'll take it, but can I have a name engraved on it?" "Yes, you can." "Pen and engraving, how much does it come to?" "×× dollars ×× cents." "Here is ×× dollars." "Thank you. Here is your change and receipt."

(b) "May I see that fountain pen?" "This one, you mean?" "That's right. Thanks. I'd like to take it, but can you engrave for me a name on it?" "Yes, we can." "How much shall I pay altogether?" "×× dollars ×× cents." "Here you are, ×× dollars." "Thank you. Here's the change and receipt."

# 第21天

郵局經常擠滿了人。他們在買郵票、明信片、信封或寄包裹、信件、印刷品。有些人在滙款、發電報；也有些人在拿留局待領信件。對大家來説，郵局確是個十分方便的地方。

## 【說明】

"擠滿了人"： be thronged（或 crowded）with people

"郵票"： postage stamp; stamp

"明信片"： postcard

"信封"： envelope

"包裹"： parcel

"印刷品"： printed matter

"滙款"： remit money; make a remittance

"電報"： telegram。"發電報" send a telegram。

"留局待領郵件": letters poste restante

## 【譯例】

(a) The post office is always thronged with people buying stamps, postcards and envelopes, or sending parcels, letters and printed matters. Some are remitting money or sending telegrams, and others are taking their letters poste restante. The post office is really a place very convenient to the people.

(b) There are always crowds of people in the post office where they buy stamps, postcards and envelopes; or send parcels, letters and printed matters. Some come to make remittances or send telegrams; and others are here to fetch their letters poste restante. In fact, the post office is quite a convenient place to the people.

# 第22天

有時我在郵局寫信。我把信放在信封裏，在信封上寫明地址，貼好郵票，把它投到信箱裏去。如果我要寄航空掛號信，辦事員會把信稱一稱，在郵票上蓋個戳記，同時給我一張收據。

## 【說明】

"地址": address。"寫明地址": write the address; address

"寄信" post a letter; mail a letter。前者是英國語，後者是美國語。

"掛號信": registered letter

"航空信": letter by air, air letter; airmail letter, airmail

"稱（重量）": weigh

"戳記" chop。"在郵票上蓋個戳記" put a chop on the stamps,

或 cancel the stamps。cancel 是 "蓋銷" 的意思。

**【譯例】**

(a) Sometimes I write letters at the post office. I put the letter into an envelope, address it, put a stamp on it and drop it into the letter-box. If I want to send a registered air letter, I'll give it to the clerk who weighs the letter, cancels the stamps on it and writes out a receipt.

(b) The post office is the place where I sometimes write my letters. When I finish writing the letter, I put it into an envelope and write the address on it. Then I stick a stamp on the letter and drop it into the mailbox. If my letter is to be registered and sent by airmail, the clerk will weigh it, put a chop on the stamps and give me a receipt.

# 第 23 天

我在香港求學，常常接到各地親戚朋友的來信。我是在郵局領取待領郵件的。這郵局靠近我的大學。我每天進去看兩次：一次在去學校的時候，另一次在回住所的時候。

**【說明】**

"進去看" 可用前面看到過的 drop in。"我每天進去看兩次" I drop in there twice a day。

"一次在去學校的時候，另一次在回住所的時候"：once (when I am) on my way to school and another on my way back to my lod-gings

**【譯例】**

(a) I study in Hongkong. I often receive letters from my relatives and friends in other places. I get my letters poste restante at the post office near our college. I drop in there twice a day: once when I'm on my way to school and another time on my way back to my lodgings.

(b) I'm studying in HongKong. Many relatives and friends of mine often write letters to me. Close to our college there is a post office where I take my letters poste restante. Every day I drop in there twice: once on my way to school and another time on my way back to my lodgings.


# 第24天


"這封快信寄新加坡，郵費多少？""我得查一下。噢，是××元。你還需要甚麼？""既然來了，我要一打大的信封。""一共是××。"

【說明】

"快信"：express letter

"郵費"：postage。"這封快信要多少郵費？"："What's the postage on this express letter？"或"Could you tell me how much this express letter is？"

"你還需要甚麼？"："Did you want anything else？"或"Was there anything else？"這裏動詞用過去時，實際上是指現在的事情，但在口語裏用過去時要比用現在時的語氣更爲婉轉客氣，能作類似用法的動詞還有 wonder, think, hope 等。

"既然來了"：while I'm here, 或 while I'm about it, 這裏 it 指郵局。

(a) " What's the postage on this express letter to Singapore, please? " " I'll have a look. Well, it's ×× dollars. Did you want anything else? " " Yes, while I'm about it, I'll have a dozen large envelopes. " " That comes to ××. "

(b) " Could you tell me how much this express letter to Singapore is? " " I think I'd better look that up. Well, it's ×× dollars. Was there anything else? " " Yes, while I'm here, I'd like to have a dozen large envelopes. " " That will be ×× in all. "

# 第25天

" 這封信是寄柏林的。請你稱一稱，告訴我要多少郵費。 " " 你的信寄柏林，要用德文寫地址。" " 好的。這樣可以嗎？ " " 可以的。郵費是××。 "

## 【說明】

" 德文 "：German。" 用德文寫地址 "：Write the address in German。

" 這樣可以嗎？ "：" Will this do? "或" Will this be OK? "

## 【譯例】

(a) " I want to send this letter to Berlin. Please weigh it for me and tell me what is the postage required? " " As the letter is going to Berlin, will you please write the address in German? " " Very well. Will this do? " " All right, sir. The postage is ××. "

(b) " This is a letter to Berlin. Will you please have it weighed and tell me how much the postage is? " " Your letter is going to Berlin, isn't it? Then the address should be written in German. " " All right. Will this be OK? " " Yes, sir. ×× , please. "

# 第26天

"我要把這個包裹寄到法國去，要多少郵費？" "我得查一下。" "你看需要掛號嗎？" "噢，那可由你選擇。如果裏面有貴重物品，掛號比較好。"

## 【說明】

"選擇"：option; 形容詞是 optional。"那可由你選擇" 可以說 You may have ( 或 make ) your option, 或 It's optional。

"貴重物品"：valuables, 原是形容詞，作名詞常用複數。

"掛號比較好" 可用 You'd better…, 或 It's better to…等句型。

## 【譯例】

(a) " What's the postage for this parcel to France? " " I'll just make sure. " " Do you think it necessary to have it registered? " " Well, it's optional. If it contains valuables, you'd better do so. "

(b) " Could you tell me how much this parcel to France is? " " I'll have to check. " " Should I register it? " " Well, if it contains valuables, yes. You may have your option. "

# 第27天

"午安, 太太。" "午安。我有些印刷品要寄, 不知要多少郵費。"

"我給你稱一稱。""我想寄掛號的。""好的。郵費是××，掛號費是××，一共是××。"

"掛號"：register；名詞是 registration。"我要寄掛號的"可以說 I want to have them registered。"掛號費"是 registration fee。

【譯例】

(a) " Good afternoon, ma'am. " " Good afternoon. I have some printed matters to mail. I want to know how much I should pay. " " I'll have to weigh them. " " I think I'll have them registered. " " All right. The postage is ××, and the registration fee is ××. The total is ××. "

(b) " Good afternoon, ma'am. " " Good afternoon. Here are some printed matters I want to mail. Can you tell me what the charge is. " " Let me weigh them. " " I want to have them registered. " " All right, ma'am. Then the postage is ×× and the registration is ××. That will come to ××. "

# 第28天

"我想滙一筆錢到美國去，該怎麼滙？用郵政滙票呢還是銀行滙票？""滙多少錢？""一百塊錢。""我看數額不大，郵滙比較方便。""那麼，請給我一張滙款單子，好嗎？""可以的，那邊櫃台上有。"

【說明】

"滙一筆錢" 可照前例說 make a remittance, 或 send ( 或 remit ) some money。

"郵政滙票 " : postal order

"銀行滙票 " : bank draft

"滙多少錢 " : "How much do you wish to send? " 或 "What's the amount you want to send? " amount 是 "數額 " 或 "數量 "。

"滙款單子 " 是 "空白的申請表 " application form, 或 application blank.

【譯例】

(a) "I'd like to remit some money to the States. How should I send it, by postal order or by bank draft? " " How much do you wish to send? " " The amount is one hundred dollars. " " I think a postal order is more convenient since it is not a big sum. " " Let me have an application form then. " " You'll find some on the counter over there."

(b) " I want to make a remittance to the States. How had I better send it, by postal order or by bank draft? " " What's the amount you want to send? " " One hundred dollars. " " The best way to send it is by postal order, which is more convenient for small sums. " " May I have an application blank, please? " " Yes, there are some on the counter over there. "

# 第 29 天

"我要兌現這張40元的郵政滙票。" "你是受款人嗎?" "是的。這是我的身份證。" "請你在滙票上簽個名。" "好的。" "錢在這裏。" "謝謝。"

【說明】

"兌現": cash, 這裏是作動詞用; 作名詞用是"現金"。

"受款人": payee

"身份證": I. D. card

"簽名": sign one's name, 或 put one's signature to。

## 【譯例】

(a) "Here is a postal order of forty dollars, please cash it." "Are you the payee?" "Yes, I am. This is my I. D. card." "Please sign your name to the order." "All right." "Here is the money." "Thank you."

(b) "I want to have this postal order cashed. The amount is forty dollars." "Are you the payee?" "Yes, I am. Here is my I. D. card." "Will you please put your signature to the order?" "All right." "Here is the money." "Thanks."


# 第30天

"航空信可直達橫濱嗎？""不可以。航空信只到東京，然後再按普通郵件投遞。""這樣太慢，不行。我還是打個電報吧。每個字多少錢？""每字××。""請你給我一張電報單子，好嗎？""好的，這裏有。""謝謝你。"

## 【說明】

"不可以"照字譯是 No, you can't; 但如說 I'm afraid not, 或 I don't think so, 語氣就比較婉轉。

"投遞": deliver; 名詞是 delivery。"按普通郵件投遞"可以說 be delivered as ordinary mail, 或 go by ordinary delivery。

"電報單子": telegraph form

256

## 【譯例】

(a) " Can air letters reach Yokohama directly? " " I'm afraid not. The letters will go by air as far as Tokyo and then by ordinary delivery. " " It won't do then. I'll have to send a telegram. What's the rate per word? " " It's ×× per word. " " Please give me a telegraph form. " " Here you are. " " Thank you. "

(b) " Can air letters reach Yokohama directly? " " I don't think so. The airmail goes to Tokyo only and then it will be delivered as ordinary mail. " " It's too slow. I'll send a telegram instead. What's the charge per word? " " ×× per word. " " May I have a telegraph form? " " Yes, here you are. " " Thanks. "

# Words and Expressions

| | |
|---|---|
| clerk [klɑːk; 美 kləːk] | 辦事員 |
| passport | 護照 |
| arrival form | 來客登記表 |
| give accommodation [əˌkɔməˈdeiʃən] | 安排住宿 |
| porter | 搬運工人 |
| luggage; baggage | 行李 |
| single (double) room | 單人（雙人）房間 |
| ventilate | 通風 |
| patronize [ˈpætrənaiz] | 光顧 |
| vacant room; vacancy [ˈveikənsi] | 空房間 |
| service charge | 侍應費，服務費 |
| trunk call; long-distance call | 長途電話 |
| reserve; make a reservation for | 預訂 |

| | |
|---|---|
| recommend | 介紹 |
| bill | 帳單 |
| department store | 百貨商店 |
| consumer goods | 消費品 |
| provisions | 食品 |
| stationery (shop) | 文具(店) |
| grocery [´grousəri] | 雜貨；雜貨店 |
| household utensils [ju(ː)´tenslz] | 家庭用具 |
| overcoat | 大衣 |
| ready-made | 現成的 |
| have something made to order | 定做 |
| tailor | 裁縫 |
| size | 尺寸；大小 |
| try on | 試穿 |
| wear well | 經穿 |
| collar | 衣領 |
| escalator [´eskəleitə] | 自動樓梯 |
| high-heeled shoes | 高跟鞋 |
| pinch | 夾脚 |
| accompany [ə´kʌmpəni] | 陪同 |
| dispensary [dis´pensəri]; pharmacy [´fɑːməsi]; chemist's [´kemists] | 藥房 |
| purgative [´pəːgətiv]; cathartic [kə´θɑːtik] | 瀉劑 |
| bookstore; bookseller's | 書店 |
| fountain [´fauntin] pen | 自來水筆 |
| change | 找頭 |

| | |
|---|---|
| receipt [ri´si:t]; invoice | 發票 |
| postage [´poustidʒ] | 郵費，郵資 |
| postage stamp; stamp | 郵票 |
| postcard [´poustkɑ:d] | 明信片 |
| envelope[´enviloup] | 信封 |
| parcel [´pɑ:sl] | 包裹 |
| printed matter | 印刷品 |
| address (n. or v.) | 地址(名)；寫地址(動) |
| letter box; mail box | 信箱 |
| registered letter | 掛號信 |
| air letter; airmail | 航空信 |
| chop | 戳記 |
| express letter | 快信 |
| valuables [´væljuəblz] | 貴重物品 |
| postal order | 郵政滙票 |
| bank draft [drɑ:ft] | 銀行滙票 |
| application form | 申請單子 |
| cash (n. or v.) | 現金(名)；兌現(動) |
| payee [pei´i:] | 受款人 |
| I. D. card | 身份證 |
| sign one's name | 簽名 |

# Exercise 9

Translate the following into English:

1. 旅館的辦事員給我一間附有浴室的房間。他告訴我租金，一切安

排很快就都弄好了。（第1天）

2. 我挑了一間朝南的房間。這房間很舒適。我可以在此好好休息。
   （第1，2天）

3. 我定了一間單人房間，請旅館的搬運工人把我的行李搬到房間裏
   去。這地方倒很安靜，因離鬧市較遠。（第2，3天）

4. 車站附近那個旅館是不久以前開設的。房間很清潔，租金也公道，
   怪不得有許多人都去光顧。（第3，4天）

5. 甲：你們有空房間嗎？

   乙：是的，後面還有一間。

   甲：我想先看一下。

   乙：好的。請跟我來好嗎？（第5天）

6. 甲：你們有兩間單人房間嗎？

   乙：不，我只能給你一間。

   甲：每天收費多少？

   乙：××元，侍應費在內。

   甲：價錢倒是公道的，但我要兩間。（第6天）

7. 甲：我的名字叫保羅·瓊斯，前天定了一間雙人房間。

   乙：讓我看一看。噢，對的，找到了，230號房間，前面二樓。請
   你登記一下好嗎？

   甲：好的。（第7天）

8. 甲：我正在找房間。

   乙：我可以介紹你到公園旅館去。

   甲：這旅館價錢貴嗎？

   乙：不，一點也不貴。單人房間每天只××元。

   甲：那倒是公道的。（第8天）

9. 甲：你看這個房間怎樣？

   乙：看來倒是不差，只是有點不大通風。這窗面向甚麼？

甲：面向一條小巷，但離鬧市聲 (noise of the traffic) 較遠。

乙：是的，這裏倒是靜的。（第 4，9 天）

10. 旅館辦事員知道我就要離開，他把帳單交給我，我請他叫一輛出租汽車，結帳以後我離開了旅館。（第 10 天）

11. 百貨商店是銷售多種商品的 (multiple) 商店，出售各種消費品；也可在那裏定製各種衣服。（第 11，13 天）

12. 甲．我打算買一件白色的尼龍襯衫。

乙：尼龍貨目前恐怕沒有。

甲：能給我定一件嗎？

乙：我想可以的。如果你留個地址，我會與你聯繫 (contact)。（第 12 天）

13. 我的朋友詹尼前天想買些東西，她要我同她一起去，我們到百貨公司去，她買了一件現成的大衣和幾樣食品。（第 11，13 天）

14. 甲：這件雨衣甚麼價錢？

乙：××元。

甲：有沒有便宜些的？

乙：很抱歉，再便宜的沒有了。（第 14 天）

15. 甲：你可讓我看看那隻熱水瓶嗎 (thermos bottle)？

乙：當然囉，太太。

甲：這是甚麼價錢？

乙：××元。

甲：東西倒是好的，但我沒打算買這麼貴的。我不想買這個了。（第 14 天）

16. 我在百貨商店乘自動樓梯到 5 樓，在那裏找到了成衣部。我打算買一件上裝，但找不到一件合意的。（第 15 天）

17. 甲：我想看看皮鞋。

乙：要甚麼尺碼的，先生？

甲：十號的。

乙：這雙怎麼樣？

甲：噢，這雙太大了。

乙：那麼讓我替你找一雙小一些的。

甲：謝謝你。

18. 甲：你陪我一道到藥房裏去一趟好不好？

乙：好的，你打算買些甚麼呢？

甲：我想去配個藥方，另外還想買些別的東西。

乙：好，我們就走吧。（第17，18天）

19. 甲：你幫我挑選一件禮物給我哥哥好嗎？他明天要過生日了。

乙：買些甚麼呢？

甲：我想還是到百貨商店去看看。

乙：好吧。我陪你去。（第17，19天）

20. 下星期日我的伯父要過生日了。我同我的朋友瑪麗一道到百貨公司看看有甚麼中意的東西，最後我挑了一隻很漂亮的大酒杯（tumbler），並在上面刻了我最好的祝福。（第19，20天）

21. 你可以在郵局買到各種郵票、明信片和信封、你也可在這裏寄包裹、信件、印刷品或發電報。（第21天）

22. 郵局辦事員把我的一封航空掛號信稱一稱，告訴我要貼多少郵票。我貼好郵票，把信交給他。他在郵票上蓋個戳記並開了個收據給我。（第22天）

23. 我在靠近我的大學一個郵局裏領取留局待領郵件。我挑選這個郵局是因為除了星期天之外，我每天可順便進去看兩次。（第23天）

24. 甲：請問這封信寄曼谷郵費多少？

乙：我來查一下。你還要甚麼嗎？

甲：不要甚麼了，謝謝。（第24天）

25. 甲：我想把這包裹寄巴黎。

262

乙：你的包裹旣然寄巴黎，地址應該用法文寫。

甲：噢，是的。你說得對，讓我來改一改。（第25天）

26. 甲：這封寄泰國的信要掛號。

乙：讓我先來稱一稱。

甲：寄到外國的信件，掛號費是多少？

乙．掛號費是××，郵費是××，一共是××。（第26，27天）

27. 甲：我要滙500元給新加坡一家工廠。

乙：你要塡一張滙款申請單。

甲：寄滙票要掛號嗎？

乙：可由你選擇，但掛號比較好。（第26，28元）

28. 我問郵局辦事員滙100元到日本去怎麼寄較好。他說數額不大，郵滙比較方便。（第28天）

29. 甲：這是日本寄來的一張200元滙票。

乙：是的，現在可以兌現。你有身份證嗎？

甲：沒有，我忘記帶了。

乙：請你把身份證帶來。（第29天）

30. 甲：我要拍個電報，請你給我一張電報單子好嗎？

乙：好的，先生。這是張空白的電報單子，請把電文寫在上面。

甲；我想把這電報作爲急電拍發，每個字多少錢？

乙：每字××。

甲：這是電文，有20個字。

乙：是的，正好20個字。那麼一共是××。（第30天）

# 第 10 月
# 經濟、商業、貿易

## 第 1 天

只有社會接受新思想，經濟、科學、技術才有發展的可能。

**【說明】**

" 經濟 "： economy

" 技術 "： technology

" 只有社會接受新思想…才有發展的可能 "： Only when society accepts new thoughts is the development…made possible. 注意：only 放在句首起强調作用，所以主句裏的主謂語要倒裝。在簡單句裏也如此，如 Only in this way can we accomplish the task, Only thus will the problem be solved; 偶然也有人這樣說 Only then he realized his mistake, 但總不如說 Only then did he realize his mistake 爲正常。另外，這個句子也可譯作 The development…is impossible until society accepts new thoughts, 或 It is not until society accepts new thoughts that the development…is made possible。

**【譯例】**

(a) Only when society accepts new thoughts is the development of economy, science and technology made possible.

(b) It is not until society accepts new thoughts that the development of economy, science and technology is made possible.

264

# 第2天

工業的發展在很大程度上依賴技術的進步，但更多的是靠那些從事這方面工作的人的自覺性。

## 【說明】

"工業"：industry

"在很大程度上依賴…"：depend very much upon…

"技術的進步"：technical progress, 或 progress of techniques

"從事"：be engaged (in)。"從事這方面工作的人"：those (who are) engaged in that field。field 是"方面"；也可簡單地說 those concerned。concerned 是"有關的"的意思。

"自覺性"：awakening

## 【譯例】

(a) The development of industry depends very much upon technical progress, but it depends even more upon the awakening of those engaged in that field.

(b) The development of industry is dependent not only upon the progress of techniques but even more upon the awakening of those concerned.

# 第3天

在缺乏自然資源的國家裏，不確保原料進口，工業就不能發達。同時，更要盡可能鼓勵出口貿易。

"自然資源": natural resources。"缺乏自然資源"可說 lack in natural resources, 或 have but poor natural resources。

"確保": secure, 是動詞也是形容詞。"不確保原料進口"是 "如果原料進口不確保"的意思, 要說 if the importation of raw materials is not made secure, 或 unless the importation of raw materials is secured。

"發達": thrive, prosper; 形容詞是 thriving, prosperous。"工業就不能發達": industry cannot thrive, 或以 country 作主語說 a country cannot hope to have a prosperous industry。

"鼓勵": encourage

"出口貿易": export trade

【譯例】

(a) In the case of a country having but poor natural resources, industry cannot thrive if the importation of raw materials is not made secure. At the same time, it is necessary for such a country to encourage her export trade as much as possible.

(b) Unless the importation of raw materials is secured, a country lacking in natural resources cannot hope to have a prosperous industry. At the same time, she must make every effort to encourage her export trade.


# 第4天

儘管人口激增, 現代科學技術還是帶來了產品供給超過需要的局面。生產過剩的結果, 那些推動消費的人, 比如說, 推銷員之類的身價就提高了。

【說明】

"儘管"： in spite of。"儘管人口激增" in spite of the rapid increase in population。

"帶來"： bring about

"局面"： situation。"產品的供給超過需要的局面"： a situation in which the supply of products exceeds the demand for them。

"生產過剩"： overproduction

"消費"： consumption; consume 是動詞; consumer 是 "消費者"。

"推動"： stimulate; stimulator 是 "推動者"。

"推銷員"： salesman; 也可作 "售貨員" 解。

"身價"： value; 也可作 "價值" 解; 用作動詞可作 "重視" 解。

【譯例】

(a) Modern science and technology have brought about a situation in which the supply of products exceeds the demand for them in spite of the rapid increase in population. As a result of overproduction, those people who stimulate consumption, such as salesmen, have come to be more valued.

(b) With the progress of science and technology today, the supply of products has come to exceed the demand for them. As a result of overproduction, the value of the stimulators of consumption, for instance, salesmen, has been raised.

# 第5天

對於和平利用原子能作出一些貢獻是我們青年的權利，也是我們的義務。我們必須明白現在已經進入了原子能時代。

## 【說明】

"原子能"：atomic energy; atomic power。"和平利用原子能"：peaceful use of atomic energy, 或 application of atomic power to peaceful purposes。application 是 "應用" 的意思。

"貢獻"：contribute (to 或 towards); 名詞是 contribution, "作出貢獻"：make contributions (to 或 towards), contribute (to 或 towards)。

"是我們青年的權利，也是我們的義務" 如前所見，可作三種譯法：1. 用 both…and…作連詞：be both the right and the duty of us young men; 2. 用 not only…but also…作連詞：be not only the right but also the duty of us young men; 3. 用 as well as 作連詞：be the duty as well as the right of us youths; 後一種說法要把 duty 放在前面; us young men ( 或 youths )，這裏 young men 是 us 的同位語。

## 【譯例】

(a) It is not only the right of us young men but also our duty to contribute something towards the peaceful use of atomic energy. We must realize that we are now in the age of atomic energy.

(b) It is the duty as well as the right of us youths to make contributions to the application of atomic power to peaceful purposes. We must be aware that we have now entered the atomic age.

# 第6天

雖然不景氣，但物價仍然很高。你想這不是個奇怪的現象嗎？

## 【說明】

"不景氣"：business depression, 或 depression in business

"物價仍然很高" 可以說 prices remain high, 或 prices are still as high as ever。

"奇怪的現象"：a strange phenomenon。"你想這不是一個奇怪的現象嗎？"：Don't you think (that) it is a strange phenomenon? 注意：think, believe, imagine, fancy, suppose, expect 等動詞,後面如跟以 that 引起的賓語從句，其否定詞 not 習慣上要放在主句裏而不放在從句裏，如 "我想天不會下雨" 說 I don't think it will rain 比說 I think it will not rain 普通得多；"我相信他明天不會來" 說 I don't believe he will come tomorrow 比說 I believe he will not come tomorrow 普通得多。

## 【譯例】

(a) Don't you think it is a strange phenomenon that prices are still as high as ever in spite of business depression?

(b) Though the depression in business is prevalent, prices remain high. Don't you think it a strange phenomenon?

# 第7天

要緩和通貨膨脹，就必須停止貨幣供應量的膨脹超過一個國家的實際生產能力；停止陷入只能由不兌現貨幣來提供資金的巨額赤字。

**【說明】**

"緩和"： slow down

"膨脹"： inflate; 名詞是 inflation。"通貨膨脹"： currency inflation, inflation

"貨幣供應量"： supply of money, 或 money supply

"一個國家的實際生產能力"： the real ability of a country to produce

"停止"： stop。注意： stop 後跟動名詞是及物動詞,作"停止"解; 後跟不定詞是不及物動詞, 作"停下來而…"解, 就是"停止了別的事情而從事…"的意思, 如 He stopped laughing（他停止笑）, He stopped to see the sights（他停下來看風景）。

"陷入"： run into; get into

"不兌現貨幣"： fiat dollar; fiat money

"提供資金"： finance; 名詞要作"財政"或"金融"解。

"赤字"： deficit。"只能由不兌現貨幣來提供資金的巨額赤字": huge deficits that can be financed only with fiat money, 或 huge deficits to be financed only with fiat dollars。

**【譯例】**

(a) The way to slow down currency inflation is to stop inflation of the money supply beyond the real ability of a country to produce and to stop running into huge deficits that can be financed only with fiat dollars.

(b) In order to slow down inflation, it is necessary to stop inflating the supply of money beyond the real ability of a country to produce, and to stop getting into huge deficits to be financed only with fiat

270

money.

# 第8天

過去商人和製造商通常是受輕視的。如今人們認爲他們所從事的
工商業是應受尊重的工作。

## 【說明】

"過去"指古代, 可說 in former times, in ancient times, 或 of
old。

"商人": businessman; merchant; 後者指大商人。

"製造商": manufacturer

"輕視": despise; look down upon

"應受尊重的工作": respectable occupation

"認爲": regard (as); consider。"認爲是應受尊重的工作" re-
gard…as respectable occupations; 改成被動是 be regarded as respectable occupations, 或 be considered (to be) respectable occupations。

## 【譯例】

(a) The businessmen and manufacturers of old were usually despised, but nowadays the commerce and industry in which they are engaged are regarded as respectable occupations.

(b) Although merchants and manufacturers were usually looked down
upon in former times, the commerce and industry for which they go in
are now considered to be respectable occupations.

# 第9天

要是兩國之間沒有相互了解，那麼貿易就不可能那樣迅速地發展起來。

## 【說明】

"相互了解"：mutual understanding。"要是兩國之間沒有相互了解…"：這是對過去事實作相反的假設，所以要用表示過去情況的虛擬條件從句來譯 If there had been no mutual understanding between these two countries…，或 If it had not been for the mutual understanding between these two countries…；也可用 but for 譯成 But for the mutual understanding between these two countries…；另外還可用 countries 作主語說 If these two countries had not understood each other so well…。

"迅速發展" make rapid progress，或 make big strides

## 【譯例】

(a) If there had been no mutual understanding between these two countries, trade between them would not have made such rapid progress.

(b) But for the mutual understanding between these two countries, trade between them would not have made such big strides.

# 第 10 天

要生產能在外國暢銷的貨物就絕對要研究該國人民的風俗習慣。

## 【說明】

272

"暢銷的貨物"：goods that can find a ready sale, 或 articles that would be quite easily salable

"風俗"：customs

"習慣" 指 "生活方式"，要說 ways, manners。

## 【譯例】

(a) In order to produce articles that can find a ready sale in a foreign country, it is absolutely necessary to study the manners and customs of the people of that country.

(b) If we are to make goods that would be quite easily salable in a foreign country, it is important for us to study the ways and customs of the people living in that country.

# 第 11 天

賣方條件極為寬厚，適合各方顧客的需要；譬如給與 3 個月的信用賒帳；如在14天內付現金，則可享有百分之二的折扣等。

## 【說明】

"賣方"：seller; supplier; 後者通常指 "供應廠商"。

"條件"：terms

"寬厚"：generous

"適合"：be adapted to。 "適合各方顧客的需要" be adapted to the needs of various customers。

"信用賒帳"：credit。 "給與 3 個月的信用賒帳"：credit is allowed for three months, 或以 they 作主語說 they allow（或 grant）a credit for three months。

"付現金": pay cash,或 pay in cash; 改為名詞詞組是 cash payment, 或 payment in cash。"在 14 天內付現金則可享有百分之二的折扣": cash payments within fourteen days are subject to a discount of two per cent。subject to 是 "可以受到⋯", 如 The prices are subject to change at any time(價目可隨時更動), 或 "以⋯為條件", 如 This can only be done subject to the consent of the manager (這事情只有在經理同意的條件下才可以做)。

**【譯例】**

(a) The sellers' terms are extremely generous and adapted to the needs of various customers. For example, credit is allowed for three months and cash payments within fourteen days are subject to a discount of two per cent.

(b) The sellers' terms, which are extremely generous, are adapted to the needs of different customers. For instance, they grant a credit for three months and allow a 2 % discount to those who will pay in cash within fourteen days.

# 第 12 天

工廠通知買方, 人造纖維可以在八月份裝運, 但必須以工廠在發信日起半個月內接到訂單為條件。

**【說明】**

"買方": buyer

"人造纖維": polyester staple fibre

"裝運": dispatch, 可作動詞或名詞。

"訂單" 是 "定貨單", 即 order。"以工廠在發信日起半個月內

接到訂單爲條件 " subject to the factory receiving the order within fifteen days from the date of the letter。

**【譯例】**

(a) The factory informed the buyers that the polyester staple fibre could be dispatched in August subject to the factory receiving the order within fifteen days from the date of the letter.

(b) The buyers were informed that if the factory could receive the order for the polyester staple fibre within fifteen days from the date of the letter, they would dispatch the goods in August.

# 第 13 天

新發明的產品節省時間，免除不便，定能滿足消費者的需要。爲了推廣這種產品，所定價格在二月份之內打九折。

**【說明】**

"新發明的"：newly invented

"不便"：inconvenient; 名詞是 inconvenience。"節省時間免除不便" save time and inconvenience（或 trouble）。

"滿足消費者的需要"：satisfy the demands of the consumers, 或 meet the needs of the consumers

"推廣"：popularize

"九折"：a 10% discount, 或 a discount of ten per cent。"打九折" 以 price 爲主語可說 the price is subject to a special discount of ten per cent, 或以 we 爲主語說 we allow a 10% discount。

(a) Our newly invented product can save time and inconvenience and will definitely satisfy the demands of the consumers. As we desire to popularize this product, the price fixed is subject to a special discount of ten per cent  during the month of February.

(b) Our newly invented product, which can save time and trouble, will surely meet the needs of the consumers. We allow a 10 % discount on orders received during the month of February in order to popularize this product.

# 第 14 天

我們生產地毯已近30年, 行銷全世界, 顧客均感非常滿意。因此, 我們確信產品的質量與做工也會得到你們的讚許。

## 【說明】

"地毯": carpet

"非常滿意": be fully satisfied (with); 改為詞組是 to the full satisfaction of…。

"做工": workmanship

"讚許": approve (of); 名詞是 approval。

## 【譯例】

(a) We have been producing these carpets for almost thirty years. They have been sold throughout the world to the full satisfaction of our customers. Therefore, we are sure that both the quality and the workmanship of our products would meet with your approval.

(b) For almost thirty years we have been making these carpets, which have been sold all over the world. As our customers are fully satisfied with the quality and the workmanship of our products, we believe they will also meet with your approval.

# 第 15 天

"你們能夠保證這種機器的質量嗎?""是的，我們所提供的機器可以經受得起經驗的考驗。我們大多數顧客在過去10年裏都一直在用它。"

【說明】

"保證": guarantee

"考驗": test, 是動詞也是名詞。"經受得起經驗的考驗" stand （或 satisfy）the test of experience。

"一直": consistently。"在過去10年裏都一直在用它" have used it consistently for the past ten years, 或 have been using it these ten years。

【譯例】

(a) " Can you guarantee the quality of this machine? " " Yes, the machine we offer you will stand the test of experience. The majority of our customers have used it consistently for the past ten years. "

(b) " Can you guarantee that this machine is of good quality? " " Oh, yes, you may be assured that the machine will satisfy the test of experience. Most of our customers have been using it these ten years. "

# 第 16 天

"我們知道貴公司生產多種不同的產品。哪些產品是你們特別想出口的呢?""噢,我們想擴展電子產品的市場,由晶體管到電腦的各種東西。請光臨敝公司看貨。"

## 【說明】

"公司": firm; company

"電子產品": electronic product

"晶體管": transistor

"電腦": computer

"看貨": see the stock; stock 是"存貨"的意思。

## 【譯例】

(a) "We know your firm produces a variety of products. What particularly are you interested in exporting?" "Well, we are trying to expand the markets of our electronic products, everything from transistors to computers. Just come to our firm and see the stock for yourself."

(b) "I am aware that your firm produces different kinds of products, but what are you most interested in exporting?" "We are looking forward to expanding the markets of our electronic products, everything from transistors to computers. Please come to our firm and look at them.

# 第 17 天

按合同出售棉花的數量是50噸。由於供應不足,賣方不能按時執行訂單，但應允在３個月內交貨。

**【說明】**

"合同"：contract。"按合同出售棉花的數量"：the quantity of cotton sold under contract; 也可說 the contract quantity of cotton。

"供應不足"：shortage of supply

"執行訂單"：execute（或 fill）an order; 在美國通常用 fill。

**【譯例】**

(a) The contract quantity of cotton is fifty tons. As there is a shortage of supply, the sellers are unable to execute the order in time but have promised to effect delivery within three months.

(b) The quantity of cotton sold under contract is fifty tons. The sellers find it difficult to fill the order in time owing to the shortage of supply. However, they have promised delivery within three months.


# 第 18 天


由於能源缺乏，工廠的生產量降低了30％，因此賣方在十月份之前不能接受訂單。

**【說明】**

"能源"： energy。"能源缺乏"： shortage of energy ，或 energy shortage。

"生產量"：output capacity

(a) Owing to the shortage of energy, the output capacity of the factory has been reduced by 30%. It is, therefore, impossible for the sellers to accept any further orders before October.

(b) As the shortage of energy has reduced 30% of the output capacity of the factory, the sellers are therefore unable to take any more orders before October.

# 第 19 天

買方要求賣方加速生產纖維板，以便同其他貨物一起交8月15日開行的貨櫃船啓運。如賣方不能交貨，則買方將不得不取消訂單。

【說明】

" 纖維板 "：fibreboard

" 加速 "：speed up。" 加速生產纖維板 " speed up the production（或 manufacture）of fibreboards。

" 啓運 "：ship，這裏是動詞。" 交8月15 日開行的貨櫃船啓運 "：be shipped by a container ship sailing the 15th August

【譯例】

(a) The sellers are asked to speed up the production of fibreboards so that they may be shipped with other goods by a container ship sailing the 15th August. If they fail to deliver them, the buyers will be compelled to cancel the order.

(b) The buyers suggest that the manufacture of fibreboards be speeded up so that they may be shipped with other goods by a container ship which sails the 15th August. If the delivery is delayed, they will have to cancel the order.

280

# 第20天

　　賣方指出貨物是按貨價加運費價格出售；爲此，買方而不是賣方應該對運輸中所受的損失負責。

**【說明】**

　　"按貨價加運費價格出售"：be sold on C&F terms; C&F 是 Cost and Freight, 與 C. I. F. (Cost, Insurance and Freight) 不同，不包括貨物在運輸途中的保險費。

　　"運輸"： transport; transit。"運輸中所受的損失"：damage occurring during the transport, 或 damage incurred during transit（或 shipment）；incur 是 "遭受" 的意思。

　　"負責"： be responsible (for)

**【譯例】**

　　(a) The sellers pointed out that the goods had been sold on C & F terms, and for that reason the buyers, and not the sellers, were responsible for the damage occurring during the transport.

　　(b) As the goods had been sold on C & F terms, the sellers were of (the) opinion that it was the buyers, and not the sellers, that were responsible for the damage incurred during transit.


# 第21天

　　部分按合同出售的羊毛內衣已於5月15日交新月輪啓運。由於季節即將來臨，賣方接到要求將其餘部分在9月上旬裝運。

"部分"可說 a part of 或 part of, 但兩者意義略有不同: a part of 是 "一小部分"指一半以下; part of 是 "一部分"可指一半以下, 也可指一半以上。注意這兩個詞組後面的名詞或代詞如爲單數, 那麼動詞也爲單數; 如爲複數,那動詞也是複數,如 (A) part of the cotton is sold. (A) part of the carpets are sold。

"羊毛內衣": woollen underwear

"新月輪": s. s. " Crescent "; s. s. 是 steamship。

"9月上旬": the first part of September

【譯例】

(a) A part of the woollen underwear sold under contract is known to have been shipped by s. s. " Crescent " on the 15th of May. As the season is coming soon, the sellers are requested to deliver the remainder of the goods in the first part of September.

(b) Though part of the woollen underwear sold under contract was shipped by s. s. " Crescent " on the 15th of May, the sellers are requested to dispatch the remainder of the goods in the first part of September as the season is coming soon.

# 第22天

如果運費急劇上漲, 賣方有權提高貨物的價格。

【說明】

"運費": rate of freight。"如果運費急劇上漲…": If the rate of freight should rise sharply…; 也可把 if 去掉而把 should 放在句

首說 Should the rate of freight rise sharply; 改成詞組可說 in case of a sharp rise in the rate of freight。

"提高"：raise; increase

【譯例】

(a) If the rate of freight should rise sharply, the sellers could have the right to increase the price of the goods.

(b) The sellers will have the right to raise the price of the goods in case of a sharp rise in the rate of freight.

# 第23天

賣方常不能準時交貨，使買方受到很大不便。爲此買方強調迅速交貨的重要性，並指出這種延誤如再發生，買方將不得不向其他方面定貨。

【說明】

"準時"：on time。"常不能準時交貨"：often fail to deliver goods on time, 或 have been unpunctual in delivering the goods; unpunctual 是 "不準時", 後面要用介詞 in。

"強調"：stress; emphasize。"強調迅速交貨的重要性"：stress the importance of prompt delivery, 或 emphasize the necessity of prompt delivery。

"再發生"：repeat

"向…訂貨"：place an order with…, 或 give an order to…

【譯例】

(a) The sellers often fail to deliver goods on time. The delay has caused considerable inconvenience to the buyers. For this reason, the buyers stress the importance of prompt delivery and point out that they will be obliged to place their orders with other firms if such a delay is repeated.

(b) The sellers have been unpunctual in delivering the goods, much to the inconvenience of the buyers, who therefore emphasize the necessity of prompt delivery, stating that if the delay is repeated, they will have to find another source of supply.


# 第 24 天


"買方爲甚麼拒絕收貨?""據說他們收到的貨物與他們定貨時看中的樣品並不相符。""那怎麼辦呢?""或是把貨物調換,或是取消訂單。"

## 【說明】

"貨"除了 goods 之外,如爲"船貨",可說 cargo。

"樣品": sample。"定貨時看中的樣品"可理解爲"導致他們定貨的樣品", the sample which has led to their placing the order, to 是介詞; 也可說 the sample which has induced them to give the order。

"符合": correspond to; be in accordance with; be the same as; be up to 都可以說。

"調換": replace; change

## 【譯例】

(a) "For what reason do the buyers refuse to accept the cargo?"

284

" They say the cargo received does not correspond to the sample which has led to their placing the order. " " What is to be done then? " " Either the goods are to be replaced or the order is to be cancelled. "

(b) " Why wouldn't the buyers accept the goods? " " Because they say the goods delivered are not up to the sample which has induced them to give the order. " " What shall we do then? " " We shall have to replace the goods or to cancel the order. "

# 第25天

由於經濟困難，買方致函賣方要求延期到年終付款，賣方則不願改變雙方協議的付款辦法，因此拒絕了買方的請求。

## 【說明】

" 經濟困難 " ： financial difficulty

" 延期 " ： defer; delay

" 協議 " ： negotiation

" 付款辦法 " ： terms of payment。 " 雙方協議的付款辦法 " ： the terms of payment (which have been) agreed upon during the negotiations。

" 拒絕 " ： reject

## 【譯例】

(a) The buyers are placed with a financial difficulty and are writing to the suppliers for permission to defer payment of their account till the end of the year. But the suppliers are not willing to change the terms of payment which have been agreed upon during the negotiations, so the buyers' request is rejected.

(b) The buyers ask the suppliers in a letter for permission to defer payment of their account to the end of the year owing to a difficult financial problem. The suppliers, however, refuse to change the terms of payment agreed upon during the negotiations. Accordingly, the buyers' request is rejected.

# 第26天

買方要求降低價格百分之五，但賣方堅持如買方希望取得減價的好處，必須把定貨的數量提高至100噸。

## 【說明】

"降低"：reduce；名詞是 reduction；也可說 decrease。

"好處"：profit,是名詞也是動詞。"希望取得減價的好處"：wish to profit by the lower price。

## 【譯例】

(a) The buyers ask for a reduction of five per cent in the price, but the sellers insist that the buyers should raise their order to one hundred tons if they wish to profit by the lower price.

(b) The buyers demand of the sellers to reduce 5% in the price. The latter, however, ask the former to increase the order to 100 tons if the reduction is to be made.

# 第27天

"請你給我一份註明價格和付款辦法的詳細目錄好嗎？" "好

的。""你們的價格是否可以稍爲減低一些?""對不起,這是我們的最低價格。"

### 【說明】

"目錄": catalogue。"註明價格和付款辦法的詳細目錄": catalogue with details of the prices and terms of payment。

"最低價格"除了 lowest price 之外;也可說 rock-bottom price。

### 【譯例】

(a) "Will you please give me a copy of your catalogue with details of the prices and terms of payment?" "Yes, here you are." "Can you reduce the prices somewhat?" "Sorry to say, these are our rock-bottom prices."

(b) "May I have a copy of your catalogue with details of the prices and terms of payment?" "Certainly, sir, here you are." "Do you think it possible to reduce the prices somewhat?" "To our regret, we can't make any reduction, because these are our lowest prices."

# 第28天

"你們的價格好像高了些。""不會的。請貴公司將我們的價格與別的公司比較,相信貴公司會發覺我們的價錢確實十分公道。"

### 【說明】

"不會的": 可說 not at all, 或 by no means

"將我們的價格與其他公司比較": compare our prices with those of the other firms ( 或 companies ); those 是替代 prices。

"公道": moderate; reasonable

(a) "It seems to me that your prices are somewhat too high."
"Not at all. Compare our prices with those of the other firms. We are confident that you will find that our prices are really very moderate."

(b) "Your prices seem to be somewhat too high." "By no means. You may compare our prices with those of the other companies; we are sure that you will find our prices very reasonable."

# 第29天

買方在徵得賣方同意之前，無權轉讓合同上的權利和義務。

## 【說明】

"轉讓": transfer。 "無權轉讓": have no right to transfer, 或 be not entitled to transfer, entitle 是 "給…權利" 的意思。

"義務": obligation

"同意": consent。 "在徵得賣方同意之前": before they obtain the consent of the sellers; 改成詞組可說 without the prior consent of the sellers, prior consent 是 "事前同意" 的意思。

## 【譯例】

(a) The buyers have no right to transfer their rights and obligations under the contract without the prior consent of the sellers.

(b) The buyers are not entitled to transfer their rights and obligations under the contract before they obtain the consent of the sellers.

288

# 第30天

買方發現在第12號箱中有80雙短襪完全損壞, 毫無價值, 無法收納, 所以通知賣方向承保的××保險公司索賠。

## 【說明】

"短襪": socks。"長襪"是 stockings。

"損壞": spoil

"保險": insure; 名詞是 insurance。"保險公司"是 insurance company。

"承保": undertake the insurance。"向承保的××保險公司索賠": claim the value ( 或 compensation ) from the × Insurance Company, which has undertaken the insurance ( 或 which has insured them, them 指"短襪" )。

## 【譯例】

(a) As the buyers found that eighty pairs of socks contained in case No. 12 were entirely spoilt and absolutely useless, they refused to receive them and asked the sellers to claim the value from the × Insurance Company which had undertaken the insurance.

(b) Among the articles contained in case No. 12, the buyers found eighty pairs of socks entirely spoilt and absolutely without any value. For this reason, they refused to accept them and advised the sellers to claim the compensation from the × Insurance Company which had insured them.

# Words and Expressions

economy [i'kɔnəmi] 經濟

technology [tek'nɔlədʒi] 技術

industry 工業

natural resources [ri'sɔ:siz] 自然資源

prosperous ['prɔspərəs]; 發達的
  thriving

encourage [in'kʌridʒ] 鼓勵

export trade 出口貿易

in spite of 儘管; 不顧

bring about 帶來; 造成

consume (v.); consumption (n.) 消費

stimulate 推動; 刺激

salesman 售貨員

atomic energy, atomic power 原子能

application 應用; 適用; 申請

contribute (to) [kən'tribju:t]; 貢獻
  contribution [ˌkɔntri'bju:ʃən]

(business) depression 不景氣

currency inflation; inflation 通貨膨脹

fiat ['faiæt] dollar; fiat money 不兌現貨幣

finance (n. or v.) [fai'næns] 財政;金融(名);提供資金(動)

deficit ['defisit] 赤字; 虧空

| | |
|---|---|
| businessman; merchant | 商人 |
| in former times; in ancient [ˊeinʃənt] times; of old | 古時 |
| manufacture(r) [ˏmænjuˊfæktʃə (rə)] | 製造 ( 商 ) |
| despise; look down upon | 輕視 |
| occupation [ˏɔkjuˊpeiʃən] | 職業；工作 |
| custom | 風俗 |
| seller | 賣方 |
| buyer | 買方 |
| term | 條件 |
| generous [ˊdʒenərəs] | 寬厚的 |
| credit | 信用賒賬 |
| discount | 折扣 |
| pay (in) cash | 付現金 |
| polyester [ˏpɔliˊestə] staple fibre | 人造纖維 |
| dispatch | 裝運 |
| invent (v.); invention (n.) | 發明 |
| inconvenient [ˏinkənˊviːnjənt] | 不便的 |
| popularize [ˊpɔpjuləraiz] | 推廣；普及 |
| carpet | 地毯 |
| workmanship | 做工 |
| approve (of) (v.) [əˊpruːv]; approval (n.) [əˊpruːvəl] | 讚許；贊成 |
| guarantee [ˏgærənˊtiː] | 保證 |
| test (v. or n.) | 考驗 |
| firm; company [ˊkʌmpəni] | 公司 |

| | |
|---|---|
| electronic [ilek´trɔnik] | 電子的 |
| transistor [træn´sistə] | 半導體，晶體管 |
| computer [kəm´pju:tə] | 電腦 |
| stock | 存貨 |
| contract [´kɔntrækt] | 合同 |
| shortage [´ʃɔ:tidʒ] | 不足 |
| execute（或 fill）an order | 執行訂單 |
| output | 產量 |
| fibreboard [´faibəbɔ:d] | 纖維板 |
| speed up | 加速 |
| ship (n. or v.) | 船(名)；啓運(動) |
| transport (v.) [træns´pɔ:t]; (n) [´trænspɔ:t] | 運輸 |
| be responsible (for) | 負責 |
| (a) part of | 部分 |
| woollen underwear | 羊毛內衣 |
| rate of freight [freit] | 運費 |
| on time | 準時地 |
| stress; emphasize [´emfəsaiz] | 強調 |
| place an order with | 向…訂貨 |
| sample [´sɑ:mpl] | 樣品 |
| correspond to; be in accordance with; be up to | 與…相符 |
| replace | 調換 |
| financial difficulty | 經濟困難 |
| defer; delay | 延期 |
| negotiation [ni͵gouʃi´eiʃən] | 協商；協議 |

| reduce (v.); reduction (n.) | 降低；減少 |
| profit (n. or. v.) | 利益；好處(名)；有益於(動) |
| catalogue [ˈkætələg] | 目錄 |
| rock-bottom price | 最低價 |
| moderate [ˈmɔdərit]; reasonable (price) | 公道的（價格） |
| transfer (v.) [trænsˈfəː]; (n.) [ˈtrænsfə] | 轉移；轉讓；調動 |
| entitle [inˈtaitl] | 給…權利 |
| obligation | 義務 |
| socks; stockings | 短襪；長襪 |
| insurance [inˈʃuərəns]; insurance company | 保險；保險公司 |

# Exercise 10

Translate the following into English:

1. 只有使用新機器我們才能希望增加生產。（第1天）

2. 技術的進步可以促使（spur）工業的發展，但只有當那些從事這方面工作的人的自覺性提高了，才會有更大的發展。(第1, 2天)

3. 一個缺乏自然資源的國家一定要確保原料進口，並盡可能鼓勵出口貿易，只有這樣才能使它的工業發達起來。（第1, 3天）

4. 現代的科學技術大大地提高了生產力，結果是產品的供應超過了需要。生產過剩往往在商業上引起（give rise to）劇烈的競爭 (keen competition)。（第4天）

5. 近年來儘管人口激增，許多國家產品的供應還是超過了需要，這是現代科學技術發展的結果。（第4天）

6. 我們青年應該在和平利用原子能方面作出一些貢獻。這是我們的權利，也是我們的義務。（第5天）

7. 要免於負債我們必須停止花費比我們所賺的還要多的錢。（第7天）

8. 過去婦女通常是受輕視的。如今她們與男子處在平等的地位（on an equal footing with…）從事各種工作，也同樣在社會上受到尊重。（第8天）

9. 要是近代的科學技術不發達，那麼生產就不可能那樣迅速地發展起來。（第9天）

10. 如蒙惠顧定貨我們可給與兩個月賒賬，如半月內付現金則可享百分之二的折扣。（第11天）

11. 賣方通知買方，由於自上月來成本不斷上漲，所定價格可隨時變更。（第11天）

12. 我們相信，我們新發明的產品定能滿足消費者的需要。如蒙訂購，不勝歡迎。（第13天）

13. 貨量超過50打，我們將樂於允許2％的特別折扣，以示優待。（第13天）

14. 本公司為歷史悠久的絲織品（silk fabrics）製造商，日本及其他許多外國的使用者都熟悉我們的牌子，相信我們產品的質量定能使你們完全滿意。（第14天）

15. 本公司每天營業，不論有無購買之意，請前來參觀。（第16天）

16. 我們有意把某些產品，特別是晶體管和電腦，出口到歐洲去，不知你們能否協助我們。（第16天）

17. 由於原料缺乏，工廠生產減少，因此通知買方不能按時交付定貨；但應允盡力繼續生產，希望能在月底交貨。（第17，18天）

18. 由於貴公司未能在指定時間之內（within the specified time）交貨，我們沒有其他辦法（alternative），只好取消我們的訂單。

（第19天）

19. 一部分貨物已準備啓運；但為節省（economize）運費起見，我們已決定再過幾天同其他貨物一起裝運。（第21天）

20. 如果原料漲價，我們要求有權提高貨價，否則我們將不得不拒絕貴公司的訂單。（第22天）

21. 這項買賣（trade）迅速交貨乃屬必要。我們曾一再向你們指出，如果這種延誤再度發生，我們將不得不另找供貨來源。（第23天）

22. 該貨約定應於上旬交付，但到月底才運去。延遲交貨使買方深感不便。（第23天）

23. 我們遺憾地奉告，到貨與樣品不一致，因此我們拒絕接受。（第24天）

24. 經仔細考慮你們8月8日的來信，我們已經決定應允你們延期到本月底付帳。（第25天）

25. 我們可報（quote）的價格以訂購500打以上為前提。如貴公司希望取得減價的好處，請增加訂購達到這一數字（figure）.（第26天）

26. 從貴公司所寄目錄看來，我們發現所訂價格好像高了些。如果價格合適，我們願意向你們訂購雨衣400件。（第27，28天）

27. 如果貴公司把我們的價格與其他公司比較，深信貴公司會了解我們的報價相當合理。（第28天）

28. 按照合同，如果賣方不能按時交貨，買方有權取消訂單。（第29天）

29. 我們感到很抱歉，發現在第20箱內所有長褲都受到損污(stain)。大部分都是由於海水浸濕。（第30天）

30. 要了解通貨膨脹，我們必須首先了解甚麼是在"膨脹"。這既不是物價，也不是工資（wages）而是通貨的供應量。當通貨的供應量超過了一個國家實際生產能力，通貨膨脹了，貨幣就開始貶值（depreciate）。（第7天）

# 第 11 月
# 書籍、學習、學習英語

## 第 1 天

詞典有點像手錶，如果是靠不住的話，還不如不要爲好；但即使是最好的詞典也不能望其完全正確。

### 【說明】

"有點像"：be something like; somewhat resemble; may be likened to

"靠不住"：undependable; unreliable

"完全正確"： perfectly correct; 改成名詞詞組是 complete accuracy。

### 【譯例】

(a) A dictionary is something like a watch. If it is unreliable, we had better not keep it. Even from the best one we know, we can't expect complete accuracy.

(b) A dictionary may be likened to a watch. You had better not keep an undependable one. We can't expect even the best dictionary we know to be perfectly correct.

## 第 2 天

雖然出版了大量的書籍，但確實值得一讀的却極少。

## 【說明】

"出版"：publish

"大量的"：a large number of; a lot of; a great many 都可以說。

"值得一讀"：worth reading。"值得一讀的書却極少"：very few books are worth reading。注意：worth 後面的動名詞一定屬於主動語態，但其意義却是被動的，如 The film is worth seeing（這電影值得一看），不可說 being seen, This book is worth buying（這本書值得買），不可說 being bought。

## 【譯例】

(a) A large number of books are published, but very few of them are really worth reading.

(b) Though a lot of books are published, very few of them are worth reading.


# 第3天

書桌上有兩本英語書，一本是園藝書，另一本是文學書。如果你要的話，兩本都可借給你。

## 【說明】

"一本…，另一本…"：one…, the other…

"園藝"：gardening。"園藝書" a book on gardening, on 在

這裏是 "關於" 的意思; 改成句子可說 a book deals with gardening,
或 treats of gardening; deal with, treat of 是 "論及" 的意思, 注意
用不同的介詞。

"文學": literature

"如果你要的話" 是 "如果你喜歡的話", 可譯作 if you like,
或 if you wish。

**【譯例】**

(a) There are two English books on the desk; one deals with gardening and the other with literature. I'll lend both of them to you if you
like.

(b) You will see two English books on the desk. One of them treats
of gardening and the other of literature. I'll lend you both of them if you
wish.

# 第 4 天

*昨天我買了這本英語小說。因為很有趣, 所以一直看到深夜。*

**【說明】**

"看" 是 "閱讀", 要說 read, 不可說 see, 或 look at。"一
直看到深夜": read till late at night。

"因為很有趣, 所以一直看到深夜" 可以說 As it is very in-
teresting, I read it till late at night, 或 It is very interesting, so
I read it till late at night。注意:用了 as 便不用 so, 用了 so 便不
用 as, 不可照漢語習慣兩者都用。

**【譯例】**

298

(a) I bought this English novel yesterday. As it is very interesting, I read it till late at night.

(b) I got this English novel yesterday. It is so interesting that I read it till late at night.

# 第5天

前幾天借給你的《飄》如果看完了，請還給我好嗎？因為我弟弟想看。

## 【說明】

"飄"：（書名）Gone with the Wind

"看完" 可說 have finished (reading), have done with, 或 be through with; 後者是美國語。

## 【譯例】

(a) If you have finished "Gone with the Wind" which I lent you the other day, please return it to me as my younger brother wants to read it.

(b) Have you done with "Gone with the Wind" which I lent you some days ago? If so, please return it to me, because my younger brother wishes to read it.

# 第6天

隨着年齡的增長，重讀青年時代我們所喜愛的書籍是個樂趣，這點我們不可忽略。

## 【說明】

"隨着年齡的增長": as we grow older; 如看作"晚年"的話, 可說 in later years。

"重讀": read again; reread

"忽略": neglect; ignore

## 【譯例】

(a) Let's not neglect, as we grow older, the pleasure of rereading books which we liked when we were young.

(b) Books we liked when we were young should not be ignored in later years, but should be read again for the pleasure they give.

# 第7天

我20歲時曾讀過這本書, 當時感到沒有意思。隔了10年之後, 前幾天重讀此書, 爲書中的深刻含義而驚嘆, 並確信這是一本經典之作。

## 【說明】

"沒有意思"是"沒趣", "無味"的意思, 譯作 uninteresting, dull, insipid, 或 tedious 都可以。

"隔了10年之後": after an interval of ten years, 或單說 after ten years 也可。

"深刻含義": deep (或 profound) meaning。"爲書中的深刻含義而驚嘆": be surprised at the deep meaning contained in the book。

"確信": be sure that…, be convinced that…, 或 firmly believe that…。

"經典之作": classic; classical work

## 【譯例】

(a) I read this book when I was but a lad of twenty, and got the impression that it was dull and uninteresting. The other day I read it again after an interval of ten years and was surprised at the deep meaning contained in it. At the same time I was sure that this was a true classical work.

(b) When I read this book at the age of twenty, I thought how insipid it was. But the other day, after ten years, I read it again and was surprised to find how deep its meaning was, and at the same time I was convinced that such a book was a classic.

# 第 8 天

秋天到了, 這是讀書最好的季節。好, 開始學習吧。

## 【說明】

"到了": has come, 或 has set in, 要用現在完成時態。"秋天到了, 這是讀書最好的季節"照字譯是兩句, 但也可寫成一句說 Autumn, the best season for reading, has come。the best season for reading 是 autumn 的同位語; 另外還可說 We are now in autumn, the best season for reading。

"好": 這是語氣詞, 表示請求或命令, 可譯作 now。

## 【譯例】

(a) Autumn, the best season for reading, has come. Now let's start studying.

(b) We are now in autumn, the best season for reading. Now for our studies!

# 第 9 天

不管我們多忙, 每天最少看兩小時有益的書是合宜的。

## 【說明】

"不管我們多忙": however busy we may be。注意 busy 的位置, 不可放在 be 後面; 也可說 no matter how busy we are, 這種說法語氣要更強些。另外還可說 even if we are busy 或 busy as we are, 後一句裏的 busy 要放在句首。

"有益的": good; useful

"合宜的" 在這裏可譯作 desirable; 動詞是 desire "期望"。
"看兩小時有益的書是合宜的": It is desirable for us to read a good book two hours a day; 也可說 It is desirable (或 to be desired) that we should read a good book two hours a day。注意 desirable, 或 desire 後面跟從句要用虛擬語氣的 should, 或動詞原形。

## 【譯例】

(a) However busy we may be, it is desirable for us to read a good book at least two hours a day.

(b) It is to be desired that one (should) read a useful book at least two hours a day, no matter how busy one may be.

(c) Even if we are busy, it is desirable that we (should) read a good book at least two hours a day.

# 第 10 天

一個人不管多忙，只要有心，就能安排時間讀書。

## 【說明】

"一個人"這裏指任何人，可用 you。

"只要有心" if you have a mind to do so; 也可說 if you really intend to, 或 if you are going to, to 後面省掉了動詞 read。

"安排時間"是"找到時間"的意思，要說 find time。"安排時間讀書": find time to read,或 find enough time for reading。

## 【譯例】

(a) However busy you are, you can find time to read if you have a mind to do so.

(b) No matter how busy you are, you can find enough time for reading, if you really intend to.

(c) Even if you are busy, you will be able to find time for reading, provided you are going to.


# 第 11 天

光是看許多書是沒有用的。還是精讀幾本好書爲好。

## 【說明】

"光是": merely

"是沒有用的": be useless, 或 be of no use; be of little use

"精讀": read carefully;改爲名詞詞組就是 careful reading;也

可說 peruse; 名詞是 perusal。

【譯例】

(a) It is useless merely to read a great many books. You had better read a few good books carefully.

(b) Merely reading many books is of little use. It is better to read a few good books with care.

(c) The perusal of a few good books is more useful than the careless reading of many books.

# 第 12 天

即使一本書有點難懂，但是只要反覆讀上幾遍就能理解了。

【說明】

"即使有點難懂"：even though（或 even if）it is a little difficult，或以 we 作主語說 even though we find it a little difficult。

"反覆"：over and over again; time and again

"能理解"：come to understand; come 後接不定詞作 "終於⋯" 或 "開始⋯" 解，如 He came to understand that he was wrong（他終於理解到自己錯了），Tractors have come to be widely used（拖拉機已開始被廣泛使用）。

【譯例】

(a) Even though we find a book a little difficult at first, we shall be able to understand it after reading it over and over again.

(b) If you read a book time and again, you will come to understand it, even if it is a little difficult.

304

# 第 13 天

"我雖努力學習，但至今並無多大進步。" "當然啦，一下子要學好是困難的。"

## 【說明】

"至今"：up to now, 或 up to the present; so far, 或 thus far。"至今並無多大進步"：so far I haven't made much progress, 或 I haven't got on very far yet.

"一下子" 是 "在短時間內" 的意思，可說 in a short while, 或 in so short a time; 也可說 within a short time。"一下子要學好是困難的"：It is difficult to learn well in a short while, 或 You can't expect to learn well in so short a time; 也可用一句成語說 Rome was not built in a day（羅馬不是一天建成的）。

## 【譯例】

(a) " I'm studying very hard, but so far I have not made much progress. "" Of course, you can't expect to learn well in so short a time. "

(b) " Though I have been doing my best in my studies, I have not got on very far yet. " " Don't worry. Rome was not built in a day. "

# 第 14 天

看書先要看序言。這樣就能最好地利用這本書。看序言確是個好辦法。

## 【說明】

"看書"是"當你看書時"的意思，要說 when you read a book; 也可理解為"如果你要看書的話"if you want to read a book.

"先"：first; first of all; the first thing

"序言"：preface; foreword

"最好地利用"：make the best use of; make the most of

## 【譯例】

(a) When you read a book, try to read the preface first of all. By doing so, you can make the best use of the book. Reading prefaces is indeed a very good habit.

(b) If you want to read a book, you had better read the preface the first thing. This will help you (to) make the most of the book. To read prefaces is really a good habit.

# 第 15 天

有些人說即使拼命地讀書，結果還是忘記，因此他們感到很喪氣。他們似乎把讀書看作儲蓄了。

## 【說明】

"拼命地"：with great effort, with all one's exertions。"即使拼命地讀書"：even if they read with great effort

"感到喪氣"：be discouraged; 如與前面"說"字連起來，也可譯作 say with regret。

## 【譯例】

(a) Some people are discouraged because they forget what they

306

have learned in books even if they read them with great effort. It seems to them that reading is like saving money.

(b) There are some people who say with regret that they soon forget what they have read with all their exertions. They may be thinking that reading is a kind of saving.

# 第 16 天

據說人大約到了70歲，記憶力就開始衰退，頭腦也不靈活，但青年時期牢牢地掌握的知識即使上了年紀也不容易忘記。

## 【說明】

"據說"：it is said, 或 people say

"人大約到了70歲"：when a man becomes as old as about seventy, 或單說 about seventy 也可。

"記憶力衰退"：one's memory weakens, 或 one's memory begins to fail

"頭腦"可譯作 mind, 或 head。"頭腦不靈活"one's mind gets stiff, 或 one's head gets hardened。

"青年時期"這裏是狀語，可說 in one's youth, 或 while (one is) young。

"牢牢掌握的知識"：knowledge that was deeply soaked（或 was firmly established）in one's mind。soak 是"吸收"；establish 是"確立"。

"即使上了年紀"：even in one's old age; 改成句子可說 even though one is old。

"忘記"除了 forget 之外；也可說 obliterate。"不容易忘記"

如以 knowledge 爲主語要說 is not so easily obliterated, does not go away so easily, 或 does not easily fade out, fade out 是 "消失" 的意思。

## 【譯例】

(a) It is said that when a man becomes as old as about seventy, his memory begins to fail and his mind gets stiff, but the knowledge that was firmly established in his youth is not so easily obliterated even though he is old.

(b) People say that at about seventy a man's memory gets weakened and his head gets hardened, but the knowledge that was deeply soaked in his young mind does not easily fade out even in his old age.

# 第 17 天

眞想能像看中文書那樣輕鬆地看外文書。

## 【說明】

"眞想…" 是表示一種願望,可照前面看到過的 I wish (that) … 這個句型來表達; 注意從句裏的動詞要用虛擬語氣。

"輕鬆地" 是 "容易地" 的意思, 可說 easily, 或 with ease。"像看中文書那樣輕鬆地看外文書" read foreign books as easily as I do Chinese books ( 或 ones ) , do 代替前面的動詞 read 以免重複出現。

## 【譯例】

(a) I wish I could read foreign books as easily as I do Chinese books.

(b) How I wish I could read foreign books with as much ease as I do Chinese ones!

# 第 18 天

最近 5 年我一直在學習英語，但要不費力地進行讀和寫還沒有把握。有沒有甚麼學英語的有效方法呢？

## 【說明】

"最近 5 年我一直在學習英語"：這裏的動詞 study（或 learn）要用現在完成進行時說 I have been studying English for the last five years（或 these five years）。

"還沒有把握"是"還不能確信自己有能力⋯"的意思，可譯作 be not yet confident of one's ability to⋯，或 do not yet feel competent enough to⋯，feel competent enough to⋯是"有足夠的能力"的意思。

"有效"：effective。"有沒有甚麼學英語的有效方法呢？""Isn't there any effective method of learning English?"也可以 you 作主語說 Will you tell me how to learn it in an effective way?

## 【譯例】

(a) I have been studying English for the last five years, but I am not yet confident of my ability to read and write it with ease. Isn't there any effective method of learning English?

(b) Although I have been learning English these five years, I do not yet feel competent enough to read and write it easily. Will you tell me how to learn it in an effective way?

# 第 19 天

我勸你邊查詞典，把某一本英語書從頭到尾讀完它。

## 【說明】

"勸"：advise。"我勸你"：I advise you to…，也可用動詞祈使語氣說 Try to…。

"查詞典"：consult a dictionary；refer to a dictionary

"邊"這裏是"不時地"的意思，可以說 from time to time，或 occasionally。

"把某一本英語書從頭到尾讀完它" read some English book through，或 read through some English book；也可說 read some English book from cover to cover。

## 【譯例】

(a) I advise you to read some English book through, even though you may have to consult a dictionary from time to time.

(b) Try to read through some English book, though you may occasionally have to consult a dictionary.

(c) Read some English book from cover to cover, referring to your dictionary from time to time.

# 第 20 天

英語是國際性的商業用語，所以對那些想從事對外貿易的人來說是必不可少的。

"國際性的": international

"對外貿易": foreign trade。"從事對外貿易": engage in foreign trade, 或 take up foreign trade。

"必不可少的": indispensable (to)

【譯例】

(a) English is an international commercial language. It is quite indispensable to those who wish to engage in foreign trade.

(b) English is really indispensable to those who wish to take up foreign trade, because it is an internationally used commercial language.

# 第21天

一個有學問的人至少要精通一門外國語, 這是最重要的。在這一點上英語可以說最符合這個目的, 因為英語在世界上用得最廣泛。

【說明】

"有學問的": educated

"精通": master 或 gain the mastery of; be proficient in, proficient 是"精通", 後面要跟介詞 in。

"在這一點上"可不譯出。

"英語可以說…": English can be said…, 或 it can be said that English…

"目的": purpose。"最符合這個目的": be most fitted (或 suitable) for this purpose。

【譯例】

(a) It is the first requisite for an educated person to master at least one foreign language. It can be said that English is most fitted for this purpose, because it is the most widely used language in the world.

(b) The first requirement for an educated person is to become proficient in at least one foreign language. Being the most widely used language, English can be said to be most suitable for this purpose.

# 第22天

外國語這東西越是實地使用，進步就越快。不要怕錯，要經常地說說寫寫。

【說明】

"這東西"：可不必譯出。

"使用"：make use of。"越是實地使用" The more practical the use you make of…或 The oftener you make practical use of…。

"進步"除了 progress 之外，也可說 improvement。"進步就越快" the more rapid will be your progress（或 your progress will be）；也可說 the more proficient you will become in it。

"不要怕錯"：Don't be afraid of making mistakes; 如要加強語氣，可加一個 ever，如 Don't ever be afraid of making mistakes, afraid 後面要用介詞 of。

"經常地"：constantly。"經常地說說寫寫" go on speaking and writing it constantly。

【譯例】

(a) The more practical the use you make of a foreign language, the more rapid will be your progress. Don't ever be afraid of making mistakes, go on speaking and writing the language constantly.

(b) The oftener you make practical use of a foreign language, the more proficient you will become in it. I advise you to go on speaking and writing it constantly without being afraid of making mistakes.

# 第23天

你越早學一種語言，進步就越快，所以你最好盡可能在年輕時開始學英語。

## 【說明】

"越早…越快…"： The earlier…, the sooner…

"最好"除了可譯作 had better 之外；也可說 I advise you to…。

## 【譯例】

(a) The earlier you begin to learn a language, the sooner you will improve in it. So you had better begin learning English as early as possible.

(b) I advise you to begin learning English as early as you can, for the earlier you begin to learn a language, the sooner you will become proficient in it.

# 第24天

學習講外國語最好的辦法是到講這種外國語的國家去。但到外國

313

去要花許多錢，這不是我們大家都能採取的辦法。於是其次的最好辦法是要設法與住在這裏的外國人交談。

**【説明】**

"學習講外國語最好的辦法"：the best way to learn（或 method of learning）to speak a foreign language

"到外國去"：go abroad。"到外國去要花許多錢"：it costs us a lot of money to go abroad

"採取"：adopt; "這不是我們大家都能採取的辦法"可以說 this method cannot be adopted by all; 也可說 it is impossible for all of us to adopt this method。

"於是"：therefore, then, 或 it follows then that…

"其次的最好辦法"：the next best way; the second best method

"與…交談"：speak with; converse with

**【譯例】**

(a) The best way to learn (how) to speak a foreign language is to go to the country where the language is spoken. But it costs us a lot of money to go abroad and it is impossible for all of us to adopt this method. It follows then that the next best way is to try to speak with foreigners living here.

(b) The best method of learning (how) to speak a foreign language is to go to the country where the language is spoken. But this method cannot be adopted by all, for it costs a lot of money to go abroad. The second best method, therefore, is to try to converse with foreigners staying here.

# 第25天

由於漢語和英語是完全不同語族的語言，要是我們不了解這兩種語言之間的差異，那就一定學不好英語。

【說明】

"語族"：linguistic family

"要是不了解"： if we don't understand, 或 unless we understand

"學好"是"精通"的意思，master。"一定學不好英語"： can never master English。

【譯例】

(a) As Chinese and English are languages belonging to entirely different linguistic families, we can never master English unless we understand the differences between the two languages.

(b) As Chinese belongs to a linguistic family entirely different from that of English, it will be impossible to master English without a knowledge of the differences between Chinese and English.

# 第26天

即使我們的英語已經學得相當好了，還是常會用錯 "yes" 和 "no"。這是因為漢語與英語不僅存在着語法上和表達方法上的不同，而且存在着思想方法上的根本不同。

【說明】

"即使我們的英語已經學得相當好了"可以說 even when we have learned English fairly well; 也可說 even when we have a fair knowledge of English。

"常會用錯 ‘ yes ’和 ‘ no ’ "： be apt to make mistakes in using " yes " and " no " ,或 often fail to distinguish between yes and no when they use them

"表達方法 "： way of expression; expression

"根本的 "： fundamental。 "根本的不同 "： fundamental dif-ference, 如用形容詞 different, 則要說 fundamentally different。

"思想方法 "： way of thinking

## 【譯例】

(a) Even when we have learned English fairly well, we are apt to make mistakes in using " yes " and " no " . This is because between Chinese and English there is a fundamental difference, not only in grammar and expression, but also in the way of thinking.

(b) Even those Chinese people who have a fair knowledge of English sometimes fail to distinguish between yes and no when they use them. The Chinese and English languages are fundamentally different in the way of thinking, to say nothing of grammar and expression.

# 第27天

"他英語說得非常流利，但有點美國口音。 ""那也許因爲他的老師是美國人吧。 "

## 【說明】

"流利 "： fluent。"英語說得非常流利 "除了說 speak English very fluently 之外； 也可說 speak English well and fluently。

316

"口音"：accent。"有點美國口音"： with a slight American accent。

"那也許因爲… "： That's probably because…

## 【譯例】

(a) " He speaks English well and fluently, but with a slight American accent. " " That's probably because his teacher was an American. "

(b) He speaks English very fluently, but has a slight American accent. " Perhaps his teacher was an American. "

# 第 28 天

她說英語像個美國人，這是不足爲奇的，因爲她生在美國，並在那裏度過少女時期。

## 【説明】

"像個美國人"可譯作 like an American; 也可說 as if she were an American, as if 後面動詞 were 是虛擬語氣。

"這是不足爲奇的"可說 It is no wonder that…, It is little wonder that…, 或 No wonder that…; 也可說 It is quite natural that…。注意： natural 後面的從句要用虛擬語氣的 should。

## 【譯例】

(a) It is no wonder that she speaks English as if she were an American, for she was born in the States and spent her girlhood there.

(b) As she was born in the States and spent her girlhood there, it is quite natural that she should speak English like an American.

# 第29天

因爲英語老師勸我們用英語寫日記，所以我打算今年就來寫。

## 【說明】

"英語老師" 通常說 a teacher of English, 但說 English teacher 也是可以的, English teacher 也可解釋爲 "英國教師"。爲避免混淆, 作 "英語教師" 解時可重讀 English, 如 ［ˈiŋgliʃ ˌtiːtʃə］; 作 "英國教師" 解時則兩個詞平均重讀, 如 ［ˈiŋgliʃ ˈtiːtʃə］。若用於書面, 在有可能被誤解時, 還是用 a teacher of English 爲佳。

"日記"：diary。"用英語寫日記"：keep a diary in English。

"打算" 可說 think, intend; 如有 "決意" 的意思, 也可說 make up one's mind。

## 【譯例】

(a) A teacher of English advised us to keep a diary in English, so I think I will do so this year.

(b) I intend to keep a diary in English this year, as one of our teachers of English advised us to do so.

(c) Following the advice of my teacher of English, I have made up my mind to keep a diary in English this year.

# 第30天

我之所以能看懂這許多英文書全靠學習英語。不管將來會遇到甚麼困難, 我決心繼續學英語。

## 【說明】

318

"靠"這裏作"歸功於"解，要說 owe…to。"我之所以能看懂這許多英文書全靠學習英語"：I owe my ability to read so many English books entirely to the study of English; 這句話也可譯作 Studying English is the only thing that has made me able to read so many English books.

"將來"是狀語 in the future, 或 in future

"遇到"：meet with; undergo。"不管遇到甚麼困難"：whatever difficulties（或 hardships）I may undergo。

"決心"：be determined, 或 be resolved。"決心繼續學英語"：be determined to continue（或 pursue）my study of English。

## 【譯例】

(a) I owe my ability to read so many English books entirely to the study of English. Whatever hardships I may undergo in the future, I am determined to continue my study of English.

(b) Studying English is the only thing that has made me able to read so many English books. Whatever difficulties may lie before me, I am resolved to pursue my study of English.

# Words and Expressions

| | |
|---|---|
| resemble [ri´zembl] | 像，類似 |
| unreliable [´ʌnri´laiəbl]; undependable | 不可靠的 |
| publish | 出版 |
| worth reading | 值得一讀 |
| gardening | 園藝 |

| | |
|---|---|
| literature | 文學 |
| till late at night | 直到深夜 |
| neglect; ignore | 忽略 |
| insipid | 無味的 |
| tedious | 使人厭煩的 |
| profound | 深刻的，深奧的 |
| classic; classical work | 經典之作 |
| desirable [di´zaiərəbl] | 合宜的，合乎需要的 |
| be convinced that… | 確信 |
| merely | 光是 |
| peruse [pə´ru:z] | 細讀，精讀 |
| up to now; up to the present; so far; thus far | 至今 |
| preface [´prefis]; foreword | 序言，前言 |
| with great effort | 拼命地 |
| be discouraged [dis´kʌridʒd] | 感到喪氣 |
| mind | 頭腦 |
| knowledge | 知識 |
| be confident of | 有把握，確信 |
| effective | 有效的 |
| international | 國際上的 |
| foreign trade | 對外貿易 |
| indispensable [ˌindis´pensəbl] | 必不可少的 |
| requirement; requisite [´rekwizit] | 必需品 |
| purpose [´pə:pəs] | 目的 |
| progress [´prougres]; improve- | 進步 |

ment [im′pru:vmənt]

| | |
|---|---|
| go abroad | 出國 |
| master (n. or v.) | 主人(名)；精通，學會(動) |
| fundamental [ˌfʌndə′mentl] | 根本的 |
| way of thinking | 思想方法 |
| fluent | 流利的 |
| accent | 口音；重音 |
| diary [′daiəri] | 日記 |

# Exercise   11

Translate the following into English:

1. 甲：你看這本詞典怎樣？

　　乙：這是本好詞典，但也像其他詞典一樣，不能望其完全正確。
　　（第1天）

2. 近年來出的書愈來愈多了，但恐怕只有一小部分值得一讀。（第
　　2天）

3. 書架上有兩本小說，一本是中文的，另一本是英文的。如果你要
　　的話，可以挑選一本。（第3天）

4. 昨天從我的朋友那裏借了一本小說。因為很有趣，我一個晚上就
　　把它看完了。（第4天）

5. 甲：上星期你借的那本小說看完了沒有？

　　乙：看完了。

　　甲：你覺得怎樣？

　　乙：很有趣。我看得幾乎忘記吃飯。（第5天）

6. 這是我年輕時愛讀的一本書。雖然時隔20年現在重讀起來依然樂

趣盎然。（第6天）

7. 有些書在年輕時看常覺得沒有多大意義；但隨着年齡的增長，重讀這些書可能為書中的深刻含義而驚嘆。（第6，7天）

8. 經典之作含義深刻，我們年輕時閱讀往往不大理解。（第7天）

9. 甲：我太忙，沒有時間看書怎麼辦？

   乙：不管你多忙，每天至少看一二小時的書是必要的。（第9天）

10. 你說你太忙，沒有時間看書，但我想只要你有心，就能安排讀書時間。（第10天）

11. 有些人看許多書而不加區別（without discrimination），這是沒有用的。我們還是精讀幾本有用的書為好。（第11天）

12. 這句句子比較長也比較難，但你只要把它仔細分析（analyse）一下就能夠理解了。（第12天）

13. 要一下子學好一件事是困難的，所以決不要因為進步不快就放棄學習。（第13天）

14. 儘管我進步不大，我還是要努力學習。我相信只要有心，一定能學好。諺語說：羅馬不是一天建成的。（第10，12，13天）

15. 甲：你有沒有看過那本書的序言？

    乙：沒有，我還未看過。

    甲：看序言有好處，它能幫助你最好地利用一本書。（第14天）

16. 有些人感到很喪氣，因為學了的東西常常會忘記。當然啦，讀書與儲蓄是不同的。（第15天）

17. 他今年70歲，記憶力並未衰退，頭腦也靈活。這大概是由於他身體健康的關係。（第16天）

18. 我已經學了6年英語，但還不能像看中文那樣輕鬆地看英語書。不知怎麼樣才能把英語學好。（第17，18天）

19. 你試把這本英語書從頭到尾看完它，遇到生字就查詞典。（第19天）

20. 那些想從事對外貿易的人必須學習英語，因爲在國際商業上，英語用得最廣泛。（第20，21天）

21. 我要學一門外國語。因爲英語最有用，所以我想一定要精通它。（第21天）

22. 在學習英語的過程中（in the course of），我不怕犯錯誤，經常說說寫寫，所以進步比較快。（第22天）

23. 他在父親的指導下很早就開始學英語。他現在能說能寫，精通這門語言。（第23天）

24. 學外國語最好的辦法是與外國人交往（have intercourse with）。如果你沒有機會到外國去，那麼要盡可能與住在這裏的外國人交談。（第24天）

25. 學習英語要注意英語與漢語的差異。如果我們老是想照漢語的方法來表達思想的話，那就永遠學不好英語。（第25天）

26. 如果別人用否定的疑問句問你，答句是肯定的（affirmative）要用 " yes "，否定的（negative）則用 " no "。（第26天）

27. 甲：你覺得他英語說得怎樣？

    乙：他說得非常流利，但口音不像英國人。

    甲：對了，他是在美國出生的，所以說的是美國音。（第27，28天）

28. 用英語寫日記是練習英語寫作的好辦法。經過相當時間一定會取得很好的成績。（第29天）

29. 不管我前面有甚麼困難，我決心學好英語。我現在雖然懂得不多，但只要我繼續努力，我相信是會成功的。（第30天）

30. 甲：你學英語多久了？

    乙：我從1977年以來，一直在學英語。

    甲：就你學習只有兩年多一點的時間來說，我想你已經學得相當不差了。

乙： 謝謝你的讚揚（compliment），但我還得更努力。

甲： 你有機會在實際場合練習英語嗎？——我的意思是實際運用你的英語與外國人交談。

乙： 有的，我常常設法與住在這裏的外國人交談。

甲： 好的，我祝你學習英語成功。

# 第 12 月
# 行為、思想、修養

## 第1天

只有一點點學問也許是危險的，但只要自己認識到那僅僅是一點點學問就沒有甚麼危險了。

### 【說明】

"也許"可用情態動詞 may 來表示。

"學問"：learning; knowledge。"一點點學問是危險的"：A little learning is a dangerous thing。這句話是文學家蒲伯 (Pope) 說的，譯文就是用這句話。

### 【譯例】

(a) A little learning may be a dangerous thing, but it is not dangerous at all if only you ( 或 we ) realize it is little.

(b) A little learning may be dangerous; but as long as you know it is little, it is not dangerous at all.

## 第2天

任何人都懂得人生是短暫的，而且時間是過得很快的，但只有賢者才知道應該幹些甚麼。

## 【說明】

"任何人" 說 everybody, everyone, anyone 都可以。

"懂得" 除了 know, be aware 等之外；也可以說 can see。

"賢者"： the wise; wise 原是形容詞， 這裏作名詞用， 是複數，前面要有定冠詞 the。"只有賢者才知道…"： It is only the wise that know…; it…that 是個強勢式， 語氣比 The wise know…為強；例如 I need help（我需要幫助）這個句子，如要強調 help 可說 It is help that I need（我所需要的是幫助〔不是別的東西〕），如要強調 I, 可說 It is I that need help（需要幫助的是我〔不是別人〕），that 是關係代詞。前一句的 that 可改用 which, 後一句的 that 可改用 who 但都不及用 that 普遍。

## 【譯例】

(a) Everybody can see that life is short and time passes quickly, but it is only the wise that know what they ought to do.

(b) Anyone is aware that life is short and time flies, but only the wise know what ought to be done.

# 第3天

的確有些人經常把"和平"掛在嘴上，但這並不意味着他們是真正熱愛和平的。

## 【說明】

"的確…，但是…"： It is true that…but…; 或以 true 作插入語說 True, …but…。

"經常" 可不譯出，因為動詞一般現在時就可以表示經常的動作。

"把和平掛在嘴上"：have peace on their lips; 也可簡單地說 talk about peace。

"眞正熱愛和平"：truly love peace; 也可說 be true lovers of peace.

## 【譯例】

(a) It is true that some people talk about peace, but that does not mean that they truly love peace.

(b) True, some people have peace on their lips, but this does not necessarily mean that they are true lovers of peace.


# 第4天

今天我們生活的世界實際丄是一個世界，所以對於地球任何一個地方所存在着的貧困、飢餓和不幸都不能漠不關心。

## 【說明】

"我們生活着的世界"：the world in which we live; 也可把 in 放在 live 後面而把 which 省去，如 the world we live in。

"實際上"：actually, really. "實際上是一個世界"：is actually one world; 也可把 one world 改成 a unified world。

"地球任何一個地方"：in any part of the world, 或 in the remotest corner of the earth; remotest 是"最遙遠"的意思。

"貧困、飢餓和不幸"：poverty, starvation（或 famine）and misfortune（或 misery）

"漠不關心"：除了 be indifferent to 之外；也可說 be unconcerned about。

327

(a) The world we live in today is really a unified world, so we cannot be indifferent to the poverty, famine and misfortune in any part of the world.

(b) Since the world in which we live today is actually one world, we can no longer be unconcerned about the poverty, starvation and misery in the remotest corner of the earth.

# 第 5 天

恐怖主義是甚麼貨色，如今連初中學生都知道。

## 【說明】

"恐怖主義"： terrorism

"貨色"這裏是指不好的事物，可譯作 stuff; rubbish; trash。

"初中學生"： junior-secondary-school student, junior-high-school student。"連初中學生都知道"： even a junior-secondary-school student knows

## 【譯例】

(a) Today, even junior-secondary-school students know what kind of stuff terrorism is.

(b) Even a junior- secondary-school student of today knows what terrorism is all about.

# 第 6 天

每次選舉我總是去投票的,因爲我相信參加選舉既是人民的權利,也是義務。

## 【說明】

"選舉": election

"投票": vote; cast ballot, ballot 是"選舉票"。"總是去投票"可譯作 never fail to cast one's ballot; 也可說 make it a rule to cast one's ballot。

"參加選舉"這裏指"投票", 可說 vote。

"既是…也是…" not only…but also…; 也可用前面見過的 as well as 這個詞組, 注意其用法。

## 【譯例】

(a) I never fail to cast my ballot in every election, for I believe that to vote is not only the right of the people but also their duty.

(b) As I believe that to vote is the duty as well as the right of the people, I always make it a rule to cast my ballot in every election.

# 第7天

不要當面恭維人家, 也不要在背後說人家壞話。這兩件都不能說是好事。

## 【說明】

"當面": in one's presence, 或 to one's face

"恭維": flatter; fawn on

"在背後": in one's absence, 或 behind one's back

"說壞話": speak ill of

"這兩件都不能說是好事": neither of them can be said to be good (或 laudable); laudable 是 "值得稱讚" 的意思。

## 【譯例】

(a) Do not flatter anyone in his presence or speak ill of him in his absence. Neither of these things can be said to be good.

(b) Do not fawn on others to their faces or speak ill of them behind their backs. Neither of these things can be said to be laudable.


# 第8天

當朋友向你提醒你的缺點時，重要的是你不但要樂意地，而且要感謝地接受他的忠告。世上再也沒有比聰明並肯幫助人的朋友更可貴的了。

## 【說明】

"提醒": remind (of)。 "向你提醒你的缺點": remind you of your faults (或 mistakes)，不可說 remind your faults; 改成被動要說 You are reminded of your faults, of 不可漏掉。

"重要的是…": it is important for you to…

"接受": take; accept

"肯幫助人的": helpful

"可貴": valuable

## 【譯例】

(a) When a friend reminds you of your faults, it is important for you to take his advice not only pleasantly but thankfully. Nothing in the world is more valuable than a friend who is wise and helpful.

(b) If you are reminded of your mistakes by a friend, you should accept his advice thankfully as well as pleasantly. Nothing in the world is so valuable as a friend who is wise and helpful.


# 第 9 天

把自己的錯誤看得比人家的輕得多，這是奇怪而又是經常發生的事，所以我們一定要抱公正無私的態度。

## 【說明】

"輕"是"輕微"或"微不足道"的意思，可用 slight 或 trivial. "比人家的輕得多"：far more slight（或 slighter）than those of others, 或 much more trivial than those of other people; those 是代替前面出現過的 mistakes 或 faults。

"奇怪而又是經常發生的事"可譯作 curious but common, 或 a curious but not uncommon phenomenon。

"公正無私的"：impartial, 或 unbiased。"抱公正無私的態度"：be impartial, keep unbiased。

## 【譯例】

(a) It is a curious but common phenomenon that our own mistakes should seem to us far more slight than those of others. Therefore, we must always be impartial.

(b) It is curious but not uncommon for our own faults to seem to us much more trivial than those of other people. It is therefore necessary that we should always keep unbiased.

# 第 10 天

你如果不馬上改正你行爲的話，以後一定會後悔莫及。

## 【說明】

"行爲"：conduct。"改正你的行爲"：improve your conduct, 或 mend your ways。

"後悔"：repent, 後面可以跟 of 或不跟 of, 如 repent (of) one's mistake。"後悔莫及"：find it too late to repent (of) one's mistake。

## 【譯例】

(a) If you do not improve your conduct at once, you will surely find it too late to repent of it afterwards.

(b) Mend your ways immediately, or you will surely find it too late to repent some day.

# 第 11 天

我曾反覆勸他檢點自己的行爲，但都徒勞了。就是牧師也說服不了那個頑固的人。

## 【說明】

"反覆"除了 over and over again, time and again 之外; 還可說 again and again 或 repeatedly。

"徒勞"：be useless; be all to no purpose; 也可用 in vain。

"牧師"：priest

"說服": persuade; prevail on

"頑固的": obstinate; stubborn; headstrong

## 【譯例】

(a) I repeatedly advised him to mend his ways in future, but my efforts were in vain. Even a priest would not be able to persuade that obstinate man.

(b) Although I advised him again and again to improve his conduct in future, it was all useless. Even a priest would be unable to prevail on that stubborn fellow.


# 第 12 天

請別誤會，我並不是在批評你。我只是想幫助你認識你所犯的錯誤。

## 【說明】

"誤會": misunderstand。 "請別誤會": Don't misunderstand me, 或 Don't take me wrong。

"批評": criticize; comment on

"認識": see; realize

"犯錯誤": make ( 或 commit ) a mistake

## 【譯例】

(a) Don't misunderstand me. I am not criticizing you. I am only thinking of helping you realize the mistake you have made.

(b) Please don't take me wrong. I am not commenting on you. I am only trying to help you see the mistake that you have committed.

# 第 13 天

再也沒有比看到年輕人游手好閒，不務正業更令人討厭的了。

## 【說明】

"游手好閒"： idle about; fool around

"不務正業"： do no decent work; 改成詞組是 without doing any decent work; decent 是 "正派" 的意思; 也可說 have no proper business; 改成詞組是 without any proper business。

"令人討厭的"： disgusting; repugnant; repulsive。"再也沒有比…更討厭的了"： nothing is so disgusting as…, 或 nothing is more repugnant than…; 也可以說話人 I 作主語說 I hate more than anything else…。

## 【譯例】

(a) Nothing is so disgusting as the sight of a young man idling about and doing no decent work.

(b) I hate more than anything else the sight of a young man fooling around without any proper business.

# 第 14 天

學問會使人聰明，但傻瓜搞學問却反而會更傻。你對這句諺語有何高見？

## 【說明】

"使人聰明"： make a man wise; 也可理解為 "成為聰明人"

譯作 make a wise man。

"傻瓜"：fool; foolish man。"傻瓜搞學問却反而會更傻"是 "學問使傻瓜反而更傻"的意思，可說 learning makes a fool all the more a fool; 改成被動是 a fool is made all the more a fool by it (learning)。

"高見"：your opinion; your idea。"對這句諺語有何高見?"： "What is your opinion about this proverb?"或"Let me hear your opinion about this proverb?"也可說"What do you think about (或 of) this proverb?"

### 【譯例】

(a) Learning makes a man wise, but a fool is made all the more a fool by it  What is your opinion about this proverb?

(b) Learning makes a wise man, but it makes a fool all the more a fool. What do you think of the above proverb?

(c) A man is made wise by learning, but a foolish man is made all the more foolish by it. Let me hear your opinion about this proverb.

# 第 15 天

的確，一個人應該有足夠的勇氣直率地說出自己的信念；但另一方面也必須慎重，在沒有必要的時候不要發表自己的意見。

### 【說明】

"勇氣"：courage

"直率地說出"：speak up; speak out; 如理解為"向公衆發表"也可譯作 say before the world。

"信念": belief

"慎重": discreet; 名詞是 discretion。

"發表意見": express one's opinion, state one's views。"不要發表自己的意見": not express one's opinion, 或 refrain from expressing one's opinion; refrain (from) 是 "抑制" 的意思。

## 【譯例】

(a) It is true that a man should have courage enough to speak up about his own beliefs, but on the other hand he should have discretion enough to refrain from expressing his opinion when it is unnecessary.

(b) It is true that one must be bold enough to say before the world what one thinks, but on the other hand one must be discreet enough to refrain from stating one's views when it is unnecessary to do so.


# 第 16 天

做你想做的事是不錯的；但有時不做你想做的事也是必要的。

## 【說明】

"做你想做的事": do what you want。"做你想做的事是不錯的" 可說 It is not a bad thing to do what you want, 或 It is right that one should do what one wants。"不做你想做的事也是必要的": It is necessary that one should refrain from doing what one wants to do。注意主句中有 right, necessary 等詞時，從句要用虛擬語氣，如 It is right（或 proper）that we should help others, It is necessary that he should act at once。

336

(a) It is not a bad thing to do what you want, but it is sometimes necessary for you to refrain from doing what you want to do.

(b) It is right that one should do what one wants, but it is sometimes necessary that one should refrain from doing what one wants to do.

# 第 17 天

一件事情，因爲自己不想做而不做，這可能是容易的，但有時做些自己不愛做的事情也是必要的。

## 【說明】

"因爲自己不想做而不做"：not to do a thing because we don't want to, 最後一個 to 是代表不定詞 to do; 但在動詞 like 之後常常不帶 to, 如 You may go if you like。

"…也是必要的"：it is necessary for us ( 或 you ) to…; 也可譯作 you are required to…。

## 【譯例】

(a) It may be easy for us not to do a thing because we do not want to, but it is sometimes necessary for us to do a thing that we do not like.

(b) Although it may be easy for you not to do a thing because you do not want to, you are sometimes required to do a thing that you do not like.

# 第 18 天

許多人把自由誤解爲放縱，這實在是很大的遺憾。他們不懂得自由的意義。

## 【說明】

"這實在是很大的遺憾"：It is a matter of great regret that…, It is to be deeply regretted that…, 或以說話人 I 爲主語說 I deeply regret that…。

"誤解"：mistake

"放縱"：licence。"把自由誤解爲放縱"：mistake freedom for licence, 或 confuse freedom with licence; confuse 是 "混淆" 的意思; mistake…for…是 "把…錯認爲…", 如 mistake A for B ( 把甲錯認爲乙 ); confuse…with…是 "把…與…混淆", 如 confuse one thing with another ( 把一件事與另一件事混淆起來 ), 注意介詞的用法。

"不懂得自由的意義"：do not know what freedom means; 也可說 misinterpret the meaning of freedom; misinterpret 是 "曲解" 的意思。

## 【譯例】

(a) It is a matter of great regret that many people mistake freedom for licence. They do not know what freedom means.

(b) I deeply regret that many people confuse freedom with licence. They misinterpret the meaning of freedom.

338

# 第 19 天

　　有些人説自己的需要能滿足得越多，我們就越幸福；但另一些人却主張我們摒棄的東西越多，我們的生活就越好過。

## 【説明】

　　"滿足"：satisfy; gratify。"自己的需要能滿足得越多，我們就越幸福"：The more wants we satisfy, the happier we shall be。

　　"主張"：maintain; hold；deem

　　"摒棄"：dispense with。"摒棄的東西越多，我們的生活就越好過"：The more things we dispense with, the better off we shall be; be better off 是"境況較好"的意思；也可説 The more things we can go without, the more comfortably we shall live, go without 是"沒有也行"的意思，如 If there isn't one left, I shall go without（如果一個也沒有，那就不要也行）。

## 【譯例】

　　(a) Some people say that the more wants we gratify, the happier we shall be, while other people maintain that the more things we dispense with, the better off we shall be.

　　(b) Although some people say that the more wants we satisfy, the happier we shall be, other people hold that the more things we can go without, the more comfortably we shall live.

# 第 20 天

　　沒有錢的人可以説是窮的，但只有錢而沒有別的東西可以説更窮。

339

記着：窮人不一定總是不幸的，富人也不一定總是幸福的。

## 【說明】

"沒有錢的人"：a man who has no money, 或 a man without money

"只有錢而沒有別的東西"：has nothing but money; 改成詞組是 with nothing but money。

"記着"除了 remember 之外；也可說 bear in mind。

"窮人"：the poor; poor 作名詞用是複數，與 poor people 意義相同；同樣，the rich 可指複數的"富人"。

"不一定"：not always; not necessarily。"富人也不一定總是幸福的"：nor are the rich people always happy; nor 放在句首主謂語要倒裝，這在前面已經說過了。

## 【譯例】

(a) A man who has no money may be said to be poor, but a man who has nothing but money may be said to be even poorer. You must bear in mind that the poor are not always unhappy, nor are the rich always happy.

(b) Though a man without money may be said to be poor, a man with nothing but money may be said to be poorer. Remember well that poor people are not necessarily unhappy, nor are rich people always happy.


# 第21天

財富猶如糞土，堆積起來會散發出惡臭，撒開來却可肥沃土地。

340

## 【說明】

"財富"：wealth

"糞土"：dung。"猶如糞土"：be like dung, 或 can be likened
（或 compared）to dung。

"堆積"：heap up。"堆積起來"是"如果被堆積起來"的意思,
要說 if it is heaped up, 或 if heaped up。

"惡臭" nasty smell。"散發出惡臭" send forth（或 emit）nasty
smell; 也可說 smell bad。

"撒開"：sprinkle。"撒開來"與"堆積起來"一樣, 要說 if
it is sprinkled, 或 if sprinkled。

"肥沃土地"：fertilize the land

## 【譯例】

(a) Wealth is like dung: if heaped up, it sends forth a nasty smell;
if sprinkled, it fertilizes the land.

(b) Wealth may be likened to dung: if it is heaped up, it smells
bad; if it is sprinkled, it fertilizes the land.

# 第22天

俗語說"金錢能推動世界", 但我認為應該是才能能推動世界。
沒有才能甚麼事也完成不了。

## 【說明】

"我認為"：I think, 但如說 I should think 則更好,加了一個
情態動詞 should 就可表示說話人對自己所表示的意見不作主觀肯定,

語氣比較謙遜; 也可說 I should like to say。

"甚麼事也完成不了": can hardly accomplish anything, 或 can accomplish nothing

## 【譯例】

(a) A proverb says that money moves the world, but I should think that ability moves the world. Without ability we could hardly accomplish anything.

(b) There is a proverb saying that money moves the world, but I should like to say that it is ability that moves the world. If we have no ability, we can hardly accomplish anything.

# 第23天

一個人不管多麼有錢, 總是想有更多。人的貪婪確是無止境的。

## 【說明】

"一個人不管多麼有錢" 如前所見可有幾種譯法: 1. However rich a man is ( 或 may be ) …; 2. Rich as a man may be…; 3. No matter how rich a man is…, 以上三種說法以後一種語氣最強。

"貪婪": avarice, greed, 或 greediness

"是無止境的": know no bounds; be endless。"人的貪婪確是無止境的": Human avarice indeed knows no bounds; 也可說 There are no bounds to human avarice。注意 bounds 要用複數。

## 【譯例】

(a) However rich a man is, he will surely want to be still richer.

Human avarice indeed knows no bounds.

(b) Rich as one may be, one is sure to desire to become still richer. There are indeed no bounds to human avarice.

# 第24天

不能相信別人的人是不幸的，但不相信自己的人則更不幸。

## 【說明】

"相信"：believe，後面可跟 in 或不跟 in，但兩者意義有區別：believe others 是 "相信別人的話"；believe in others 是 "相信別人可靠"，所以這裏要說 believe in others。"不能相信別人的人是不幸的" 可照字譯說 Those who cannot believe in others are unhappy;也可譯作 If people cannot believe in others, they are unhappy。

## 【譯例】

(a) Those who cannot believe in others are unhappy, but those who cannot believe in themselves are still more unhappy.

(b) If people cannot believe in others, they are unhappy. But if they cannot believe in themselves, they are still more unhappy.

# 第25天

在學校裏成績優良，未必就會在社會上有所作爲。另一方面，所謂有所作爲也未必意味着一個人的眞正成功。

"在學校裏成績優良"可理解為"因為學業成績優良"譯作 because one's school record is excellent（或 outstanding）。

"有所作為"：success（或 advancement）in life；動詞是 succeed。
"未必就會在社會上有所作為"：one does not necessarily succeed in this world。

"所謂"：so-called, 作形容詞用。

"未必意味着一個人的眞正成功"：not always mean true advancement as a human being；也可說 be not equivalent to real success as a human being；be equivalent to 是"等於"的意思。

## 【譯例】

(a) One does not necessarily succeed in this world because one's school record is excellent. On the other hand, the so-called " success in life " is not always equivalent to real success as a human being.

(b) It does not necessarily follow that you will succeed in this world simply because your school record is outstanding. On the other hand, the so-called " success in life " does not always mean true advancement as a human being.


# 第 26 天


雖然不能説只要努力就一定會成功, 但那部分努力也決不會完全白費的。

## 【說明】

"努力"：effort; 作動詞要說 make efforts。

344

"一定"除了 surely, certainly 之外; 也可說 invariably。

"雖然不能說…但…" : We can't say that…, but…, 或 Although it does not necessarily follow that…

"白費" : be useless; be in vain

【譯例】

(a) Although it does not necessarily follow that your efforts will invariably bring you success, those efforts will never be completely useless.

(b) We can't say that you will surely succeed if only you make efforts, but you can be sure that your efforts will never be entirely in vain.


# 第27天

回首前塵, 使我不得不感到吃驚的是, 以前有許多事情都是由於環境使然的。這種環境只能説是純粹的機緣。

【說明】

"前塵" : one's past life。"回首前塵" : look back ( 或 reflect ) upon one's past life。

"環境" : circumstances。"由於環境而發生的" : happen due to circumstances。

"純粹的機緣" : pure chance

【譯例】

(a) Looking back upon my past life, I cannot but be surprised to find how many things happened due to circumstances considered as nothing but pure chance.

(b) When I reflect upon my past life, I cannot help being surprised to find how many happenings were due to circumstances that cannot be regarded as other than pure chance.


# 第28天

有些人似乎過於熱衷地趕時髦。他們認爲要是自己不能走在時代尖端，就是不幸的。

## 【說明】

"過於熱衷"：be too eager

"時髦"：fashion。"趕時髦"：follow the fashion

"走在時代尖端"：be ahead of one's times

## 【譯例】

(a) It seems that some people are too eager to follow the fashion. They think they are unhappy when they cannot be ahead of their times.

(b) Some people seem to be so eager to follow the fashion that they think themselves to be unhappy if they cannot be ahead of their times.


# 第29天

相當多的人依然抱着外國貨總比本地貨好這種觀念。

"相當多": quite a few; not a few; some few

"抱着"（意見、觀念等）: entertain。"依然抱着…這種觀念": still entertain the idea that…; 也可用 idea 作主語說 There still remains the idea that…。

"外國貨": foreign goods; imported goods; goods（或 articles）of foreign make; make 在這裏是名詞,作"製造"解。

"本國貨"domestic goods, 或 goods of domestic make

【譯例】

(a) Quite a few people still entertain the idea that articles of foreign make are always better than domestic ones.

(b) There still remains among some few people the idea that imported goods are invariably superior to those of domestic make.

# 第30天

許多人的景況確實比戰前好多了，但遺憾的是相當多的人似乎只想到自己的利益。

【說明】

"戰前": before the war, 或 in the pre-war days

"景況好多了": be（或 become）much better off, lead（或 live）a much better life。在"許多人的景況確實比戰前好多了"這句話裏, "景況"是主語, 但在英語裏可不必照譯, 可用 many people 作主語說 Many people have certainly become much better off than

347

they used to be before the war, 或 A lot of people are leading a much better life than they were in the pre-war days.

**【譯例】**

(a) Many people have certainly become much better off than they used to be before the war, but regrettably, not a few of them seem to be thinking only of their own interests.

(b) It is true that a lot of people are leading a much better life than they were in the pre-war days, but, to our regret, quite a few of them seem to think only of their own interests.

# Words and Expressions

| | |
|---|---|
| learning; knowledge [ˈnɔlidʒ] | 學問 |
| actually | 實際上 |
| starvation; famine [ˈfæmin] | 飢餓；飢荒 |
| be unconcerned about | 不關心 |
| terrorism [ˈterərizəm] | 恐怖主義 |
| election | 選舉 |
| cast ballot; vote | 投票 |
| flatter; fawn on | 恭維 |
| speak ill of | 說壞話 |
| in one's presence; to one's face | 當面 |
| behind one's back; in one's absence | 背後 |
| remind (of) | 提醒 |
| helpful | 有幫助的，肯助人的 |

| | |
|---|---|
| valuable | 可貴的 |
| impartial [im´pɑ:ʃəl]; unbiased [´ʌn´baiəst] | 公正的 |
| conduct [´kɔndəkt] | 行爲 |
| repent | 後悔 |
| prevail on; persuade [pə´sweid] | 說服 |
| obstinate [´ɔbstinit]; stubborn [´stʌbən]; headstrong | 頑固的 |
| misunderstand | 誤會 |
| criticize; comment [´kɔment] on | 批評; 評論 |
| idle about; fool around | 游手好閒 |
| do no decent [´di:snt] work; have no proper business | 不務正業 |
| disgusting; repugnant [ri´pʌgnənt]; repulsive | 令人厭惡的 |
| courage [´kʌridʒ] | 勇氣 |
| speak up; speak out | 直率地說出 |
| discreet | 愼重的 |
| express one's opinion; state one's views | 發表意見 |
| refrain (from) | 抑制，忍住 |
| licence [´laisəns] | 放縱 |
| mistake (n. or v.) | 錯誤(名); 認錯，弄錯(動) |
| confuse | 混淆 |
| misinterpret [´misin´təːprit] | 曲解，譯錯 |
| satisfy; gratify | 滿足 |
| maintain [men´tein]; hold; deem | 主張 |
| dispense with | 摒棄; 沒有…也行 |

| | |
|---|---|
| wealth | 財富 |
| heap up | 堆積 |
| nasty [ˈnɑːsti] smell | 惡臭 |
| fertilize | 使肥沃 |
| accomplish | 完成 |
| avarice [ˈævəris] | 貪婪 |
| know no bounds | 無止境 |
| success（或 advancement）in life | 有所作爲 |
| be equivalent to [iˈkwivələnt] | 等於 |
| make efforts | 努力 |
| look back; reflect | 回顧 |
| circumstance [ˈsəːkəmstəns] | 環境 |
| follow the fashion | 趕時髦 |
| be ahead of one's time | 走在時代尖端 |
| quite a few; not a few; some few | 相當多的 |
| entertain [ˌentəˈtein]（意見、觀念等） | 抱着 |

# Exercise 12

Translate the following into English:

1. 如果只有一點點學問而自己却不知道是一點點，那是很危險的。（第1天）

2. 我不需要這些書。我要的是一本詞典，你能介紹給我一本好的詞典嗎？（第2天）

350

3. 有些人經常把和平掛在嘴上,但我說他們愛的却並不是和平。( 第 2 , 3 天 )

4. 現在世界上不少地方還存在着貧困、飢餓和不幸。我們既然生活在同一個世界上, 對這些現象就不能漠不關心。( 第 4 天 )

5. 恐怖主義在世界上很多地方都存在着, 這種主義是甚麼貨色我們大家都是清楚的。( 第 5 天 )

6. 甲: 這次選舉你有沒有去投票?

   乙: 有的, 每次選舉我都去投票。

   甲: 你爲甚麼這樣重視選舉?

   乙: 因爲我想這是我的權利, 也是義務。( 第 6 天 )

7. 她既不當面恭維人家, 也不背後說人家壞話。從這兩點來說她是值得稱讚的( praiseworthy )。( 第 7 天 )

8. 朋友提醒我們的缺點, 我們應該感謝他。的確, 向我們提忠告的朋友要比恭維我們的朋友好得多。( 第 7 , 8 天 )

9. 喜歡人家恭維而不喜歡人家提忠告是常見的現象, 所以我們應該經常抱謙虛謹慎( modest and prudent )的態度。( 第 9 天 )

10. 有些人只愛人家恭維而不願接受人家的忠告,最後他們犯了錯誤, 後悔已是不及。( 第 7 , 8 , 10天 )

11. 也有小數頑固的人, 他們相信自己總是正確的。你永遠說服不了他們, 到頭來( in the long run )他們非失敗不可( be doomed to failure )。( 第11天 )

12. 他誤會我了。我好意幫助他認識所犯的錯誤, 但他却認爲我在說他的壞話。( 第 7 , 12天 )

13. 我批評他游手好閒不務正業, 但他說他找不到就業的機會。( 第 12, 13天 )

14. 怎麼( How comes it that… )學問會使人聰明而傻瓜搞學問却反而會更傻? 你想這是甚麼道理? ( 第14天 )

15. 甲：她直率地說出自己的想法，這倒是很有勇氣的。

    乙：是的。但我想在沒有必要的時候還是不說爲是。（第15天）

16. 有的時候我們不能做自己想做的事；也有的時候我們必須做自己不願做的事，這是常有的事。（第16，17天）

17. 許多人不懂得自由的意義。他們以爲旣然有自由就可以做任何自己愛做的事情，這確是個很大的錯誤。（第17，18天）

18. 他把自由與放縱相混，以爲可以爲所欲爲，這實在是一件使人遺憾的事，他曲解了自由的意義。（第18天）

19. 有些人認爲錢愈多就愈幸福，你的高見以爲如何？（第14，19天）

20. 我以爲有錢的人不一定是幸福的，無錢的人也不一定是不幸的。（第20天）

21. 甲：把財富比作糞土，你看是否恰當？

    乙：我不大看得出兩者的相似之處。

    甲：財富像糞土，因爲堆積起來會發惡臭，撒開來却可以肥沃土地。（第21天）

22. 我以爲才能比金錢更重要。沒有才能世界上甚麼事也完成不了。（第22天）

23. 學無止境，不管你多麼有學問，也應該設法取得（acquire）更多的知識。（第23天）

24. 受人幫助的人是有福的，但以助人爲樂的人却是十分值得稱讚的。（第24天）

25. 只相信別人當然是可笑的（ridiculous），但只相信自己也是很危險的。（第24天）

26. 雖然不能說學校裏成績優良就一定會在社會上有所作爲，但努力學習也決不會是完全白費的。（第25，26天）

27. 回首前塵我們往往會發現許多事情都是由於當時某些環境造成的。如果沒有這些環境，我們可能不會是現在這個樣子。（第27

天 )

28. 說外國貨總比本地貨好自然是錯誤的；但如果本地貨的確比外國貨好，那我們相信就不會再有人抱這種想法了。（第29天）

29. 許多人的景況比以前好多了；但有些人對現狀似乎還不滿足，認爲自己不能像富人一樣過生活是不幸的。（第28，30天）

30. 我們能夠從羣衆那兒學到許多有用的東西，他們甚至可以敎一些東西給最有學問的人。如果有機會的話，你可以要求他們告訴你所見過的和知道的事情。千萬不要爲了向別人問你不知道的事情而感到羞愧。有一次有人向一個有學問的人問起他是怎樣取得那麽多知識的。他答稱：" 向每個人請敎。"（ ask information of ）

# Key to the Exercises
## (For reference only)

# Exercise 1

1. A: Excuse me. What time is it?
   B: It's twenty-five minutes past two. (或 two twenty-five).
2. My watch doesn't keep time. It gains one minute every day.
3. A: How do you go to school, on foot or by bus?
   B: The school is not far from my house. I always go on foot.
4. A: How long does it take you to go to school?
   B: It's only ten minutes' walk.
5. His house is on the outskirts. It takes him a long time to go to the station.
6. The park is not far from here. It won't take you long to get there by bus.
7. There is still half an hour before the film begins. Let's drop in here for some coffee.
8. A: When will the film begin?
   B: Oh, there is still plenty of time.
9. Yesterday he went hurriedly to the station, because he wanted to catch the 2:15 train.
10. He missed the last train because he was five minutes late.
11. A: When shall we reach our destination?
    B: So long as it doesn't rain, we shall be able to get there before noon.
12. I'm not very well today. Maybe I caught cold last night.
13. All his family never go to bed later than ten o'clock every evening.
14. A: What time will you come tomorrow?
    B: Not earlier than eight o'clock, I'm afraid.
15. That student is very punctual. He is never late for school.

16. A: How does he work at the factory?

    B: He is a good worker. He works hard and never asks for leave.

17. We are in the nick of time. If we had come three minutes later, we should have missed the train.

18. He was here just now. If you want to see him, you can wait for him here.

19. Time passes swiftly. It's three years since I began to study English. I'll make good use of my time to learn it well.

20. A: Will he be back tomorrow?

    B: No, he will not come back till next week. This week he will not be free.

21. It's four months since my brother began to study English every third day under an English teacher.

22. On Sunday I went to see a friend and didn't come back home till after supper.

23. A: When were you born?

    B: I was born in 1948. I'm thirty-two years old.

24. A: How old are you?

    B: I'm fifty years old.

    A: Is that so? It seems to me that you are only forty.

25. Yesterday I met a schoolmate of mine after an interval of twenty years. He was so old that I could hardly recognize him.

26. I told him that we had studied at the same school twenty years before.

27. He saw my father twenty years ago. At that time he was only a teenager.

28. His elder brother is in his early forties and is older than he by four or five years.

29. A: How old is your grandfather?

    B: He is already over seventy.

    A: Really? He looks younger than his age.

30. His father is getting on in years, but he is still in good health. He will be eighty on the coming birthday.

# Exercise 2

1. A: How will the weather be tomorrow?
   B: The weather forecast says it will be raining tomorrow.
2. It's fine today, but it's a bit too cold for the time of year.
3. It's already three o'clock. I wonder why he hasn't come yet.
4. Spring is early coming this year. The peach blossoms on the outskirts have already come out. I remember they had not yet opened by this time last year.
5. It's spring now. The weather is warm. There are more and more flowers in the park day by day.
6. Spring is charming. Shall we go for a walk in the park?
7. It's really too foolish of us not to go out to enjoy ourselves on such a fine day.
8. How hot the weather is today! What about going for a swim at the seaside?
9. Nothing is more pleasant than to have a spring outing in the countryside on such a warm and sunny day.
10. A: Do you think it will rain today?
    B: Yes, you'd better take your raincoat with you.
11. He has been studying English off and on for three years, but he has made little progress.
12. We are going to make an excursion to the countryside next week, but it has been raining since yesterday. I wonder when it will clear up.
13. A: When will the concert take place?
    B: It'll take place next Wednesday, rain or shine.
14. Last week we went for a spring outing. On our way back we were caught in a heavy rain and everyone of us was drenched to the skin.
15. It rained last night. The air is pure and fresh this morning. How I wish to take a walk in the fields!
16. According to the radio, it'll be cloudy this afternoon, and will drizzle towards evening.
17. It's drizzling. I wonder when it'll clear up.

18. The rainy season has set in. It has been drizzling off and on for the last few days, and the air is very damp.
19. A: The broadcast says we are in for drizzle.
    B: It'll be all right so long as it doesn't rain heavily.
20. Winter has begun earlier this year. It seems we are in for a long spell of cold weather.
21. Last night we couldn't sleep a wink as her baby was crying all night.
22. Do you know a typhoon has approached this region? The heavy rain last night was probably due to the typhoon.
23. It's very muggy. Everybody is sweating all over. This is the hottest day I have known since I came here.
24. A: Look, the sky is clouding all over. We are going to have a heavy rain soon.
    B: It's good that the temperature will go down after the rain.
25. It rained cats and dogs last night. According to the weather forecast, there will be still more showers in a day or two. I'm afraid too much rain will do harm to the crops.
26. I have been to many summer resorts, and I think the Mediterranean coast is the best among them.
27. Summer is much cooler in the countryside than in town, so I hope I shall be able to go there for the summer.
28. It's snowing very hard. The temperature is falling. Perhaps it'll freeze tomorrow. Though the weather is cold, it's the best season for skating and skiing.
29. After the snow the road is very slippery. Watch your step when you go out, or you will fall.
30. I don't mind running some distance every day, for running is a very good exercise. After a period of training I believe I'll feel quite fit.

# Exercise 3

1. A: How are you?
   B: I'm very well, thank you.

A: I haven't seen you for a long time. Are you busy with your work or something?

B: I was away on business. I got back only yesterday.

2. A: He didn't come to work yesterday. Is he ill?

    B: Yes, he was running a temperature, but he is better today.

3. Last month he went to Japan to spend his holidays and didn't come back till last week. He looks much better than I saw him last.

4. He happened to be not at home when I went to see him the day before yesterday. I told his family that I would go again if I had time.

5. A: When did he come?

    B: He has been here for half an hour.

    A: Oh, I'm sorry to have kept him waiting.

6. Mr. Cook, may I introduce to you Mr. Smith? Mr. Smith is interested in English history. He hopes to consult you on a few questions.

7. A: Would you please introduce me to your friend Mr. Cooper?

    B: Yes, I would be glad to. But he is busy now. Just wait a moment, please.

8. I can't find the book you gave me yesterday. I don't for the life of me remember where I have put it.

9. I came across Mr. Burton, one of my secondary-school teachers, in the street the day before yesterday. It's more than ten years since I saw him last.

10. Paul is a man of his word. He never breaks his promises, so everybody trusts him.

11. We have lived together since childhood. We have studied in the same school and are now working in the same factory.

12. Through the introduction of my friend, I got acquainted with Peter, the librarian. We have been good friends ever since then.

13. I'm very grateful to you for the kindness you have shown me since I came here. I hope to come here again very soon. I'll come to see you then.

14. I have sent him a present as a token of my gratitude for the help he has rendered me.

15. I shall be very glad if you will go with me for a drive in the country tomorrow.

16. A: Do you feel like going for a drive in the country?

    B: No, I don't think I will. I'm busy. I can't afford the time. Thank you all the same for your kindness.

17. A: Well, it's time we left.

    B: Can't you stay a little longer?

    A: We are going to the movies at two.

    B: If so, I won't keep you.

18. I went to her house to say good-bye to her. She happened to be not at home. I told her family I'm leaving by the 7:00 train tomorrow.

19. A: What time are you leaving?

    B: I'm catching the 6:20 train.

    A: I'll come to the station to see you off.

    B: It's very kind of you to do so.

    A: Not at all. It's the least I could do.

    B: Thank you very much.

20. A: I wish you a pleasant journey, John, and hope you will come again soon.

    B: I hope so too. Thank you very much for coming to see me off.

21. A: Have you ever been in Macau?

    B: Yes, I have been there once.

    A: When did you go there?

    B: I went there two years ago.

22. A: Hello.. This is Smith here. May I speak to Mr. Jones?

    B: I'm sorry, Mr. Jones is not in.

    A: When do you expect him back?

    B: He said he would be in around three.

    A: All right. I'll ring again at about half past three.

    B: Very well.

23. Please ask Mr. Jones to call Smith at four o'clock. My number is 556843.

24. A: Paul, will you please call Peter and tell him I shall not be able to go to the reception tomorrow because I'm not feeling very well?

B: All right.

25. Will you please ask Mary whether she will attend the reception to be given next Sunday in honour of the foreign teachers?

26. I went to his house, but he was not there. Then I phoned his office. The answer was that he had returned home. So I couldn't find him.

27. In case of an emergency, you can ring him up. He may be very busy, but I believe he will help you.

28. It's possible that the letter was wrongly addressed, so it didn't reach me.

29. A: Would you mind returning these books for me to the library when you go there?
    B: Not at all.

30. A: I'm afraid I must be going now. My train leaves at 5:30.
    B: I won't keep you then. Please give my best regards to your father when you get home.
    A: Thank you very much. I'll pass it on. Good-bye.
    B: Good-bye.

# Exercise 4

1. In spring the weather here is very changeable. It is sometimes hot and sometimes cold, so it is very easy for the people of poor health to get ill.

2. If you pay attention to exercise and take good care of yourself, surely you will get better.

3. I know that exercise is good for health, so I make it a rule to take exercise every day.

4. A: How many hours must an adult sleep every day?
   B: I think it best for him to sleep eight hours a day. Lack of sufficient sleep will affect his health, you know.

5. He has regular habits. He gets up early every morning and pays attention to exercise and nutrition.

6. I believe it very important to have regular habits. My younger brother is getting stronger day by day just because he keeps good

habits.

7. My son was very weak before, but now I'm glad to see him gaining weight day by day.

8. He has been a victim to insomnia. Owing to the lack of sufficient sleep, he is in bad health.

9. A: She is very delicate, and it is also useless for her to take medicine. What do you think she should do?

   B: I should advise her to pay more attention to exercise.

10. A man with a healthy constitution will not be an easy prey to tuberculosis.

11. Some people were born weak. But if they pay more attention to exercise, they will become stronger.

12. We must realize that if we are in good health it is not necessary (for us) to be too much afraid of illness.

13. Even a slight cold should not be overlooked, because a slight disease may turn into something serious if no care is taken.

14. One often doesn't realize so much the importance of health when one is in condition ( 或 good health).

15. I used to suffer from constipation. The doctor advised me to take more vegetables and more exercise every day. Now I am glad to have got over the trouble.

16. He has heart disease and has often been subject to fits of attack. The doctor has advised him not to take any strenuous exercise.

17. Smallpox is terrible. Formerly a great many people died of this disease, but now we can prevent it by means of vaccination.

18. Yesterday I felt dizzy and chilly. The doctor wrote me a prescription. I took the medicine and was somewhat relieved.

19. I took his temperature and found that he was running a high fever. I sent him to the hospital at once to see what the trouble was.

20. He was indisposed and had a violent headache. The doctor said he was ill of ( 或 with) influenza and had to be hospitalized.

21. A: What's wrong with you?

   B: I'm dizzy and feel sick.

   A: Let me take your temperature. You are running a high fever. Probably you have got flu.

362

22. The doctor says that his illness is not serious and will be all right after a few days' rest.

23. A: What does the doctor say?

B: The doctor says that he has got appendicitis and will have to be operated on.

24. She suddenly fell sick yesterday evening. The doctor diagnozed her illness as heart disease and decided to admit her into the hospital.

25. A: I have stomach trouble. Sometimes it aches terribly.

B: Why don't you go to see the doctor then? The earlier you do something about it, the better.

26. A: He has been ill for the best part of a month.

B: What's wrong with him?

A: Probably he has caught some infectious disease.

27. What a large number of people die of cancer every year! I hope that with the development of medicine it will be easier to cure this terrible disease.

28. The patient has got cancer. The doctor says it is a hopeless case. No medical treatment is of any use to him.

29. Even though we don't feel indisposed, we had better go to the hospital once in a while to have a physical examination to see whether there is anything the matter with our health.

30. At one time he was so ill that there seemed to be little hope of his recovery. But fortunately after Dr. Jones' careful treatment he has got better day by day and is now even healthier than ever before.

# Exercise 5

1. Our room is on the fifth floor. On the opposite side of the street is a park, where we can see various kinds of trees and flowers.

2. We went up to the top of the hill which commands a very fine view of the surrounding country.

3. Our house is just opposite the park. In front of our house are planted a few cherry-trees, so you can't miss it.

4. A: You have a TV set, haven't you?

B: Yes, we have a TV set and also a radio set, a refrigerator, in fact everything.

5. Though the air is fresh and the surroundings are peaceful in the country, many people are not quite used to country life for the lack of modern conveniences.

6. His brother used to work in the country, so he is used to country life.

7. He can speak English, so can his sister; but his elder brother can speak Japanese as well as English.

8. The air in the city is very dirty and the dust is full of disease germs, so it is very easy (for us) to get some infectious diseases.

9. One of my friends used to live in a residential quarter in the suburbs, but now he has removed into ( 或 to) a new flat in our neighbourhood.

10. The plan was scheduled to be fulfilled in another month, but owing to the shortage of manpower it will not be completed till the end of this year.

11. The waste liquid and gas from the factories have caused the pollution of air and water. If no suitable measures are taken, it is certain that people's health will be seriously endangered.

12. More and more people find that the air in large cities is very dirty, so they are anxious to make their abodes in some place where the air is fresh.

13. If there are modern conveniences, it is certain that many people would rather make their abodes in the country, where the air is much better than that in the city.

14. We must make great efforts to protect the environment against pollution.

15. Life was naturally hard in primitive society, but there seemed to be very few factors that endangered the health of the people. From this point of view, we almost envy primitive society.

16. Last summer she spent a whole week in Hawaii and went swimming nearly every day. She said that was the pleasantest time in her life.

17. Do you think it an enjoyment to sleep soundly in a comfortable bed after a hot bath?

18. A: If you are willing to share potluck with us, we shall be very glad.

B: Thank you very much. It's very kind of you. But I still have something to do in the morning, so I must be away.

19. The southerners usually have rice as their staple food, but sometimes they also take steamed buns, noodles and other things made from flour for a change of taste.

20. A: Have a cigarette, please.

B: No, thanks. I've already stopped smoking.

A: Why do you give it up?

B: The newspaper says smoking is one of the chief causes of lung cancer.

21. A: How do you like my new jacket? Does it look all right?

B: Yes; and it goes well with your trousers, too.

22. I usually go for a haircut every two weeks. Some people have their hair cut once a month, but most of them go to the barbershop once every three weeks or so.

23. A: Is the principal in?

B: Yes, he is. Do you want to see him?

A: Yes, I would like to have a talk with him.

B: I don't think that will do today. He is having a meeting just now.

24. If your friend is very busy, you had better not call on him unexpectedly, because by doing so you will put him to trouble.

25. I went to see a friend yesterday. He kept me waiting for one whole hour. That was really the most unpleasant thing.

26. He insisted on going out in the rain, but his mother advised him not to, because it would be harmful to his health if he got wet.

27. Her son insisted that he be allowed to swim in the river. She, however, would not permit him to, because the river was so deep that he might be in danger of losing his life if nobody took care of him.

28. Everybody agrees that swimming is a very good exercise, but the beginners must be very careful in order to avoid any possible risk.

29. It has been two years since he went abroad to study. As he is far

away from home, he always finds it a great pleasure to receive letters from his family.

30. If we live under constant strain, our health will be affected. So it is sometimes necessary for us to relax.

# Exercise 6

1. My nephew is very fond of painting. He never fails to paint one or two hours every day. But he can't paint very well yet.

2. He likes movies very much. He says he never fails to see a movie at least once a week.

3. Somehow he doesn't like mathematics. On the other hand he takes great interest in music, and never fails to play the violin at least an hour a day.

4. A: What do you do on Sundays?
   B: I usually go to the movies with my family. Sometimes I also play chess with my friends.

5. It is five years since I began to play the violin. But sorry to say, I am not much of a musician.

6. My avocation is learning English. I want to buy an English grammar book. Which do you think is the best?

7. I always read some novels in my spare time. Sometimes I also read some English novels. But because of my poor knowledge of English I find it difficult to fully understand them.

8. It is really very interesting to read novels. Sometimes I'll even forget my meals if I am not reminded.

9. He is, as it were, a movie fan. He never fails to go to the movies whenever he finds time. Some pictures he would even see two or three times.

10. He neither smokes nor drinks. Only he is fond of taking coffee. He finds it an enjoyment to have a cup of coffee after each meal.

11. His son neither studies nor works. Only he indulges in playing cards. I am afraid he will be quite useless to his family.

12. If you knew English, you would be able to read "Robinson Crusoe"

in the original.

13. If I were to enter the university, I would study medicine.

14. If this novel were to be translated into English, those who know English would surely be very much interested in it.

15. A: Are you a footballer or a basketballer?

    B: No, I am neither a footballer nor a basketballer, but I like to play both of these games.

16. Though his father is getting on in years, he walks like a young man. It is said that he was a top-notch sportsman forty years ago.

17. He said to me, "There will be a basketball match tomorrow. If you want to watch it, I'll get the ticket for you."

18. He told me that he had been good at sports in his youth, and it was nothing for him to swim five miles at a stretch.

19. In recent years table tennis has become more and more popular. Many young people are very good at playing this game. My younger brother also wishes that he could learn how to play it.

20. A: Do you like skating?

    B: Yes, I have been learning it for four years.

    A: Then you must be a good skater.

    B: Far from it!

21. It is probably no exaggeration to say that English is one of the most important languages in the world as far as its usefulness is concerned.

22. His elder brother is good at playing go. Last week he took part in a contest and came out first.

23. A: Judging from your level of English, you must be a returned student.

    B: No, I haven't been abroad, but I like to study English very much. I'm still very far from (being) good at it.

24. Judging from her remarks, she seemed to have no ear for music. I guess she can't play the violin.

25. I desired that my son should be an engineer, but he would like to study physics. As a physicist, he is by no means remarkable.

26. What a beautiful poem! I think this is the best poem he has written. Have you ever seen such a masterpiece?

27. Last night as there was nothing important, my friend Jenny invited

me to attend a concert. But sorry to say, I have no musical sense, so I didn't enjoy it very much.

28. I went camping with a few of my schoolmates this day week. The weather in the mountains was very changeable. But as we had made careful preparations in advance, we were having a very pleasant time.

29. A: Do you dance?

   B: No, I have never learned.

   A: I'll teach you then. If only you would try, I believe you'll surely be a good dancer.

30. A: What's your hobby?

   B: I like music very much.

   A: Then you must be a musician.

   B: Far from it. I'm only an amateur.

   A: Do you play any musical instrument?

   B: Occasionally I play the accordion. I'm also interested in playing the violin, but to my regret, neither of them can I play very well.

# Exercise 7

1. Travelling is a pleasure. I advise you to go on a journey whenever you have enough money.

2. In former times travelling was a very unpleasant thing because of the lack of good communication facilities. People very often had to go on foot, so it took a long time to go to a distant place.

3. Nowadays we have various means of fast communication such as the train and airplane. You will find it very convenient to go to any place in the world.

4. A: Have you ever been here before?

   B: No, this is the first time I come to visit your country.

   A: What's your impression?

   B: Well, I find everything new to me. It's just like jumping from my own country into a new world.

5. I shall have to go to Peking on business in the near future. I haven't

made up my mind yet whether I'll travel by train or by plane.

6. I met Peter last week. He told me he had just returned from England. He went there to visit his relatives.

7. I went to the airport yesterday afternoon to see Mr. Cook off. He was going to London on business.

8. It is true that travelling by plane is much quicker than by train, but you will surely feel tired when you look down from the plane and can only see the sky, the clouds or the surface of the earth far below.

9. I don't like travelling by plane. I would like to go by train instead. Though the train is slower than the plane, I can see the sights on my way.

10. I want to reach my destination as quickly as possible. So I think the best way is to travel by plane.

11. We boarded the plane. Very soon the plane took off. In a few minutes we were above the clouds. Sometimes we could see the land far below between the clouds.

12. There is no direct bus service from here to the airport, so I think we had better take a taxi.

13. A: It's overcast today. Do you think it is flying weather?
    B: So long as there is no fog and no storm, I don't think they'll cancel the flights.

14. Our ship is sailing at a high speed. The sea becomes rougher and our ship begins to pitch and roll. Some passengers get seasick easily, while others are not afraid of the rough sea. They still walk up and down the deck.

15. I am a bad sailor. When I went to Japan last year, the sea was very choppy and I felt quite uncomfortable.

16. Today the sea is calm and the ship doesn't toss. I find it very delightful to take a sea trip.

17. A lot of ships are coming in and going out here every day. Some moor at the wharf, while others anchor at the harbour, passengers will have to get ashore by steam launch or by boat.

18. A: Haven't you travelled around the American continent?
    B: No, I have never been there. I really wish I could have a chance

to see it.

19. As I didn't have enough time, I had to travel by plane. If I had made a bus-and-train tour, I would have enjoyed the fine views on my way.

20. I was to go to Japan last month as a member of the delegation. But they made a change in the plan at the last moment, so I didn't go with it.

21. I haven't been to Europe, so I know nothing of European customs. I am going to consult Jenny. She might give me some suggestions.

22. One dark night they boarded a boat, crossed the river and came to a small country town, where they put up for the night.

23. After a long journey we arrived at a small hill by the lake. The beauty of the scenery was beyond all description.

24. There were many people rowing on the lake. Some were singing and some were playing the accordions or other musical instruments. They seemed to be very happy.

25. We climbed up the hill. The sun was setting at that time. We gazed at the distant sails on the river. The fine view was really beyond description.

26. Recently a friend of mine arrived in Hongkong. He desires to see the sights of the city. I have promised to show him around when I have time.

27. There are always many people strolling on the streets on Sundays to enjoy their day off. There are also some who come from other places to see the sights of the city or do some shopping, so the streets are more crowded than usual.

28. A: What animals interest you most in the zoo?
B: The monkeys. They are always very amusing to both old and young.

29. This is my first visit here. I have done much sightseeing. I am deeply impressed with the beauty of the scenery here.

30. The other day I went to visit the museum. I went with a group of friends — it was an excursion. I had been there before but there was much I wanted to see again. We were shown around by a curator, who gave us all necessary explanations. The visit was a great success.

We learned a good deal and had a very pleasant time.

# Exercise 8

1. This road leads to the commercial centre. Therefore it is always congested. It is even worse on Sundays.
2. The bus was crowded with excursionists going to the beach. As I could not find any seat, I had to keep standing all the way to the terminus.
3. There are a lot of cars in the streets. You must be very careful and cross the street only under the green light. Otherwise you may be run over by a car.
4. I suppose it will take me some time to go from one end of the city to the other. There is no direct bus service, so I'll have to change buses on my way.
5. This bus is for the suburbs. It's already so packed that we can't get in. We had better wait for the next one.
6. I boarded a trolley bus and occupied a back seat. I told the conductor where I wanted to go and paid for a ticket. Soon I arrived at my destination.
7. There is a lot of traffic in the streets, especially during the rush hours. You must be very careful when you cross the street.
8. Get in quickly. We are already late. If there is a traffic jam, we won't be able to get there on time, I'm afraid.
9. When I got back from school, I had to share the taxi with a stranger as the buses were packed like sardines.
10. It is a slow train, which stops at all the stations on its way. Hence it will take much more time than an express to reach our destination.
11. Most passengers change trains or get off at big stations or junctions. Those who want to leave at small stations must take a slow train because a fast train doesn't make stops there.
12. A: The train ought to be in already. I wonder why it is behind time.

    B: Probably it is delayed by the storm. Otherwise it won't be late.

13. With the increase in the number of motorcars in recent years, traffic accidents have happened quite frequently. We can't help worrying about our safety when we go out.

14. It is said that the plane is delayed by unfavorable weather. I hope nothing has gone wrong with it.

15. A considerable number of houses near the commercial centre have been pulled down. Hence the streets in the neighbourhood can be widened.

16. Luckily I have found lodgings in the neighbourhood of our factory. Though it is convenient for me to go to work from now on, I'll have to pay twice as much rent as before.

17. Owing to bad weather, our plane was late by two hours. But as it landed safe and sound, we heaved a sigh of relief.

18. I asked a passer-by if he happened to know a gentleman by the name of Smith. He said he couldn't tell me as he himself was a stranger there.

19. Please remember to ring up my uncle after you receive this letter and tell him that I have arrived in Hongkong safe and sound.

20. A: I want to fly to Geneva on or about the first.
    B: I'll just see what there is.
    A: By the way, I don't like a night flight.
    B: All right, sir.

21. A: I want to catch the 11:15 train.
    B: We'll be all right if there are no hold-ups.

22. A: Will you please tell me how I should go to the station?
    B: You had better take the No. 18 trolley bus from here down to the City Hall, where you change for a No. 5 bus to the station.

23. A: I have got to catch my plane, which takes off in an hour.
    B: I believe you will be able to arrive at the airport in some forty minutes. So you don't have to worry.

24. A: Does the 21 (bus) go to the general post office?
    B: The general post office? No, it only goes as far as the bridge! You want a 12.

25. A: Will you please direct me to the telegraph office?
    B: Cross the bridge over there and go straight on. When you come

to the end of the road, turn to the left and then take the second turning on your right.

26. A:  May I ask where South Street is, please?
    B:  Take the second turning on the left and then ask again.
    A:  Is it far?
    B:  No, it's only five minutes' walk.

27. A:  Excuse me, please. Could you tell me the way to the zoo?
    B:  It's some distance from here. You can take a No. 18 bus.
    A:  Where shall I get off?
    B:  Ask the conductor and he will tell you.

28. A:  Does this road lead to the seaside?
    B:  No, you are going the wrong way. Turn round and turn left at the traffic lights.

29. A:  Should I take a bus if I go to the public library?
    B:  No, it's within walking distance.
    A:  Thank you very much.
    B:  That's quite all right.

30. A:  Excuse me, sir. Can you tell me where the stadium is?
    B:  I'm sorry, but I can't. I'm a stranger here myself. I saw a policeman standing on the corner of the street. He will be able to help you.
    A:  I'll ask him then. Thank you. Good-bye.
    B:  Good-bye.

# Exercise 9

1.  The clerk of the hotel gave me a room with a bathroom attached. He informed me of the price. Soon everything was settled.

2.  I chose a room facing south. It was very comfortable. I could have a fine rest here.

3.  I booked a single room at the hotel. I asked the porter to carry my luggage to the room. The place was very quiet, for it was far from the noisy street.

4.  The hotel near the station was established not long ago. The rooms

are clean and the prices are reasonable. That's why it is so well patronized.

5. A: Have you any vacant room?

    B: Yes, there is one at the back.

    A: I want to have a look first.

    B: All right. Please come with me?

6. A: Have you got two singles?

    B: No, I can only let you have one.

    A: How much a day do you charge?

    B: x x dollars, service charge included.

    A: The price is reasonable, but I want two rooms.

7. A: My name is Paul Jones. I made a reservation the day before yesterday for a double room.

    B: Let me see. Oh, yes, here we are, room 230. First floor front. Will you register, please?

    A: All right.

8. A: I'm looking for a room.

    B: I'd recommend you to the Park Hotel.

    A: Is it an expensive place?

    B: No, not at all. The price is x x dollars per day for a single room.

    A: That's quite reasonable.

9. A: How do you like this room?

    B: Looks nice, but it's not very well ventilated. What does the window look out on?

    A: Just a small alley, but the room is away from the noise of the traffic.

    B: Yes, it's quiet here.

10. The clerk of the hotel knew that I was leaving. He gave me the bill. I asked him to call a taxi for me. Having paid the bill, I left the hotel.

11. The department store is a multiple store. It sells all kinds of consumer goods. We can also have various kinds of clothes made to order there.

12. A: I'm trying to find a white nylon shirt.

374

B: Nothing in nylon at the moment, I'm afraid.

A: Could you order me one?

B: I should think so. If you leave your address, I'll contact you.

13. My friend Jenny wanted to go shopping the day before yesterday. She asked me to go with her. We went to the department store. She bought a ready-made overcoat and some articles of food.

14. A: How much is this raincoat?

B: × × dollars.

A: Have you got anything cheaper?

B: I'm sorry we have nothing cheaper.

15. A: Will you please show me that thermos bottle?

B: Certainly, ma'am.

A: How much is it?

B: × × dollars.

A: It's certainly nice, but it's more than I was thinking of paying. I don't think I'll take it.

16. At the department store I went up the escalator to the fourth floor, where I found the ready-made clothes department. I was trying to get a coat, but I failed to find a suitable one.

17. A: I'd like to see some leather shoes.

B: What's your size, sir?

A: My size is ten.

B: What about this pair?

A: Oh, they are a bit too big.

B: Let me bring you a smaller pair then.

A: Thanks.

18. A: Would you accompany me to the chemist's?

B: Yes, what are you going to buy?

A: I want to have my prescription filled, and also to buy some other things.

B: All right. Let's go.

19. A: Would you help me (to) choose a present for my elder brother? He is having his birthday tomorrow.

B: What are you trying to get?

A: I think we'd better go over to the department store to have a look.

B: All right. I'll accompany you.

20. My uncle is having his birthday next Sunday. I went to the department store with my friend Mary to see if there was anything of interest. At last I chose a beautiful tumbler and had my best wishes engraved on it.

21. At the post office you can buy all kinds of stamps, postcards and envelopes. You can also send parcels, letters, printed matters or telegrams here.

22. The post office clerk weighed my air letter which was to be registered. He told me what the postage was. I stuck the stamps on the letter and gave it to him. He put a chop on the stamps and wrote out a receipt.

23. I get my letters poste restante at the post office near our university. I have chosen this post office because I can drop in twice a day except on Sundays.

24. A: What's the postage on this letter to Bangkok, please?

B: I'll have a look. Was there anything else?

A: No, that's all. Thank you.

25. A: I want to send this parcel to Paris.

B: Since your parcel is going to Paris, the address should be written in French.

A: Oh, yes, you are right. Let me change it.

26. A: This letter to Thailand is to be registered.

B: Let me weigh it first.

A: What's the registration fee for foreign mail matters?

B: The registration fee is x x and the postage is x x. That will be x x in all.

27. A: I want to remit 500 dollars to a factory in Singapore.

B: You'll have to fill in an application form.

A: Should I send this order in a registered letter?

B: This is optional, but it is preferable to do so.

28. I asked the clerk at the post office how I should remit 100 dollars to Japan. He said the postal order was more convenient since it was not a big sum.

29. A: Here is a postal order from Japan for a sum of 200 dollars.

    B: Yes, it can be cashed now. Have you got your I.D. card?

    A: No, I forgot to take it with me.

    B: Bring it along, please.

30. A: I want to send a telegram. Will you please give me a telegraph form?

    B: Yes, sir. Here is a blank form; please write your message on it.

    A: I think I would send it as an urgent telegram. What's the rate per word?

    B: It is x x per word.

    A: This is my message. There are twenty words.

    B: Yes, just twenty words. Then that will be x x in all.

# Exercise 10

1. Only by using the new machine can we hope to increase production.

2. Technical progress will spur the development of industry, but only when the awakening of those who are engaged in that field is raised, can a greater development be made possible.

3. A country having but poor natural resources must secure her imports of raw materials and encourage her export trade as much as possible. Only by this way can her industry thrive.

4. Modern science and technology have greatly raised the productive forces and the result is that the supply of products exceeds the demand for them. The overproduction often gives rise to a keen competition in commerce.

5. In recent years the supply of products in many countries has exceeded the demand for them in spite of the rapid increase in population. This is the result of the development of modern science and technology.

6. We youths must make contributions towards the peaceful use of atomic energy. This is our duty as well as our right.

7. In order to avoid getting into debt, one must stop spending more

than what one earns.

8. In former times women were usually despised, but nowadays they are engaged in various occupations on an equal footing with men and are respected in society as well.

9. But for the development of science and technology, production would not have increased so rapidly.

10. If you will favour us with your order, we can allow you a credit of two months, or a 2% discount for cash payment within half a month.

11. The sellers inform the buyers that as the costs have been rising since last month, the prices fixed are subject to change at any moment.

12. We believe our newly invented product will meet the needs of the consumers. We shall be very pleased to receive your order.

13. We are pleased to allow you a 2% discount for a quantity of more than 50 dozens as a special term.

14. We have been producers of the silk fabrics for quite a long time and our brands have been very popular among the users in Japan as well as in other foreign countries. We are sure that the quality of our products will meet with your full satisfaction.

15. We are open every day, and whether you are ready to buy or not, please come and look around.

16. We are interested in exporting some of our products, especially transistors and computers, to Europe. We wonder whether you could help us.

17. Owing to the shortage of raw materials, the factory had decreased production. Accordingly, they informed the buyers that they could not fill the order in time, but promised to make every effort to resume production and expected to be able to deliver the goods by the end of the month.

18. As you have failed to deliver the goods within the specified time, we have no alternative but to cancel the order.

19. A part of the goods are ready for shipment, but to economize (on) freight we have decided to ship them together with the other goods a few days later.

20. If the cost of raw materials rises, we hope to have the right to increase our prices, or we shall have no alternative but to decline your order.
21. Prompt delivery is important in this trade as we have pointed out time and again. We shall have to find another source of supply if such a delay is repeated.
22. The goods were promised to be delivered in the first part of the month, but were not shipped until the end of the month. The delay has caused considerable inconvenience to the buyers.
23. We regret to inform you that the goods delivered are not in accordance with your samples, so we refuse to accept them.
24. Having carefully considered your letter of August 8, we have decided to allow you to defer payment of your account to the end of this month.
25. Our price quoted was for orders of 500 dozens and over. If you wish to profit by the lower price, we must ask you to increase your order to this figure.
26. From the catalogue which you have sent us, we find that your prices are somewhat too high. If the prices are reasonable, we should place the order with you for 400 raincoats.
27. If you compare our prices with those of the other firms, we feel sure you will realize that our quoted prices are very reasonable.
28. According to the contract, the buyers are entitled to cancel the order if the sellers fail to deliver in time.
29. We regret to find that in case No. 20 all the stockings were stained. A great number of them were damaged by wetting from sea-water.
30. To understand inflation, we must first understand what is being "inflated". It is not prices or wages, but it is the supply of money-currency. When the supply of money exceeds the real ability of a country to produce, currency is inflated and money begins to be depreciated.

# Exercise 11

1. A: What do you think of this dictionary?
   B: It is a good dictionary, but like the other dictionaries you can't expect it to be perfectly correct.
2. More and more books have been published in recent years, but only a small part of them are worth reading, I'm afraid.
3. There are two novels on the shelf. One of them is in Chinese, and the other in English. You may choose one of them if you like.
4. I borrowed a novel from my friend yesterday. It is so interesting that I finished (reading) it in one evening.
5. A: Have you finished the novel you borrowed last week?
   B: Yes, I'm through with it.
   A: How do you like it?
   B: It's so intesting that I almost forgot my meals.
6. This is a book that I liked to read in my youth. Though twenty years have passed, I still take great interest in re-reading it.
7. We often found some books uninteresting in our youth, but when we re-read them in later years we might be surprised at the deep meaning contained in them.
8. A classical work is deep in meaning and is often not easy to understand when we read it in our youth.
9. A: I'm too busy to read. What shall I do?
   B: However busy you may be, it is necessary for you to read one or two hours a day.
10. You say you are too busy to read, but I think you can surely find time to do so if you have a mind to.
11. It is useless for some people to read many books without discrimination. We had better read a few useful books with care.
12. This sentence is rather long and difficult, but you will be able to understand it if you analyse it carefully.
13. It is difficult to learn a thing well in a short while, so never give up learning if your progress is not rapid.
14. Even though I haven't made much progress, I'll study hard all the same. I believe I can learn well if I have a mind to. The proverb says, "Rome was not built in a day."
15. A: Have you read the preface of that book?

380

B: No, I haven't.

A: It is good to read the preface, for it will help you make the most of a book.

16. Some people are discouraged because they often forget what they have learned. Of course, reading is unlike saving money.

17. He is seventy this year. His memory doesn't fail and his mind is still quick. This might be due to his good health.

18. I have studied English for six years, and yet I can't read an English book as easily as I do a Chinese one. I don't know how to learn English well.

19. Try to read this English book from cover to cover and consult the dictionary whenever you come across any new words.

20. Those who wish to engage in foreign trade must study English, because it is most widely used in international commerce.

21. I would like to learn a foreign language. As English is most useful, I think I must master it.

22. In the course of studying English, I'm not afraid of making mistakes, but go on speaking and writing constantly, so I have made more rapid progress.

23. Under the guidance of his father he began to study English very early. Now he can speak and write it and is proficient in that language.

24. The best way to learn a foreign language is to have intercourse with foreigners. If you have no chance to go abroad, then try by all means to speak with foreigners living here.

25. When we learn English, we must notice the differences between English and Chinese. We can never learn English well if we always try to express our thoughts in a Chinese way.

26. If you are asked with a negative question, you must use "yes" if your answer is in the affirmative, and "no" if it is in the negative.

27. A: What do you think of his English?

B: He speaks very fluently, but his accent doesn't seem to be that of an Englishman.

A: That's right. He was born in the States, so he speaks with the American accent.

28. Keeping a diary in English is a good way to practise writing English. You will surely achieve good results in due course of time.

29. Whatever difficulties may lie before me, I have made up my mind to learn English well. Though I know very little, I believe I can succeed so long as I continue to make efforts.

30. A: How long have you been studying English?

B: I've been studying it since 1977.

A: I think you are doing fairly well considering you have only studied for a little over two years.

B: Thank you for the compliment, but I'll have to work still harder.

A: Do you have any chance to practise your English in real situations — I mean actually using it with foreigners?

B: Yes, I often try by all means to speak with foreigners living here.

A: Good! I wish you success in your English studies.

# Exercise   12

1. It is a dangerous thing that one has only a little learning and yet doesn't realize it is little.

2. I don't want these books. It is a dictionary that I need. Could you recommend me a good one?

3. There are some people who often talk about peace, but it is not peace that they love, I should say.

4. There are still poverty, starvation and misery in many parts of the world. Since we live in the same world, we can't be indifferent to these phenomena.

5. Terrorism exists in many parts of the world. All of us know what kind of stuff terrorism is.

6. A: Did you go to cast your ballot in this election?

B: Yes, I did. I never fail to cast mine in every election.

A: Why do you pay so much attention to the election?

B: Because I think it is my duty as well as my right.

7. She doesn't flatter anyone in his presence or speak ill of anyone behind his back. Considering these two points, she is praiseworthy.

8. When we are reminded of our mistakes by a friend, we should thank him. In fact, a friend who gives us advice is much better than a friend who flatters us.

9. It is a common phenomenon that people prefer flattery to advice. It is therefore necessary that we should always keep modest and prudent.

10. There are some people who only like to be flattered and not to be advised. At last they find it too late to repent of the mistakes which they have made.

11. There are also a few obstinate people who believe themselves to be always correct and will never be prevailed upon. In the long run they are doomed to failure.

12. He has misunderstood me. It is my good intention to help him realize the mistake he has made, but he thinks that I spoke ill of him.

13. I criticized him for idling about and doing no decent work, but he answered that there was no chance for him to be employed.

14. How comes it that learning makes a man wise, but it makes a fool all the more a fool? What do you think the reason is?

15. A: She was bold enough to speak out what she thought.
    B: Yes; but I think she had better refrain from doing so when it is unnecessary.

16. Sometimes we can't do what we want to, and sometimes we have to do what we don't like. This is a common occurrence.

17. Many people don't know what freedom means. They think they can do whatever they like since they have freedom. This is really a great mistake.

18. It is a matter of great regret that he confuses freedom with licence and thinks he can do as he pleases. He misinterprets the meaning of freedom.

19. Some people think that the more money we have, the happier we shall be. What's your opinion?

20. I think he who has money is not always happy, nor is he who has no money always unhappy.

21. A: Do you think it correct to compare wealth to dung?

    B: I don't quite see the likeness of the two.

    A: Wealth is like dung because it sends forth a nasty smell if heaped up, but it fertilizes the land if sprinkled.

22. I think ability is more important than money. Without ability we could hardly accomplish anything in the world.

23. There is no limit to knowledge. However learned one may be, one must try to acquire still more of it.

24. Those who are helped by others are fortunate, but those who find pleasure in helping others are quite praiseworthy.

25. It is certainly ridiculous to believe only in others, but it is also dangerous to believe only in one's own self.

26. Though it does not necessarily follow that you will invariably succeed in life because of your excellent school record, those efforts exerted in your studies will never be completely useless.

27. Looking back upon our past life, we can often discover that many happenings were due to certain circumstances at that time. Without such circumstances we might not be what we are now.

28. It is certainly wrong to say that foreign goods are always better than domestic ones, but we believe no one will entertain such an idea if domestic goods are really better than foreign ones.

29. A lot of people are leading a better life than before, but some of them seem to be still dissatisfied with the present condition and think themselves to be unhappy if they can't live like the rich.

30. We can learn a lot of useful things from the people. They can even teach the most learned man something. If there is any chance, you may ask them to tell you of what they have seen and known. Never be ashamed to ask about what you don't understand. A learned man was once asked how he had acquired such a vast amount of knowledge. "By asking information of everyone," he answered.

英語一日一題 / 陳朴編著. --臺灣初版. --
臺北市：臺灣商務，1998〔民87〕
面 ； 公分

ISBN 957-05-1474-4（平裝）

1. 英國語言 - 句法

805.169                                    87007170

# 英語一日一題

## 定價新臺幣 360 元

| | |
|---|---|
| 編 著 者 | 陳　　朴 |
| 發 行 人 | 郝 明 義 |
| 出 版 者 | 臺灣商務印書館股份有限公司 |
| 印 刷 所 | 臺北市重慶南路 1 段 37 號 |

電話：（02）23116118・23115538
傳眞：（02）23710274
郵政劃撥：0000165-1 號
出版事業
登 記 證：局版北市業字第 993 號

- 1984 年 4 月香港初版
- 1998 年 8 月臺灣初版第一次印刷
- 1998 年 11 月臺灣初版第二次印刷

本書經商務印書館(香港)有限公司授權出版

ISBN　957-05-1474-4　（平裝）　　　　b 40161040